Good Gladys

Embrace the Dead

Martin Renaud

Cover Art: Sue Renaud
Cover Design: Martin Renaud

This is a work of fiction. All the characters, organizations and events portrayed in this book are either products of the author's imagination or are used fictitiously.

ISBN: 9780987851697

Who are these coming to the sacrifice?
To what green altar, O mysterious priest

—John Keats, 1820

CHAPTER 1

"She has no shame," thought Sauce. He stared at the small round wooden table—more specifically, at the silver cigarette lighter sized RCA digital recorder lying in the center of the table, next to his cell phone. The starburst reflection from the hanging lamp with the tassel-rimmed paisley shade over the table, his one inherited treasure from his long-dead mother, bounced off the recorder. He squinted, partly from the shattered light, partly from the chest-tightening guilt of not replying earlier to his phone messages. Dara had been out of his life for almost three years. Three gloriously, uncomplicated years.

He picked up the cell phone, then put it down again, undecided on what to do. He was still in his work clothes: suit pants, pale blue shirt, lavender tie.

On most nights he would be pulling off his tie before he crossed the threshold of his forty-year-old one-bedroom condo, impatient to shed the dregs of the day for a few mindless hours of football or baseball or whatever sport he could find on the television to pass the time before bed. He liked sports. They gave him exactly what he expected. He resented Dara for the same reason.

After three years, he had almost recovered and was seriously contemplating returning to school to complete his law degree. He had only been a couple of months away from the bar exam when he agreed to put off completion to run away with Dara to St. Martin. Six weeks, two days and several hours, that was how long their relationship lasted. A blind fury of sweet emotion that ripped apart his life, destroyed his career, distanced him from friends, and forced him into a paltry existence investigating insurance fraud cases.

"I'm in jail, Byrne! You have to help," was the entire first voice mail message. He'd seen her number on the call display but waited a week before listening to the voicemail.

"She must think I returned to my old life after she was finished with me," he thought, laughing to himself. "And she said 'Byrne.' She probably assumes that I get called that all the time by colleagues and clients." Although his full name is

Byrne Aase, he has been called "Sauce" since he was a child, even by his parents. "I couldn't have helped her anyway," he reasoned, deciding not to return her call. He knew she had the money to buy the best; why should he embarrass himself by returning her call?

Then came the second call. "I'm out, no thanks to you. Be coming by tonight to catch up," she stated. He wished he had answered the call and set her straight. He wasn't ready to see her—didn't think he would *ever* be ready to see her. Nevertheless, the reflected artificial light from the lamp bouncing off his recorder caused his heart to pound nervously, reminding him that night had arrived.

He was sure she would come. She kept her promises. The day he met her, on the corner of Seventh and Bryant, outside San Francisco's Hall of Justice, she told him they were destined to be together. She didn't say forever. Nevertheless, at the time, he heard 'forever.' He wasn't a one-night-stand kind of guy. Even in grade school, he would fall in love at the hint of a smile. He, therefore, assumed Dara had lifelong intentions, so he followed her across the street to the coffee shop. Just over six weeks later, he realized the truth and remembered her exact words. She had said what she meant to say and nothing more.

He picked up the digital recorder, hit record, and placed it into the pocket of his shirt. He was prepared this time. Whatever she says, he will be able to review it and prevent wish-fulfilling mental revisions. He developed the habit of recording important events, and transcribing them later, after his first insurance fraud case: a middle-aged, average woman with her two teen children in the back seat of her van, rear-ended on a busy intersection while stopped at a red light. It appeared to be straight-forward until he called one of the witnesses, who had kindly offered his contact information to the police at the scene. The witness was adamant that he saw the woman's back-up lights, as she reversed into the car behind her. At the insurance office the next day, however, that same witness signed a statement attesting that the woman's van had not moved until it was struck from behind. A few days later, Sauce learned it was her fifth rear-end accident in the past two years. Obvious insurance fraud. He reasoned that the witness must have been paid off. He had no evidence to prove it, though.

Since then, his recorder had bailed him out of dozens of similar situations, supplementing his memory; his recorded evidence had even forced a couple of fraud artists to confess to additional past transgressions. Dara wasn't going to get the best of him this time. He was prepared and wouldn't commit to anything until he was able to replay their entire conversation, over and over again.

CHAPTER 2

"She isn't dead. You know her, Sauce! Mummy wouldn't allow it. She's making too much money to die now!"

"I'm just repeating what I read in the Chronicle the other day."

"Sensationalism sells papers." She scoffed, throwing her brown leather, three-quarter length coat on the sofa. Dara was wearing loose fitting, generic jeans and a tight, tan silk blouse, advertising her rebelliousness and wealth in one ensemble. Her shoulder-length blonde hair was tied up in a tight bun—not one hair out of place—and her face was elaborately decorated, like a Broadway actress who wanted every facial expression to be visible from the cheap seats.

"So why me? I can't be your counsel; you must know that." Sauce stood his ground, wanting a quick end to this meeting. "You haven't called in three years. Last I saw of you was at that nightclub in Marigot when you left with those two dancers. You didn't say goodbye then, and you needn't say it now." Sauce picked up Dara's coat, about to throw it back to her.

"Stop living in the past!" She turned her back to him. "I know about your law degree. It was your perverted sense of justice wasn't it? You abandoned the bar exam, felt guilty about all the students who might have been able to attend law school in your place. You felt like you scuttled your chance and let people down, over a girl. You fool. You could have gone back, begged for forgiveness, claimed temporary, lustful insanity. They would have let you back in and you know it, so don't blame me. Besides, you're better off as an investigator. It's more your thing."

"I'm better off alone," said Sauce, throwing the coat on the floor at Dara's feet. "I'm surprised you called; you're obviously aware of my failed legal ambitions."

She casually scanned the room, then turned to Sauce with a wry smile. "Do this for me, and then tell me if you're better off alone," she challenged. "Mummy doesn't need another lawyer—hers are better than you could ever have hoped, with legal ease and loopholes, that is. But they only do what Mummy pays them to do. She's not worried about the charges and expects her lawyers to get her out of jail soon. After she's out, though, Mummy will need someone less easily influenced by her money and glamour. That's you! You never cared for my mother. She knows that she can't manipulate you. Usually that would be enough for her to write you off. Now, however, you're precisely the kind of man she wants in her corner."

"Because you'll do all the manipulating, is that it? What did you tell Gladys? A few words from you and I'll come running, maybe even work for free?"

"No, I never said you'd work for free. Name the price, it doesn't matter."

"I see what you're doing. Get me to commit to a price and then you'll own me for another six weeks." Sauce knew he was losing control of the conversation. He hoped the reference to the past would unsettle Dara long enough for him to get rid of her.

"You're wrong again." She didn't bother to mask her annoyance. "You're pretending to have changed. I know better, though. You were always trusting. I can tell you're still that person I whisked away from his tedious life for the most breathtaking adventure he could ever wish for. Take a deep breath and calm down. You should realize that I came here as your friend. I know what you are capable of, so when Mummy suggested I give you a call I realized that she was absolutely correct. You would be able to help us."

"I won't be a part of her latest publicity stunt." Sauce put his hands on his hips, and deepened his voice to demonstrate his resolve. "You've obviously been in contact with her so the reports of her missing for months were false, all part of her ruse."

"Get your facts straight. She's only been missing for five weeks. Although the word 'missing' isn't accurate in this context. Of course I know where she is. I'm her daughter! To the rest of the world she is still not quite missing, but let's say unseen. There isn't any ruse or con game or whatever other synonym your imaginative Roget's thesaurus of a mind can conjecture. She has a very good reason for staying out of the spotlight, and it has nothing to do with money. Or at least she hasn't figured out how to monetize it yet. Either way, she isn't working an angle this time. She's in serious trouble."

"I may not have changed but you sure have," Sauce said. "When we were together, you hated your mother."

"I'm surprised at you, Sauce. Hate is a nasty word. You once said it means 'having a desire to kill' or something like that. I may have disliked her work, despised it even, but I always loved her."

"Loved her money, you mean." Sauce sneered, showing his disgust. He walked toward the door, hoping that Dara would follow. "Yeah, I don't think I'll be much use to you this time."

"Remember that day we left for St. Martin?" asked Dara, sitting down on the edge of the sofa. "I took you home, just before we left, so I could pack a few clothes for the trip. You met Mummy and talked with her while you waited for me." Sauce turned and raised his eyebrows. "Good," she continued. "Do you remember the first thing you said to her?"

"No, but I hope she took offense."

"It was perfect. Mummy asked you some self-aggrandizing question like, 'How do you like the place?' You looked her in the eye and—oh, I loved your answer so much it was etched in my memory. You said, 'Bankruptcies and broken families from your thievery is all I see.'" Dara paused, and Sauce smiled. "You despised what she was doing as much as I did. But like me, you didn't hate her."

"I didn't? You don't know that," challenged Sauce. "I certainly knew enough about her, from the talk shows and celebrity gossip in the news, to hate her. 'Good Gladys, psychic to the stars' they call her. I can predict the future better than her. Believe in Gladys's ability to talk with the dead and she will stay in your life until you are out of money. Gladys is the kind of person people either love for the wrong reasons, or hate for the right ones."

"I never said you loved her. No, I agreed with Mummy that you are much more useful to us than a fawning admirer or a starched-shirt, lawyer-for-hire, yes man. You understand her." Dara smiled.

Sauce tried to resist the manipulation. "Here's the best I can do. Leave, and I'll mull it over. I promise I won't say no until I call you tomorrow."

"Better than call, you can meet me in the courtroom. Mummy has her second arraignment at noon." She stood and held out a folder to Sauce. "Here's a copy of the transcript from her first court appearance and some interview notes from her lawyers." Sauce refused to take the folder, so she set it on the little round table and picked up her coat. As she walked to the front door, she finalized her visit with a prediction. "If you read the transcript tonight, I guarantee you'll want to arrive early tomorrow to get a good seat."

CHAPTER 3

Lying in bed later that night, Sauce castigated himself for the level of intrigue and interest he felt for the coming morning. He wanted to be dismissive and hold to his earlier conviction by rejecting Dara's invitation, thereby proving her wrong. She had not been wrong, however, and barring a major earthquake or life-threatening accident he was going to be in the courtroom at noon. The worst consequence, he surmised, was that Dara might presume she had inherited the kind of extra-sensory powers her mother professed to possess.

After Dara's departure, Sauce had waited a full five minutes before curiosity took command of his behaviour. He watched as his hands untied the white string enclosing Dara's folder and removed the crisp white pages. He scanned the notes from Gladys's lawyers—four lawyers, posing similar questions in a similar tone. Each reached the same conclusion as to the likelihood of receiving a favourable verdict. Sauce was as confused by the content of the notes as he was by the extremely unlikely occurrence of agreement among four attorneys.

His first impression as he began reading, aloud as he habitually did when alone, was that Dara had mistakenly been given the wrong notes. Comment after comment, paragraph after paragraph, page after page, made use of an incorrect pronoun when addressing matters related to statements made by the defendant. "He professes his innocence; he is delusional; *nolo contendere*, no contest must be his plea; at trial the jury will surely be convinced that he is insane, and was so during the execution of the crime," Sauce read aloud.

"Poor idiot," thought Sauce on this initial perusal of the notes. "They've already decided his guilt before beginning to develop a defense." As he continued to read, he became increasingly confused about references made in the notes. The connection to Good Gladys seemed straightforward enough: her manager, Cole Beckley, died as a result of a knife wound to the chest, which he received while at work in his office. Also straightforward was the reason for detaining the accused. The man found at the scene when the police arrived was identified by Beckley's secretary as the last person to have seen him alive. Periodically, however, each lawyer would refer to the defendant by the name, *Mr.* Gladys.

Sauce couldn't make sense of the connection between the defendant being accused of murder and Gladys. No reference was made to a co-defendant, or accessory, or any such legal jargon to implicate more than one person in the matter.

Sauce re-read the notes, more carefully the second time, but didn't gain any more insight than in his initial cursory scan. He then turned to the transcript of the initial arraignment, hoping for clarification. "United States of America versus Mr. Gladys," he mumbled, reading down the first page. The names of the lawyers confirmed that the notes in Dara's package were addressing the same case. The title was fairly standard:

TRANSCRIPT OF ARRAIGNMENT AND MOTIONS HEARING BEFORE THE HONORABLE RICE S. WHEELER UNITED STATES DISTRICT JUDGE

After that, however, the proceedings were anything but standard:

The Court: For the sake of clarity alone, I will refer to the defendant as Mr. Gladys, as neither he, nor his lawyers have provided evidence of legal identification.

The Defendant: I object, your Honour.

The Court: You have no cause. I'll remind the defendant, and everyone in attendance, this is a court of law. I will not tolerate such outbursts. Mr. Gladys, that is your first and final warning. If you wish to speak, you must step up to the microphone and wait until I give you permission to address the court. Is that clear?

The Defendant: (approaches the microphone, stands still and waits, silently)

The Court: Yes, Mr. Gladys, what is it?

The Defendant: I would like to clarify, your Honour, that I have repeatedly stated my name and will submit to a lie detector, if I must, to prove to the court that I am Gladys, known and loved by millions as Good Gladys.

The Court: Yes. Thank you.

The Defendant: I would also like the court to recognize that these lawyers I am paying to assist me are merely consulting on this matter, and except for asking them for clarification on legal procedures and legal language, I will be defending myself.

The Court: Yes. Thank you. Mr. Gladys, has your council clarified the charges that have been raised against you.

The Defendant: Clarified? I don't need them to explain the charges. I've known what murder was since I was a child.

The Court: Mr. Gladys, I must caution you that the prosecution will use anything you say to support their case against you. This includes statements about your knowledge and full understanding of the meaning of the charges put forth against you. Are you prepared to enter a plea?

The Defendant: Not guilty, of course. I didn't kill anyone. I'm as much a victim as Mr. Beckley.

The Court: Yes, thank you, Mr. Gladys. You may sit, for now.

The Defendant: If you please, your Honour, call me Gladys.

The Court: Yes, thank you. I'll accept your plea of not guilty. I now turn to Mr. Farnis. What are the prosecution's intentions regarding bail and custody?

Mr. Farnis: The prosecution would like to remind the court of the severity of the charges and the hostility of the witness. We request the defendant be remanded without bail until the trial.

The Defendant: Hostile? I'll give you hostile you opossum-faced, ninety-pound miscreant. I know your kind. Mother preferred your older brother, right? Your wife hasn't let you in her bed for years; even your kids won't let you drive them to school out of embarrassment. Your body stopped producing growth hormones when you were nine! Don't give me that look! You can't intimidate me! You shriveled little …

The Court: Mr. Gladys! You were warned to remain silent until addressed by the court. Attacking the prosecution will only vitiate your case. I remind you that you have council present to assist you with this arraignment. I encourage you to seek their advice on issues raised by the prosecution, rather than say something that strengthens the prosecution's position against you.

The Defendant: Mistrial! You just told me to shut up. You can't do that; I have a right to speak. It's a free country. You can't stop me.

The Court: Bailiff, please escort Mr. Gladys out of the courtroom. You were warned.

The Defendant: (struggling) Get away from me. I didn't kill Cole, though if anyone had a right to, I sure did. I made the man, gave him everything he had. He owed me his life.

Note: The defendant repeated his claims of innocence as he was escorted out of the courtroom by the Bailiff.

The Court: Mr. Gouch, would you please approach the microphone. As legal aide to Mr.

Gladys, are you or your colleagues prepared to counter the prosecution's request for remand?

Mr. Gouch: Your Honour, we have no instructions on the matter from our client. In his interest, however, I should state that we are unanimous in requesting a continuance on the issue of bail until the mental state of Mr. Gladys has been assessed by a learned professional.

Ms. Dara Stockard: You criminals!

The Court: So, Mr. Gouch, until the second arraignment, you agree with the prosecution to have Mr. Gladys remain in custody?

Mr. Gouch: We submit to your discretion, your Honour. We concede that the charges are severe, wilful intention to inflict bodily harm causing death, and Mr. Gladys has been uncooperative with the court and his council about his identity.

Ms. Stockard: He told you his identity. He is my mother! He told you that, repeatedly. He hasn't been uncooperative.

The Court: Ms. Stockard, the warning I issued earlier was for everyone in attendance. I am charging you with contempt. Bailiff remove her from the courtroom. Ms. Stockard you will be held in the county corrections for that outburst. You will remain in custody for forty-eight hours, at which time you will be required to submit a written apology for disrupting these proceedings, before being released. I also warn you, I will not be this lenient the next time you upset the order of my courtroom.

"The man is sunk." Sauce put the folder aside. Knowing he wouldn't be able to sleep, he got out of bed, walked to the kitchen, and removed a bottle from the freezer. He poured a large vodka and tonic to settle his nerves and took a long sip. His heart rate slowed and he felt whole again. It occurred to him that his recorder was still in the pocket of the shirt he had worn earlier in the evening. He also realized the recorder was still capturing an audio version of his life and actions, not having been turned off since before Dara arrived.

He retrieved the recorder and settled on the sofa to review the recording from the moment of Dara's entrance to his pronouncement that "The man is sunk."

Ringing in his ears were Dara's words, "He is my mother."

"What the hell does that mean?" Sauce was confident that the Dara he had known would not risk a charge of contempt, unless she stood to benefit. He was intrigued.

He was also worried for the man who was caught up in Dara and Gladys's game. "They must have bribed him with a promise of money, fame, maybe even sex," Sauce considered. "But he probably has no idea what these people will do to him. These women will leave him to rot in prison, and those idiot lawyers will sit back and do nothing to stop it.

"Murderer?" he wondered. "Perhaps? A sap, more likely, taken in by Gladys's well-honed talent for manipulation and exploitation. I don't think Gladys is the murdering type; she wouldn't hesitate to profit from it, though. I can just picture the wheels turning in her scheming brain when she learned of this man's predicament. She has connections in law enforcement. They would have told her the prosecution's entire case rests on the weakest premise: last man to see the victim alive. It's an empty claim. Only the dead man knows who he met with before he died. In most situations it would be the murderer, though even that cannot be presumed. Gladys pieced the information together. That's one of her skills, making the most of the information she gathers.

"She probably told the accused she had used her psychic connection to speak with the victim, knew he was innocent, and had a plan to prevent him from being found guilty. She knows how to work people, especially desperate ones. Somehow she plans to turn this case into a marketing bonanza for a new book or stadium tour. Dara, on the other hand, knows better. What is she doing getting wrapped up in this?”

CHAPTER 4

"What's your angle, Sauce?"

"No angle. Gladys asked me to attend. I used to know her daughter, years ago."

"Ah, friend of the family. Spirit lover, huh?" Officer Hammi laughed. "I didn't pick you to mix with that extrasensory crowd."

"Yeah, right." Sauce dismissed the playful accusation. He could take a joke, especially in circumstances like this. Officer Hammi had been in college with Sauce for a couple of years before Hammi felt a calling, by way of rising tuition fees and an inability to find employment, toward law enforcement. Over the years, their friendship evolved into an exchange of information for mutual benefit. Sauce liked Hammi, despite finding him a bit too gullible for his occupation.

Today, in the main corridor outside the courtroom, it was Hammi's turn to share information. Sauce had left a message for him early that morning and asked about the defendant, details of the case, and any first impressions by the attending officers regarding the defendant's sanity. Hammi called an hour later and suggested meeting before the arraignment began. His exact words were, "I gotta tell you to your face. You probably won't believe me otherwise."

"Gladys's daughter told the defendant I might be able to help with the case. That's all." Sauce was consciously trying to avoid using pronouns until he had more evidence.

"Divine knowledge of your unique investigative powers, I bet," chided Hammi.

"Unlikely. Gladys's daughter and I had a thing some years ago. Nothing special, but you know how hard it is for a woman to say goodbye."

Hammi twirled his black pencil-thin mustache between his index finger and thumb as Sauce continued. "I wasn't going to take the case, and still may not, but these transcripts Dara gave me seem … well, kind of muddled. I hate being confused, and the court's notes are confusing. Do you have anything to help clear this up?"

"Clear it up? Sorry, Sauce. There's no clarity in this matter. She seems to be in total control. That Gladys is a piece of work."

"So she has been here, then?"

"Now let's not have miscommunication between you and me. When I say Gladys is in total control, I mean the man on trial who calls himself Gladys. I refuse to venture an opinion on his identity. I try to keep an open mind, especially when there are many unknowns, as in this case."

"So it's true, then. The defendant is claiming to be Gladys," stated Sauce incredulously. "Just when I thought I had seen it all, something like this presents itself to baffle my senses. I don't know about you but it's cases like this that make me appreciate my sanity."

"I bet you haven't heard half the story yet," Hammi said. "You wouldn't believe what's been going on in prison. I wouldn't have, had I not seen it with my own eyes."

"The prisoners are giving him a hard time?" asked Sauce with a knowing smile.

Hammi pulled Sauce over to the wall and whispered, "We've been told to keep it hush-hush. You know, from the press. So you didn't hear it from me. Anyway, these things have a way of getting out. I heard that at least one of the guards sold the story to a tabloid reporter already. We expect it to be quite a circus in the courtroom today. Judge Wheeler even requested extra security."

"Now you have me really intrigued. Why all the tension? He's just one man, albeit a slightly deranged man."

"Listen to this: even the prisoners are terrified of him." Hammi looked around for eavesdroppers, then continued. "Here's what happened. On his first day in lockup, he tells some of the prisoners to leave him be. They don't like it, right? So they start to push and shove in the cafeteria. You know, the usual thing for newbies. The guards quickly broke it up, but Gladys gets a bloody lip in the scuffle. So she or he—hell, even I'm not sure what to call him—walks up to Moskovitch. He's this massive lifer, must have a hundred and fifty pounds on Gladys. He tells Moskovitch, loud enough for everyone to hear, that in five minutes he's a dead man, then walks away. Well, all the prisoners have a big laugh about it. Then five minutes later, at the other side of the cafeteria, Gladys stands up, raises his hands, closes his eyes and counts down, five, four, three, two, one. Wouldn't you know it, when he finishes the countdown, Moskovitch grabs his chest and drops to the floor. Heart attack, the official word, but can you imagine the effect on those guys in the cells?"

"Lucky guess?" asked Sauce. "Or could Gladys have slipped the big guy something?"

"You can be sure that's what the guards thought. So they put Gladys in solitary for a few days. But the doctor said it was a blood clot in the aorta and he would have died if they hadn't got to him as soon as they did. No one could have caused it or predicted it—except Gladys, I guess. So after a couple of days the guards let him back in his cell. But then Gladys did it again!"

"Killed someone else?" snapped Sauce.

"Shh! Killed isn't quite the right word. Moskovitch survived, and no one saw Gladys do anything *to* him. But Gladys definitely seemed to know what was going to happen. At the very least he let it happen if you ask me. I heard the rumour and wanted to see for myself. We all did. Apparently, Gladys told some of the other prisoners that this time he was going to kill a guard during exercise break. Word spread like wildfire and I was called up for added security, just in case.

"The exercise area is not very big, but the other guys gave Gladys a lot of space. He just sat on one of the benches looking calm and peaceful. We stayed in the cages, out of reach, you know? We were pretty worked up, like the inmates. Then at about two o'clock, he yelled out, 'One minute.' Well that got us real tense, *real tense*. We had our hands on our pistols, and thumpers, ready for … well anything, or so we thought. The prisoners looked at us with the widest grins you'd ever seen, like they couldn't wait to see one of us drop dead. Some of them were even brave enough to approach Gladys and ask, 'Which one? Tell us which one. I wanna see him when he gets it.'

"We were terrified. And, as it turned out, rightly so!"

"You actually saw Gladys kill a guard?" asked Sauce.

"Hold your tongue!" Hammi looked around, then, noticing no one had heard, returned to his story. "Listen, I was there, so you can think whatever you like, but this guy, or girl or whatever, is not normal. The prisoners are terrified of him, as are most of the guards. I tell you, even I would rather be home today than in that courtroom near him. As I was saying, when Gladys announced 'One minute', we were all getting pretty edgy. But when he stood up, raised his hands and began counting down, ten, nine, eight—well, we almost lost it. The prisoners started counting with him, really loudly. It was so intense. Then Gladys reached five and pointed a finger at Officer Stanley. Sergeant Armstrong panicked and withdrew his sidearm, but as he unlatched the safety, the gun slipped from his fingers, dropped to the ground, and just as all the prisoners screamed 'one' the gun discharged. Stanley didn't have a chance; the bullet entered right below his jaw, turned his brain to mush."

"It … it was an accident!" exclaimed Sauce, as quietly as he could under the circumstances.

"Normally I'd agree with you. No one who was there believes it was, though. I mean, you can't predict accidents like that one. Yet Gladys did! I saw him pointing at Stanley before Armstrong even withdrew his revolver. How could he have known what was going to happen, unless he really could do the kind of things Gladys has been doing for years?"

"Gladys never pulled off something like that before," countered Sauce.

"Oh, I heard stories of her talking to dead people and finding out all about people's secrets and their vices. Dead people know all about what's happened and maybe even what's going to happen."

"Gladys was all smoke and mirrors, trust me," said Sauce. "She was all about ripping people off, getting money. This doesn't sound at all like the kind of thing Gladys would do. This guy is not Gladys."

"That's your call. You won't find one man who was in that prison who'll believe you, though. The prisoners think Gladys is like a god or something."

"I'm surprised they didn't just kill the guy out of self-preservation," offered Sauce.

"I told you, they're terrified. He's been ordering them around. Even the hard, drug-addicted lifers answer his every whim. I've never seen anything like it in all my years on the force."

"Now you're sounding like a believer. And *Gladys* just stood there, in the exercise area? You're sure he didn't move or provoke Armstrong?" asked Sauce, searching for a logical explanation.

"Like I said, the gun just slipped, dropped to the concrete, and discharged. The bullet could have gone anywhere." Hammi twitched his mustache nervously, looked around, then said, "I've got to get to my post. You'd better hurry and get a seat. We've been told to be extra vigilant, and you should, too. There's no telling what Gladys might try in there."

"So you're convinced he's Gladys now?"

"Like I said, I keep an open mind." He turned and quickly walked down the corridor toward the entrance of the courtroom.

Sauce took a seat at the back and scanned the room full of reporters and gawkers. His eyes met Dara's, briefly. Her face was expressionless, though Sauce knew she was counting his attendance among her many victories.

CHAPTER 5

Sauce leaned to one side to see past the woman with the oversized blond wig sitting in front of him. He could only see the back of the defendant's head. He watched as Dara stood and leaned over the rail to say something to the man pretending to be her mother. "She doesn't seem worried at all," he thought after seeing Dara kiss the defendant on the cheek, let out a short giggle, then sit back down.

Sauce stood obediently to the bailiffs call, "All rise, the Honourable Judge Rice Wheeler presiding." He thought it was funny that many of the reporters in the room immediately began scribbling into their notebooks as the judge proceeded to enter the courtroom. Sauce almost laughed out loud when the judge tripped on his robe just as he reached the bench, and fell forward, his forehead blessing the rail with a soft thud. This impromptu dance elicited a chorus of "oohs and ahhs" from the gallery. Sauce finally got a glimpse at the defendant's face when he turned to look at the audience as if to say, "you came for a show? Well, the show has just begun."

Sauce considered himself a pretty good judge of character, and thought that the defendant looked devious and untrustworthy. "His hair is too perfect. His suit, expertly tailored. I don't like him. He looks more like an actor than a murderer, though I guess a man can be both."

Sauce looked at the notepad of the female reporter sitting next to him. She had already scribbled details of the Judge's entrance. Sauce audibly laughed as he read the caption, "Gladys strikes first! Judge nearly killed on way to bench."

Sauce abruptly averted her gaze and looked at the judge, who was fussing with his robes and shuffling pages. "Get on with it already," Sauce thought. Judge Wheeler leaned over the bench and whispered something to the stenographer, who seemed perplexed at the delay.

"Sir?" asked the stenographer loudly enough to be heard over the murmurs from the restless crowd. Sauce had seen this behavior before. When he was in law school he had attended the trial of an alleged mob hit man. That judge seemed nervous, was slow to begin and delayed the proceedings by asking the stenographer a number of questions. Afterwards, one his professors explained that many old-school judges consider the stenographer—a *miracle worker* who could listen attentively, comprehend immediately, transpose effortlessly and all with one hundred percent accuracy—to be the smartest person in the courtroom. During a tense moment on any particular day, the judge may derive hope and comfort in those lightning fast fingers, pounding the keys rhythmically.

Looking down from the bench, Judge Wheeler frowned at the question from his stenographer. "No comfort there," thought Sauce. The judge loudly cleared his throat, lifted the gavel, and dropped it a little too heavily onto its base, filling the courtroom with unnecessary trepidation.

"Yes attention, er, um order," the Judge began softly. He cleared his throat again. Deepening his voice to a more authoritative baritone he continued. "Please, I'll be brief. The matter of the murder of Mr. Cole Beckley has been brought before this court, prematurely." He ignored the loud chatter in the gallery and continued. "When I first became a judge, a learned colleague gave me a snippet of alliterative advice that I have held onto as prophetic for days like today. He told me, 'Never brave the barristers on the bench.' I thought about that sage piece of wisdom after the initial arraignment and feared I had done precisely its opposite. I have re-examined the preliminary evidence for detaining the accused and have come to the conclusion that a wrong needs to be set right."

"May we approach the bench, your Honour," yelled out the prosecutor Mr. Farnis.

"No! Let me finish," Judge Wheeler answered. "Cases like this are wonderful fodder for ambitious young men, such as yourself." Sporadic laughter spread through the room, as Mr. Farnis was well past the age where the term "young" would apply. "Sensational headlines are all but guaranteed with a case like this. Once in a while, such headlines must be tolerated, but not this time. I have reviewed the evidence and made specific requests regarding irregularities concerning the timeline, the witness for the prosecution, and the physical evidence pertaining to the identity of the accused. All three of these lines of inquiry have led me to one conclusion.

"Regarding the timeline, I am not convinced that the investigating officers have adequately established that the accused was the last person to see the victim alive. The coroner's report allows for the murder to have been committed a full six hours prior to the visit by the accused. The only witness to account for Mr. Beckley being alive at the time of the visit was his secretary, Ms. Karen Escobar. The investigating officers confirm that after recording her initial testimony at the crime scene, they have been unable to contact or locate her. Apparently, she moved out of her apartment the day before the murder, and her current place of residence is unknown. Am I correct, Mr. Farnis, that you are unable to produce this witness?"

"We are confident your Honour that we will find her before the trial commences," he replied.

"Are you?" Wheeler asked. "I am not. Furthermore, you have accused a man you cannot identify. I have seen the fingerprint analysis and DNA screen and am more annoyed than mystified. The accused claims to be the famous Good Gladys, which of course is absurd. When I was presented with the results of the aforementioned physical evidence, I expected to learn the defendant's true identity. In fact, upon seeing the initial results, I requested a second DNA screen. What did I find from these tests? Corroboration! Is this court supposed to suspend its belief in the laws of nature, and simply agree that Good Gladys, once a forty-four-year-old, slim, five foot ten inch, beautiful brunette is now this thirty-five-year-old, six foot tall, dashing young blond man seated before us? No, it can't. And if the court cannot even accept the physical evidence as veridical, then it must conclude that tampering has occurred at some level of the investigation. You see where this leads me, I'm sure.

Tampering of evidence, lost witnesses, illogical timelines. You have no case, Mr. Farnis. My conclusion is to apologize to the accused and dismiss the case forthwith. That is all."

Judge Wheeler stood amidst a firestorm of questions from reporters oblivious to courtroom decorum, and from the prosecution who was yelling that he should be given an opportunity to present his arguments.

CHAPTER 6

Sauce bought a paper bowl of prepared crab from The Crab Station to nibble on as he wandered past the tourists on Fisherman's Wharf. This was his ritual whenever he needed to mull over a complex issue or simply avoid dealing with life in general. The aroma of freshly baked bread and steamed seafood mingled with the noise of street buskers, merciless pedestrians, traffic, and street car bells. The sensory stimulation was Sauce's mental elixir: urban confusion produced inner tranquility.

He left the courtroom immediately after Gladys's dismissal, eager to avoid being trampled by the parade of reporters scampering to be first to interview the accused on the courthouse steps. He also wanted to avoid Dara and her inevitable gloating about successfully manipulating him. He needed time. All the details he read in the documents Dara had left for him, all the details in Judge Wheeler's speech, and even Hammi's nonsensical descriptions of Gladys's adventures in prison left his brain swimming with hypotheses. The worst part was he could not fathom what his involvement was. Why had Dara contacted him? After a few hours walking through the streets, he felt confident that the case had taken a very positive turn, where he was concerned that is. Dara and Gladys did not need anything from him. They were free, so he was free. The sun was sinking as he approached the front door of his apartment, laughing at himself for his shivering anxiety after Dara's initial phone call. He was looking forward to a quiet evening watching basketball in his pajamas.

He walked through the door and was immediately greeted, "There you are! I thought I might have to wait all night for you to come home." Dara was seated on the edge of his sofa, wearing the grey pleated pencil skirt and fuchsia blouse Sauce recognized from the courtroom.

"What the devil? Why are you in my house?" He could feel the crab sidestepping up his esophagus.

"Mummy wants a word," she answered, unaffected by his temper. Sauce stood silent for a few seconds, then grunted, and walked past Dara to the kitchen freezer for his vodka.

"You must have questions, after today," Dara called.

"I can manage without answers," he yelled back.

"Aren't you curious though? Can't be easy for someone like you, not knowing what's going on. You investigate, uncover little truths, shatter little lies. You may learn something from Mummy, like it or not."

Sauce guzzled his drink and poured another. Entering the living room, he noticed Dara had not moved from the sofa. Suppressing his annoyance, he walked past her on his way to the bedroom. "We're done here. Lock up when you leave," he told her, as a conclusion to their discourse for the evening.

"Don't go in there!" she shouted, just as he was about to open his bedroom door. Sauce stopped and turned back to her. Dara looked longingly into his eyes. "Mummy says this has to be done tonight. Please meet with her. You have to understand. Mr. Beckley's murder was just the beginning. More people will die. Mummy might be next." She paused, looked down at the floor and softly added, "I might be next."

"Manipulation. Good try. Gladys has taught you well." He took a sip of his drink and walked back into the living room, stopping right in front of Dara. "You expect me to believe that *Mummy's* money can't protect the two of you? That somehow *I* can?" His raised voice cracked as he shouted out the last two words. He finished his drink and slammed the glass down on the coffee table. "I have work to do in the morning, real work. Just leave me alone."

"What work? You don't have any active cases right now." She stood up and stared into his eyes, smiling. "Mummy has ways of knowing these things. You should really see this as an opportunity. Don't be a fool. She has connections, the kind that would benefit your work."

"Aha," he snapped. "My line of work is honest, if not lucrative. Your mother is anything but honest. She turns people like me into bottom feeders: garbage can divers, widow stalkers, phone hackers, and pick-pockets. Not interested."

"You're wrong. She doesn't want to turn you. She wants to speak with you for exactly the opposite reason." She put her hands on Sauce's shoulders. "No foolin'. When Mummy realized how much trouble she was stirring, she asked me if there was anyone I knew who could be described as incorruptible. You were the only one who came to mind. That's why she asked me to track you down."

"Just tell me what she wants," he said, taking a step back.

"No. You have to hear it from her." She reached down and picked up her suit jacket from the sofa. "Suspend disbelief for a few hours, and listen to her. That's all we ask. Just listen to her."

"One condition. After this you leave me alone. No more breaking into my house. No more calling my phone. Leave me alone."

"I knew you would want to come."

CHAPTER 7

"Turn that damn thing off," Sauce snapped at the driver as the cab approached its destination. "Fly Me To The Moon" was playing on the taxi's stereo and Sauce was not in the mood. "Just let me off at the corner." Sauce paid and stepped out, weak-kneed and gasping for air due to the stuffiness of the cab combined with the car sickness he always felt when not in control.

He bent over, placing his hands on his knees. He looked down the street, one way, then the other, searching for Dara's canary-yellow Porsche. She had suggested they travel together. Sauce declined. The two very large vodkas had ruled out driving himself. After the events of the last couple of days, and his history with Dara, he figured his only option was to subject himself to the germs and odours of one of

San Francisco's overpriced road warriors. Dara had waited in her sports car at the side of the road outside Sauce's condo for his ride to arrive. Sauce figured she had orders from her mom to make sure he didn't get lost on the way.

He should've known better than to have had an expectation regarding Dara's behaviour. She probably hadn't even followed him. Cab drivers never take the most direct route when there are more lucrative options. "She's probably already had time to shower and change out of her courtroom clothes," he reasoned. He reached into the pocket of his grey rain breaker and turned his recorder on.

He crossed the street and looked at the series of gated entrances surrounded by twelve-foot hedges, spaced at regular intervals—a leafy, green walled barrier against the real world. He passed the first two ornate, black, motorized gates and pressed the call button at the third. A high-pitched "whirr, whirr" above his head attracted his attention. He looked up at the PTZ camera that had tilted and focused on his location. "Yes, that's right. It's me," Sauce mouthed at the camera inaudibly. The gate opened a couple of feet, just enough for Sauce to squeeze through, before closing again.

He approached the front door to be greeted by Dara's voice over a speaker embedded in one of the massive, twenty-foot high, white pillars on both sides of the entrance staircase. "Let yourself in and follow the lights to the library. Mummy will be along in a few minutes."

"Library?" he thought. "Who the hell has a library anymore?" He followed Dara's instructions, turned the brass knob on the massive oak door, adorned with hand-carved, mock Egyptian hieroglyphs, and entered the unlit hall. The door closed on its own as soon as Sauce took his fingers off the knob. He could see a faint glow at the end of the hall, presumably cast from the light he was supposed to follow. He scanned his surroundings: oval mirror with a gaudy, gold frame on one wall; a framed oil painting of *Footsteps in the Sand* with the familiar story printed on a descriptive card just below.

The rest of the wall space along his walk down the hall was occupied by various sized portraits of unfamiliar people wearing a variety of clothes, suggesting a long lineage of ancestors keeping watch on the current residents of the house. Sauce scoffed and raised his eyebrows. "All show. Everything's pastiche," he thought. "Gladys was born in Calgary, Alberta, or so the papers say, ran away from home to the southern states as a teenager and somehow emerged as a weather girl in Los Angeles in her early twenties. No family, no lineage, just a great body and the ability to deceive."

He turned the corner and noticed a pair of double solid in-pocket doors ahead of him that were slightly open, allowing the light he was following to spill out. He pushed on one of the doors, which responded without resistance, exiting into the wall. The library was a circular room. At its center was a massive globe measuring at least five feet in diameter, resting in a gnarled mahogany claw. Sauce read the plaque at the base of the globe.

"Beauty is truth, truth beauty," – that is all
Ye know on earth, and all ye need to know
~ KEATS

He mused, "I guess a world that believes in that is easy pickings for someone like Gladys."

At the room's tangent, farthest from the sliding doors, were floor-to-ceiling windows, framed by thick, burgundy, velvet curtains. From the windows at each side were semicircular, floor-to-ceiling bookshelves. Volumes upon volumes of books filled every inch of shelf space.

The room was symmetrical. Even the few pieces of furniture—two walnut coloured, leather sofas, two high-backed leather easy chairs and four strategically placed mahogany side tables with cabriole legs—were spaced equidistant to each other, the walls and the globe.

Sauce circled the room, testing a few of the books in the shelves for authenticity and discovered, to his delight, that most of them were faux books: leather covers over blocks of wood. On each of the side tables was a copy of one of Gladys's own books. "Most likely ghost written," he mused aloud. He lifted one and read the title: *Gladys Radiates Love*. "Say the last word backwards and at least the title would *sound* honest," he thought. He kept walking around the room until he had returned to the entrance, impatient and ready to leave. He looked out the windows and wondered if Gladys was going to make him wait all night.

Just then he felt a bump from behind. "Oh, you're here," said the man pretending to be Gladys, walking backwards into the room pulling a drink cart along. "I was just bringing in some refreshments."

He moved the cart to the center of the room, next to the globe, and proceeded to mix a couple of martinis. "Dara tells me that vodka is your drink … Oh, where are my manners?" He walked back to Sauce's side and extended a hand. "It seems I still don't have this living as a man thing down. Men shake hands when they meet, don't they?"

Sauce raised his eyebrows, shook his head and walked past his host. He took the shaker, filled one of the glasses, and drank the contents in one gulp.

"Skip the song and dance, buddy. I'm not buying it, so how about you go tell Gladys I am here, so I can hear what she has to say and go home."

"You are incorrigible. Believe what you want to believe; that has always been my advice." He walked to one of the sofas, undid a blazer button, and sat down. "Let me tell you what you want to hear," he continued. "I am a man paid by Gladys to pretend that some mystical transformation has occurred changing her from a woman to, uh," he swung both arms up and down, "to this. The reason for the pretense is obvious: money, and lots of it. People will flock to stadiums to hear the pseudo-philosophical ramblings of a medium who has done what no other mystic has accomplished. That's your point-of-view, isn't it?"

"In a nutshell. The nuttiest of nutshells!" answered Sauce while mixing another drink.

"First of all, you are not the only one in the room who needs a drink so if you don't mind …"

Sauce smiled at his victory and proceeded to pour a second glass. He brought the glass to his host and took a seat at the other end of the sofa. "I'm glad not everyone in this house is full of bullshit."

"I wasn't finished—you know for an educated man you have a lot to learn about how to treat a lady."

"And you're an expert on women, are you? You, who have been conned into this charade to the point of getting incarcerated, charged with murder—which, by the way, is not going to go away just because you are not behind bars anymore. I know the DA and he's not going to let up on you. Gladys is taking you for a ride."

"The DA has nothing on me."

"Perhaps nothing as far as Beckley's murder, but there are those two incidents in prison."

"What did I do? Nothing really."

"I suppose the heart attack guy and the doctor could have been confederates of yours—simple enough for a *psychic* who can falsify DNA results, right? But you did threaten to kill a guard."

"Oh, don't believe everything you hear from the rumour mill," he answered, chuckling. "I merely said that a guard would be next. Rampant fear did the rest."

"You pointed directly at him just before he died!"

"I pointed, from over a hundred feet away. That's all. Something spectacular always happens when I get people all worked up. I'll take credit most of the time, but I have my limits."

Sauce gulped his drink, unsure what to make of this explanation.

"As I was saying, you didn't let me finish. But thanks for the drink." He lifted the glass in the air in a mock toast and took a sip of the martini. "The second thing I was going to say was that you are wrong about me. You obviously don't believe, but the truth doesn't go away just because someone refuses to see it for what it is. I am Gladys, heart and soul. Just not in body." Sauce started to laugh, but Gladys continued undaunted.

"Do you think I like being like this? I had a great body. Men would stare at me when I entered a room—mind you I could do without some of that looking down my top or up my skirt nonsense. In general, though, I relished the attention. Now I'm stuck with this egotistical beast between my legs that won't keep still whenever a woman enters the room. I have to shave, my face I mean, every single day. I certainly did not volunteer for that. I am a victim, trying to make the best of an unusual predicament that has been forced on me."

"So we're back to that are we?" Sauce stood up, prepared to leave. "What a bloody waste of my time!" He had heard enough and walked to the drink cart to set down his glass.

"You can't leave," snapped Gladys. "We haven't even discussed why I asked you here."

"Dara asked me here, not you. Of course, you are all in this together, but count me out. Whatever the game, you'll have to find another patsy, 'cause I'm out."

"Five minutes, please." Gladys made an attempt to look needy, but his square jaw and deep set eyes ruined the effect. An even bigger mistake was approaching Sauce and putting a gentle hand on his shoulder.

"Don't touch me. I'm not that kind of guy. Even if I was, you wouldn't be my type, I'm sure."

"Sorry, force of habit. C'mon truce. How about I just tell you why you're here? Then you can leave and think about it. What do you say? Have another drink and I'll be brief."

Sauce sighed but thought one more drink couldn't hurt. He proceeded to pour vodka into the mixer.

"Progress! As I promised I'll get straight to the point. I want to hire you, as a PI."

"Do you now?" Sauce thought this was going to be just as he predicted.

"Nothing salacious. I mean there's nothing wrong with a little scandal, but I don't think you will encounter any of that kind of thing. Simple surveillance, take a few photos of public meetings, record habits, patterns, you know the routine, I'm sure."

"And who is the lucky target of my investigations."

"Dr. Reginald Jett, Professor of Organic Chemistry at the University of San Francisco. You may have heard of him."

"No," answered Sauce. "Why him?"

"He threatened Dara. I don't want to get into the particulars, so let's leave it at that. I just want you to find out where he goes each day, who he meets, that sort of thing. Simple. I've put his home address on this." Removing a slip of paper from an inside blazer pocket, Gladys handed the information to Sauce.

"So this egghead is dangerous then. Perhaps the type that might slip a shiv into the chest of your manager."

"Oh there are hundreds of lowlifes in San Francisco he could hire for that kind of mischief. Just be sure to carry your thirty-two caliber Midnight Special and you'll be fine." Gladys smiled to indicate that the last comment was a joke. "He won't suspect you are working for me. In fact, that's why I wanted you, in particular, for this assignment. Say you happen to be sloppy, and he does notice you. He may hire someone to check on your credentials. What will he learn? That you're a two-bit gumshoe, who restricts his practice to the insurance industry, with a hit and miss success record. He was in a fender-bender last week, so he'll assume you are involved in that investigation. You see, he won't suspect our relationship."

"We don't have a relationship!" snapped Sauce, after finishing his drink.

"Call me tomorrow after my interview and let me know if you are interested."

"Interview?"

"Yes, you'll want to watch. I'm going to reveal all the gruesome details that led to my current condition on the Amber Ellis Show."

"So you can cash in on those millions of gullible Americans who will clamour to stadiums and theatres for your next magical mystery tour. What if, instead of investigating this professor, I decide to stop you from bilking the public with this idiocy? You did confess to the truth earlier, remember."

"I did nothing of the kind. I told you what you were thinking; none of that was the truth. Besides, who would believe your word over the beloved Good Gladys?"

"They'll believe when they hear it in your own voice." With a broad smirk on his face, Sauce placed his hand in his pocket to grab the digital recorder. His eyes widened, and the smirk changed to a puzzled frown as he searched one pocket after another. They were all empty.

Gladys answered his questioning glare by tossing the recorder back to Sauce. "I am not a fool.

You should probably remember that for future reference."

Sauce was furious at having had his pocket picked and at being speechless about it. He stormed out of the house and down the driveway.

CHAPTER 8

"Hangovers suck," thought Sauce, lying in bed with his eyes closed. "Good thing I don't have to work. One advantage to not having a client is the ability to sleep in, then lie next to the TV for the day after a bender." Every movement sent a wave of weakness through his extremities. His stomach gurgled as gastric bubbles threatened to force him out of bed. He tried to remain still and calm.

Scattered images from the previous night projected on the insides of the lids of his closed eyes. "How the hell did I get home?" he wondered as the continuity of the details felt broken and irretrievable to his memory. He had a vague recollection of walking after he left Gladys. "Oh, God! Why did I have to remember him?" The image of that man's smile, his glistening white teeth, the dark impressive two piece suit and tie … Sauce saw the image, then immediately lost it. "What colour was that tie?" he thought, forcing himself to focus on this detail to assuage the rising wave of nausea that accompanied the memory of his visit with Gladys.

He rolled onto his side and curled his legs toward his chest, which temporarily alleviated his urge to vomit. The mental images continued: his key in the keyhole, the door opening, and the kitchen light casting shadows through the living room reminded him of his return home a few hours earlier. Suddenly, he saw it again: his mother's face projected eerily on the canvas surface of the paisley shade of her lamp. The lamp was turned off, yet her face glowed. Death hadn't changed her one bit, he thought. Her lips were turned downward in her customary grimace. She had always looked displeased with him. Her eyes seemed tiny behind the enormous, fake, black eyelashes. Her hair, mostly grey with patches of faded black dye, rose from her forehead like a wave cresting near the shoreline, threatening to destroy the dreams of lazy sun worshippers lying too close to the water.

Remembering his mother was too much for Sauce. He jumped out of bed, ran into the bathroom, and sunk his head into the porcelain basin, retching and spewing out the acid and poison.

Exhausted, he collapsed onto the cold linoleum, curled his legs, and fell back asleep.

Waking a few hours later, he felt refreshed, though annoyed with himself. "Pace yourself, next time," he thought. He wandered sleepily toward the kitchen to put on the kettle, pausing to notice the chair propped on an angle against the front door. "Oh yeah, that," he mumbled. Not much of a deterrent he reasoned but at least if someone had come in, the chair falling over might have made enough noise to wake him. "Fat chance," he countered aloud, thinking about where he had been sleeping, without an inkling as to how he ended up lying in the bathroom.

He grabbed the chair so he could return it to the kitchen and was about to continue walking when, through the corner of his eye, he saw the lamp hanging in the corner. "I couldn't have been that drunk." He carried the chair across the living room to investigate. Standing on the chair, he looked first through the bottom of the lamp, then around the sides, and finally down the top. It appeared to be unadulterated and dusty as usual. "Okay, then, maybe I was that drunk.

"It all makes sense, in a way." He carried the chair as he talked to himself. "Dara is here to wreck my life again just as she did before, and excess alcohol brought back the guilt. The power of mental association, that's all it was. I was off in St. Martin when the accident happened, so it was my fault I didn't get to say goodbye. Mom wouldn't have cared if I was here or not. Well, she might have cared—people do crazy things when they're dying."

He put the kettle on, plopped two slices of bread into the toaster, sat at the kitchen table, and opened his laptop. "First things first," he mused, determined to be proactive. He looked up the number of a local alarm company. He hated the idea of spending money he didn't have on home security, but hated even more having people enter his home whenever they wanted. "Dara will get a shock the next time she tries to break in here." He made the call and, after insisting that this was an emergency, booked an appointment for the following day.

With his tea and toast prepared, he settled on doing some research to prepare him for his next move against the "forces of evil," a term he had just adopted for Gladys and Dara. He typed "Dr. Reginald Jett" into the search bar.

"Organic chem, tenured prof, over a hundred research papers, government environmental impact advisory panel, numerous successful grad students, boring in spades. This guy is a nobody!" His eyebrows raised, however, as he came across an image of the man taken several years back at a political campaign fundraiser. The photo was one of the "casual at the table" shots photographers like to take to give the appearance of spontaneity. Sauce didn't recognize any of the people at the table with the professor. Inadvertently included in the shot was Gladys, mouth open in conversation at the table behind the professor.

"So at least I know they have probably met each other." He pondered for a few moments on this weak association, then smiled as an idea took shape that would be sure to get Dara and Gladys off his back. "At the very least," he thought, "they will think twice about including me in any future plans."

He picked up his cell phone and dialed the number showing on his computer screen. He waited for the customary greeting, then said, "Yes. Hi. I was hoping you could connect me with Professor Jett." He waited again; one ring, two, then heard a female voice give a short mechanical plea. He waited for the tone, then responded, "Hi my name is Byrne Aase. I was hoping to schedule a meeting with you to discuss, uh, a matter that may interest you." He paused to contemplate the words that would be persuasive enough to garner a response, then thought, "Oh hell, might as well come out with it!"

"It concerns recent events involving Good Gladys." He slowly recited the digits of his phone number then disconnected the call, smiling.

Just over an hour later, he was driving his red convertible TR7 toward the university. During the thirty-minute trip he gradually increased the volume on the radio to drown out the rushing sound of the wind whistling past his face through the open top of the car. He rarely thought of his mother while driving, but this morning's events rekindled memories of riding in the passenger seat while his mom drove him to school as a child. She hated the car but felt forced to drive it after winning it in a lottery just after he was born. After graduating from high school, his mom agreed to sell it to him on installments—it took him about five years to pay it off. Though it was continuously breaking down and parts were overpriced, he loved the car, mostly because he knew his mom didn't.

His thoughts kept going over old wounds, especially the ones associated with the year after Dara had changed his life. He had come home expecting to salvage his law career. Learning that his mom had died in the hospital while he was in the Caribbean plummeted him into one vodka bottle after another. Guilt ridden, yet free in a way that few people would understand, he rarely left his home, neglected his bills to the point of spending an entire month without electricity, and indulged in the one activity he could manage, drinking.

His foot pressed harder on the accelerator with each mile he passed and each memory he unearthed. Finally reaching the entrance to the university, he breathed a sobering sigh of catharsis. "I'm not going there again," he thought. "Last night was a one-off, sparked by surprise at seeing Dara. Today I take my life back!"

Sauce had been in the shower when the phone rang. He wasn't anticipating such a fast reply to his message, and less than an hour had elapsed since he'd called Dr. Jett. He scurried to wrap a towel around his body and get to the phone while it was ringing, and succeeded. Dr. Jett had time that afternoon and would meet with him. Here he was racing through the winding lane that approached the chemistry building, ready to put an end to his recent troubles.

"Oh shit," exclaimed Sauce as the sound of a siren forced him to switch his right foot onto the brake pedal. He looked over his shoulder, positioning his car near the curb as he slowed down. A police motorcycle was closing the gap and slowing down to match speeds with the sports car.

A few minutes later, Sauce was looking at a pair of sunglasses reflecting the image of a guilty man handing over his license and registration. "Do you have any idea how fast you were going?" asked the officer.

"I've been meaning to have the gauges on the dash checked," Sauce began in a futile attempt to create plausible doubt. "Usually I just follow the flow of traffic—but no one else was on the road today so I may have followed the stupid speedometer instead. I guarantee I'll have it checked as soon as I get finished with my appointment."

"Appointment? So you are not a student?"

"No, officer," answered Sauce, wondering about the relevance of the question.

"We've recently had a string of thefts from the buildings in this area: computers and chemical supplies mostly. If you have no business on campus then you will understand that I will have to report you as a person of interest."

"I *have* business on campus," said Sauce. "Just check with Dr. Jett. He'll vouch for me. We have a meeting, in …." Sauce hesitated as he looked at his watch. He was arriving thirty minutes early, partly because he *had* been speeding. Weighing the risks of prosecution for one crime versus another, Sauce completed his sentence, "… oh! A half-hour. Damn you're right! I must have been speeding."

"Stay here," said the officer. Sauce wiped sweat from his brow and watched the officer through the rear-view mirror. After a short conversation on his radio, the officer returned. He handed Sauce his identification and concluded the incident saying, "I have a major accident to see to on the causeway, so consider this your lucky day. One person's fall, is another's windfall, as my dad always said. Make sure you get those gauges fixed."

"Will do officer." Without hesitation, Sauce released the clutch and accelerated towards his destination.

He followed the signs to visitors' parking, then the path leading to the organic chemistry buildings. Having extra time, however, he decided to delay entering, preferring to enjoy the warm sun and wander around the grounds. He was aimlessly thinking about the last couple of days, struggling for insight about the reasons for Dara coming to him for help. "Could she have missed me? I must have made some kind of impression for her to call me as soon as she got into trouble." Sauce was beginning to feel good about himself, briefly, a mental treat he indulged in so infrequently that it made his head dizzy in the same way ice cream eaten too quickly results in brain-freeze.

Tripping over the exposed root of an errant Lodgepole Pine, contumacious for having to grow miles from its comfort zone, Sauce fell to his knees with an acquiescent, "Ow!"

"You okay, mister!" asked a girlish-looking boy walking nearby.

"Damn." Sauce cursed at his own fatuity. He stood and brushed the dirt from his knees. Scanning the area around him, he realized he had been walking without due care and might actually be lost.

"Thanks," Sauce replied to the student. "D'you know the direction to the organic chem building?"

"Down that hill, around Stacks, that's what we call the library, and keep straight. Shouldn't take more than five minutes."

"Thanks again," concluded Sauce. The directions proved to be accurate, as Sauce was easily able to find his destination. Entering the pastel yellow, stucco-covered building, he felt a familiar coldness on his skin that he always experienced before an exam, smelled the putrid institutional cleanser that resembled the odour of boiled pig fat, the same recognizable smell of his mom's kitchen when she was preparing a rack of ribs to be barbequed, and heard the haunting scratches of long gone sticks of chalk marring blackboards. He enquired at the office about the professor's office and was advised to wait there while the unusually short receptionist with a tiny onyx-black Ankh-shaped nose ring and pink spiked hair could determine if the professor was available. "I have an appointment," Sauce offered, to which the receptionist replied, "Everyone says that!"

Patiently he waited, trying to appear casual as the clock on the wall advertised the movement of the sun across the sky. Ten minutes, then twenty more passed before Sauce called through the plexiglass framed office window, “Was he in his office?”

“Who?” came the terse reply.

“Professor Jett, remember? You told me to wait.”

“Oh yeah. I’m busy you know!” she offered as an excuse for her forgetfulness. “How about I call his office?”

“Or you could just tell me where it is and I’ll go check myself.”

“Oh, they don’t like that. No, I’m supposed to call first. You can’t break the rules.”

Sauce exhaled loudly to signal his annoyance and leaned against the wall to continue his wait. Within a minute, however, he was greeted by a young man at the end of the hall.

“You here for Jett?” called an cxuberant British voice.

“Yeah,” answered Sauce.

“Brilliant. This way then.”

Sauce ran to the end of the hall, rounded the corner and continued walking alongside his escort.

“How’s ’e to get ’is work done with you gov’ment types constantly about?” the young man asked in a tone that simultaneously denoted annoyance and superiority.

Sauce ignored the mistaken identity and changed the subject. "Are you one of his students?"

"His best student. Won't be long and I'll 'ave learned all I can from Jett and 'ave to move on."

Sauce scanned the pimply faced imp for signs of sarcasm but saw only raw, youthful, egotistical sincerity. He thought, "At no more than five foot six and maybe a hundred pounds, this kid is obviously compensating for years of being picked on at Eton." He resisted the compulsion to laugh and continued on in silence. They stopped at a grey metal door. The sign on the wall stated that this was the correct room: R. A. J. Dept. of C.

"Enter at your own risk, my boy!" said the pugnacious one, slapping Sauce brusquely across the back of his shoulder before continuing down the hall.

CHAPTER 9

He opened the door and walked into the small rectangular anteroom. Two metal chairs were positioned against one of the clean white walls. There was little room for anything else. Sauce knocked on the inside door, checked the handle, which was locked, then immediately knocked again. He could hear shuffling on the other side of the door, which raised his expectations and his heart rate. Then he was greeted by the call, "Be right with you." Sauce recognized the voice as the same one he'd spoken with on the phone earlier.

"No hurry," he replied. He was doing a good deed, a selfless, altruistic act. The imminence of the meeting boosted his self-pride and self-control. He could hold on a few more minutes. "Just wait until this guy hears what I have to tell him. He'll be stunned that I came all this way, with no expectation of reward. People just don't do that anymore."

The door opened. "Mr. Byrne, please forgive me, but I expected you much earlier, then got caught up in reorganizing my bookshelves while I waited." Pointing at the stacks of books aligned around the floor, he added, "I kind of painted myself into a corner, as the expression goes." He laughed genuinely at himself. Sauce joined in reservedly, knowing it is impolite to let someone laugh alone.

"That's the kind of thing I would do," said Sauce. "Ah, but Byrne is my first name. Aase is my last."

"I am so sorry," interrupted Jett. "Addle minded for all things not related to my field, I'm afraid."

Sauce smiled. "No offense taken. Call me Sauce; it's sort of a nickname."

"Oh, yes. Appropriate too. I get it," he answered. "Please come in and feel free to move the books from the chair." Sauce lifted the stack of books from the armchair next to the large oak desk and looked around the floor for a suitable spot to place them. "Allow me," said Jett, grabbing the books and adding them to a larger stack leaning against the wall.

The two men sat down just as the phone rang. While Jett answered a few chemistry related questions from the caller, obviously an anxious student unprepared for an upcoming exam, Sauce looked at book titles, listening to Jett's amiable telephone demeanor and arriving at conclusions about the professor.

"What could he have possibly done to piss off Gladys?" Sauce thought. "He's just a normal guy: mid-fifties, unimposing, friendly. Not the kind of person you'd see as a threat to an international superstar, con artist."

Jett hung up the phone, leaned back in his chair with his hands behind his head and blew air through pursed lips, loudly, like the spouting of a whale. "I'm sorry about the interruption, but we're now into my scheduled office hour, you know, for student questions about an upcoming test. We will most likely be repeatedly interrupted I'm afraid."

"No, I'm sorry I'm late. Well, I *was* early in fact. The receptionist at the front office forgot to tell you I was here and left me waiting in the hall."

Jett let out a little laugh. "So it's Edith's fault. That figures. I guess in a way it's my fault too since I argued for keeping her on. You see, since she's been working in the front office, my colleagues and I have been able to get a lot more work done." Sauce laughed at the joke, feeling an unexpected sense of camaraderie. "I hope you still have time for a meeting." Sauce nodded and was about to voice agreement but was interrupted as Jett continued. "I was intrigued by your call. I am frequently asked to consult on matters related to chemical structure or identification … never on matters to do with the occult, though."

"I'm afraid you are still out on that question. I am here about a personal matter. I assumed from your response to my query that you were familiar with Gladys."

"What a hoot? She does seem to keep her audience guessing, doesn't she? No, never a dry, dull moment with that one."

"I'm sorry," said a confused Sauce.

"The trial … the death in prison … I read all about it in the papers. What a brilliant mind she must have! I have to admit, I am just as intrigued as everyone else about how she contrived the whole thing. I have a few theories about how she did it. Like you, I too tried to figure out her methods—especially since receiving your call. I didn't want you to leave empty-handed."

"Empty-handed? I didn't come here for me." Sauce paused, hoping his tone was genuine enough. "I came to warn you."

"Really?" replied Jett, sitting up in his seat and leaning toward Sauce. "I assumed you were a reporter looking for an expert's opinion on how she might have caused a blood clot in that convict, or how she manipulated a DNA test."

"No, I'm not a reporter, and frankly, I really don't care how she got out of jail. People like her always find a way. I mean, she didn't actually get put in jail did she? People are talking like she was on trial and she killed a guard, forgetting the fact that in actuality it was just some guy claiming to be Gladys."

"Corroborated by her daughter, of course," added Jett.

"Precisely! Her daughter. She's the one that got me wrapped up in this mess. I'm actually a private investigator. I only do insurance stuff, as a matter of fact. Nevertheless, Gladys wanted to hire me to follow you."

"Me? What could I have possibly done to deserve such an honour?"

The sarcastic tone projected along with this question made Sauce smile. He started to laugh as he answered, "There was some mention of you having threatened her daughter."

"Threatened to do what?" Jett asked, obviously taking the whole situation as a humourous joke. "I didn't even know she *had* a daughter, prior to the recent publicity."

"She may have only said that to coerce my complicity."

"Ah, I see. Playing on your infatuation with the young girl. Sex sells. Gladys knows that as much as anyone."

"Well now you know why I asked for the meeting. I wasn't going to play her game, regardless of what that game actually is."

"Smart. I should expect nothing less from an investigator hand-picked by Good Gladys." He gave a soft laugh, then paused and grimaced for just a second before resuming his pleasant smile. "I am indebted to you for letting me in on the ruse. Of course I have no idea what she is up to."

The phone rang and Jett hastily picked it up and started talking. "Yes … Of course, go ahead … Yes, yes, I know the question … No, not like that. Remember the week five lab on pyrimedines … Similar, yes, but not exactly."

Sauce listened to the conversation thinking, "Why couldn't I have had teachers like him in school? A teacher who genuinely wants his students to do well. Perhaps that's why Gladys is interested in him. Nice guys finish last when con artists target them."

"You should take another look at the example on page, oh just give me a second to confirm the page." Jett pointed down at the floor next to Sauce's feet, where a textbook was lying. Sauce took the cue, picked up the book, and handed it to Jett. "Ah, here, page five hundred and thirty. Work through that example. I'm sure that will help. No problem." He hung up the phone and apologized again for the interruption.

"So where were we? Oh yes, we were trying to explain why Gladys is interested in me." He waved his arm in a semicircle. "As you can see from my humble belongings, I'm not wealthy. Perhaps she wants to frame me for her next crime. I'm sure I'll have to be on my guard for anything. Her creativity is unmatched, isn't it? I mean who would have thought to frame an innocent man for a murder you committed, convince that man to present himself as you, a woman, then manage to get everyone in a tizzy to the point of having the whole thing thrown out of court?"

"So you think Gladys really killed her manager?" asked Sauce.

"Given that her profession is entirely built on manipulation, deception, and immorality, I wouldn't doubt that she is capable of orchestrating this whole sordid business, including the murder, to reap the rewards from the publicity." As Sauce's agreeable expression transformed to a doubtful, questioning gaze, Jett's demeanor projected mild concern, rather than amusement. "If you disagree, then tell me, Mr. Investigator, what's your theory?"

Sauce looked sheepishly at the professor and admitted, "I don't have a theory. In fact, I don't even care what she's up to as long as Gladys and Dara leave me alone."

"Do you think that is likely, given the circumstances? First, let's consider the fact that you have been asked to work for them. You seem to know these people better than me; are they likely to give in, just because you said no?"

"Actually, I've probably known them just as long as you have, but no, it is unlikely, I guess."

"Do you need to guess? Think about it. They are masters of manipulation. Why else would thousands of people willingly hand over their life savings to them? In your past dealings with Gladys and her daughter, have they ever convinced you to do something after you told them you wouldn't?"

"Yeah, well, if you put it that way, then I would have to say yes, repeatedly."

Jett smiled broadly and shrugged his shoulders. "The best predictor of future behaviour is past behaviour, I'm afraid."

"Damn, you're right." His head hung low as he realized how many times Dara had already beaten him over the past couple of days. He raised his head. "I did come here, though. That kind of breaks the cycle, doesn't it?"

Jett looked worried. "I'm not so sure. You seem to be quite intelligent, but Gladys has years of experience at getting rich, intelligent people, like yourself, to acquiesce to her demands."

"I'm not rich," interjected Sauce. He was also thinking he may not be especially intelligent either, but kept that to himself.

"So, perhaps she is only interested in your body," joked Jett, alleviating some of the tension Sauce was feeling. "Seriously though, she appears to have a role for both of us in her next circus act. You may be okay with that, but then you have been associated with these people for a lot longer than me, haven't you?"

"Like I already said, not really. A few years ago Dara and I hooked up for a few weeks. It was just a spontaneous getaway. Then it was over. We were both young, impetuous …"

"How were you introduced? I mean, was it at a party, through a friend?"

"No. It was on the street, outside the courthouse, while I was working on my law degree."

"You just walked up to her and hooked up, or was it more the other way around?"

"Shit! You're right! It was the other way around." Sauce scoffed, remembering what she'd said when she mentioned their first meeting the other day. *When I took you home.*

"Did you take her home to meet your parents?," asked Jett, coincidentally. "Court her in any of the traditional ways? Do any of the things that men typically do to manipulate the affections of a girl? You know, did you buy her gifts, or take her out for dinner?"

"No, she didn't meet my family, and Dara paid for everything we did. She's rich."

"Did you know that from the beginning? Did you know who she was, who her mother was?"

"She told me. Yeah I knew she was rich. You probably think I'm some kind of heel! Truth is, I probably was. I thought I loved her, at the time, well, in a way, but you may be right. I may have been deceiving myself all along. Perhaps it was just her money that attracted me."

"She is an attractive girl, too, I assume. It could have been mostly lust on your part. On hers, however, well there's no other way to put it; you were played." Jett smiled. "I don't know anything about your history, but I assume your life changed direction somewhere down the line and you abandoned law school. Your current profession, shall we say found you, rather than was chosen by you?"

"You could say that. It certainly sounds better than the truth when you put it that way."

"I'm afraid I had you all wrong, then. Please don't take this the wrong way, but I don't think they picked you because of your intelligence."

Sauce looked surprised for a second, but tears of self-incrimination projected his acceptance of the verdict. Jett continued, "They wanted a lawyer in their back pocket, and chose you years ago. Probably figured you would return from that adventure and resume law school, indebted to them for the brief reprieve from your studies. I think you should take pride in the fact that you already messed up one of their plans by abandoning law."

"Small victory, it seems."

"Quite! It seems they aren't finished with you. The last thing you should do at this point is assume to be a step ahead of them in anything you choose. We can't be sure, but even your decision to come here may fit with their plans. It's like in chess: you can never predict your opponent's next move so you plan for multiple contingencies."

"And you think there will definitely be a 'next move' in the cards for me. I'm such an idiot!"

"Now, now, don't get down on yourself. Gladys has been using people for years. Greater men than you have been duped by this woman. Look, I told you before that I was intrigued by you, and I still am. Let me help you, advise you. Together we might be able to beat them. You have to be clear-headed if you are going to get out of this with the shirt still on your back."

Sauce jumped from his chair to shake Jett's hand, then hesitated as a troubling realization captured his thoughts. "Aren't they getting what they asked for yet again? They wanted me to follow you, and in a sense …"

"Ah, but you won't be reporting back to them, now will you?"

Sauce thought about his conversation with Gladys, and as far as he could recall, there was no mention of filing reports; they just wanted him to follow Dr. Jett and learn about him.

Jett stood and rounded the desk walking toward Sauce, who politely stood to meet him. "I may know just the way to upset their apple-cart. It's time you started calling the shots. Take control. They've been pursuing you. Turn it around. Pursue them, or at least the daughter. Take her out, buy her dinner, and just when she thinks you're hers, over dessert perhaps, tell her you and I have joined forces against them."

"I see. Take control so she suspects she has won my allegiance, then shock her with the truth. It may not work, but it does sound like fun for a change. I can't wait to see the look on her face."

"Make sure it happens in a public place. Don't take any unnecessary chances. Besides, the shock may get her to say something embarrassing or incriminating and you'll want witnesses."

Sauce sensed that the meeting was at an end and was about to say goodbye.

"Ah, before you go, one other thing is kind of nagging at me," said Jett. "What did you mean earlier when you said I had known Gladys as long as you?"

"Oh, that was nothing. I just meant that like me, you had met Gladys in the past."

"Whatever gave you that idea? Did she insinuate a previous relationship between us?"

"No, no. I looked on the internet. I had to learn more about you after my meeting with Gladys, you understand. You and Gladys are in a picture together. Not necessarily together, but at least in the same picture. She's more a part of the background. I just figured you two were at the same party and were bound to have met. That's all."

"No, you are mistaken. If Gladys and I happened to attend the same party—and we can't be sure the image wasn't doctored to give that impression—we certainly didn't meet."

"I guess I jumped to the wrong conclusion then," suggested Sauce.

"In the interest of full disclosure, and because I'm sure your investigations will uncover this little detail eventually, if they haven't all ready, I should probably admit that I did attend one of her performances. When was it? Must have been about two or three months ago, just before the papers reported her missing, I believe. Now that's an interesting coincidence, don't you think?"

"You actually paid to see her?" Sauce wasn't sure what to make of this confession.

"Of course not! I didn't even *want* to see her. It was my research assistant, Derek who forced me to go. Kind of a head-strong kid—actually he's twenty-two, but that's not the point, now is it? You met him earlier; I told him to fetch you from the office when you, um, arrived."

"Yeah, I thought he seemed quite ambitious. Hardly the kind I'd expect to believe in psychics."

Jett smiled in agreement. "You're right there. He thought the whole thing was a bunch of non-sense. But his father, Hughbert Mackie, Chairman at Mosley's Bank in London, is a huge fan of Gladys's. He spends a fortune on tickets that he donates to charities wherever Gladys performs. He totally believes in the stuff, insisted his son attend Gladys's Los Angeles performance to judge for himself. Have you ever seen one of her shows?"

"No," said Sauce abruptly. "Oh shit!" The discussion of Gladys performing reminded him of something Gladys had said the previous evening. "I was supposed to set the PVR to record her today. Gladys told me she was going to be interviewed on television, but I forgot all about it until now."

Jett laughed. "Just more smoke and mirrors Sauce. That's all. You really shouldn't believe anything she says. I heard the DJs on the radio talking about that this morning on my way to the university. But it's not today; it's next week. If you had remembered you would have spent a long time searching for the correct channel. She really seems to be sending you on a wild goose chase. First telling you to follow me; then telling you she would be on TV."

"You're right, of course."

"That's why you have to act first. Get Dara alone, give her the shock of her life, and then she'll know you are not going to take any more nonsense."

"Thanks, Dr. Jett. That's advice I am sure to follow."

"Oh, please. It's not like I'm a *real* doctor," he said with a chuckle. "All the students call me Jett. You're not the only one with a nickname." He scribbled some numbers on a notepad, ripped off the page, and handed it to Sauce. "That's my cell; let me know how it goes."

CHAPTER 10

Sauce arrived home with a renewed sense of independence. "Gladys really did me a favour by telling me about Jett," he thought. He walked to the kitchen, looked into the refrigerator, and frowned at the limited possibilities for a meal. Having no desire to go out again, he settled on a box of soda crackers and a large tumbler of vodka. "A balanced meal," he joked to himself. He filled the glass, guzzled his drink, and poured another before returning the bottle to the freezer.

He returned to the living room, set his feast on the coffee table, and removed the digital recorder from his jacket pocket. He hit play and relaxed listening to his conversation with Jett, eating his crackers.

"Everything he said made sense," Sauce thought after the recording had finished. "Talk about contrast: nothing involving Dara or her mother made sense!" Despite what Jett had proposed Sauce thought he would prefer not to have anything more to do with them. Sauce sipped his vodka, put on the TV and found a baseball game to focus on. He returned to the kitchen a few times to refill his glass, enjoying his escape from reality. Before the game was over, he was sleeping soundly on the sofa.

The pounding on the door startled Sauce onto his feet, knocking the coffee table and spilling his half-empty drink onto the carpet. He was disoriented by the brightness in the room. Blinding sunlight shone through the gaps in the living room curtains. The kitchen looked like it was glowing hot, radiating a feeling of urgency for the dawn of a new day. Sauce looked at the time on his cell phone. He had slept on the couch the whole night.

He stumbled to the door. Looking through the peephole he could see the *SFAlarm* insignia on the van out front. "Oh shit!" he exclaimed after opening the door. "I forgot you were coming."

"Hello sir. Reception flagged this service call as an emergency. I could return another time, though, if now is inconvenient."

"No! No, I was just a little caught off guard. Come in, and let's get this started."

He led the technician into the living room, turned off the television, which was still on from the previous night, and offered him a seat.

"No thanks. I have another house to do today. If you would just show me all the points of entry, I'll prepare an estimate for the installation. If all you want is a basic system, alarm pad, two doors and the windows, then I should be finished in a couple of hours."

Sauce quickly gave the tour. As the technician was about to exit the front door to obtain the material he turned to Sauce and asked, "So why the emergency install? This is a pretty secure neighbourhood, and your doors and windows already have top quality hardware, in really good shape."

"My house was broken into already this week," snapped Sauce, "and I want to put a stop to it, okay?"

"What were they after, if you don't mind me asking?" asked the tech.

Sauce did not feel like discussing the situation, so he abruptly changed the subject. "You said these locks are good quality? Are you suggesting only people with poor locks need an alarm to stop break-ins?"

"The fact is no security will stop a determined thief. Locks and alarms are primarily a deterrent. Your locks, for example, are good enough to keep a large percentage of criminals out. A break-in, you say … and no scratches on the lock, no marks on the door … I'd say you have a top notch thief interested in you. Only a really good thief would be able to pick this lock without leaving a trace. The alarm won't keep someone like that out of your house, but it will alert the police once they open the door. I could also install a few motion detectors, but the result would be the same. So depending on the response time of local police, once your expert criminal enters, they would only have a narrow window to conduct a search for your valuables and get out. I figure anyone with the skill to pull off the crime would also correctly assess that the risk to reward ratio was too high. In any case, you'll know if anyone got in and out of your home without permission."

"They're not going to give up," said Sauce softly.

"If you got problems that big, man, you should be callin' the cops."

"I don't think they'll help. I have to make a phone call, excuse me." He walked to the bedroom, pulled out his phone, and selected Dara's number from the received calls folder. "Master criminals," he thought. "Probably murderers and who knows what else. Jett's right. They won't stop, so I have to get myself out of this mess."

"Sauce, how unexpected!" came Dara's musical greeting.

"Dara, I've been thinking about your mother's predicament. I think it's about time we got together to talk. You know, for real this time. No games, just you and me. How about over dinner, tonight?"

"Are you asking me on a date? How sweet!"

"Sure, how about I pick you up at about seven? We can go to Salvador's where it's nice and quiet."

"That sounds nice, but not Salvador's. Media has better food and is more intimate."

"And has a six-month waiting list," countered Sauce annoyed that even picking a restaurant results in a disagreement.

"Tell the lady at the desk my name as you book the reservation and you'll have no problem. Oh, and I'll meet you there, okay? See you at seven."

Sauce threw the phone onto his bed in anger. He turned around to see the technician in the doorway.

"Problem with the misses?" he asked.

"More like a near miss. Ever been in a relationship with someone who was so much your opposite you still regret it years later? Then no matter how many times you say you're not interested she still tries to weasel her way back into your life?"

"A real fatal attraction kind of girl," he answered. "Yeah, I know the type. Don't worry, though. With this alarm she won't get in unannounced again."

Sauce realized he divulged more information than he had wanted to this stranger. He looked at him and asked, "Did you have a question?"

"Oh, uh, yeah. On which wall did you want me to place the keypad?"

At seven-twenty that evening Sauce was impatiently waiting for Dara to arrive. He passed the time going over his plan for the evening and scanning the menu. "Look at these prices," he thought nervously. "Not one appy is less than thirty dollars! It'll take me months to get this meal off my credit card. That's the price I have to pay to get Dara and Gladys off my back, I guess. She won't see it coming. We'll talk and eat, and she'll think I am one hundred percent onboard with her mother's plan. Then after dessert, I'll tell her about my meeting with Jett, and she'll have to admit their plan for me failed. I'll finally have the upper hand."

"Upper hand?" came a voice from behind him. "What are you on about?"

Sauce turned his head and Dara was right behind him, looking gorgeous in a shimmering designer black gown. "Damn," thought Sauce, silently to himself this time as his heartbeat began to race.

"How many of those have you had?" She pointed at the empty martini glasses on the table. He had ordered a martini for each of them when he first sat down and didn't even notice he had already finished them both—and he always thought aloud once alcohol hit his system.

"You're late," he answered loudly.

"You're drunk," she shot back quietly in his ear.

"I only had the two, if you really want to know. I thought you weren't coming."

"And miss you making an ass of yourself, all alone talking to ghosts. Or perhaps you're going to tell me you've acquired my mother's gift?" She smiled at her joke and sat down.

"Can we leave your mom out of the conversation please?" suggested Sauce. "How about we make this dinner just about you and me, for once?"

"It's a lovely restaurant, don't you think?" said Dara, abruptly shifting the conversation.

Sauce looked around briefly. "I hadn't really noticed. Yeah, it's all right, I guess. Could be a bit brighter, though. Do they have to keep it so dark?"

"It's supposed to be romantic. See all the other tables? Couples. No families or whiny kids. If we went to Salvador's, like you wanted, we'd be competing with dozens of screaming brats to hear each other."

"I wonder how many of these couples would appreciate that after they had to wait months to get in, we got an express pass based on your mother's name."

"Well I see one couple that wouldn't care. See that man over by the fireplace? I'm sure he used an express pass, too. That's Mr. Mackie, the chairman of Mosley's Bank, and his wife. He probably just flew in from England. I'm sure he didn't need a reservation."

"That's Mr. Mackie? Do you know him?"

"Of course, silly. But in a place like this, it's inappropriate for me to walk up to their table and say hello. Why, you don't know him, do you?"

"I met his son." Sauce regretted this admission as soon as the words left his mouth.

"That foul-mouthed, conceited ingrate? Where did you meet him?"

Sauce felt his face go red. He rested his elbows on the table and folded his hands in front of his mouth to ensure his thoughts didn't inadvertently escape. "Damn, Sauce! What now?" he thought. He tried to think of a suitable excuse that might salvage his plan, but nothing came to mind, so he decided to skip dinner and dessert and proceed directly to the main course. "At the university, yesterday."

"So you decided to listen to Mummy. That's great! I hope you were discreet with your enquiries."

"You mean you hope I didn't mess things up for you and your mom. Well guess what? I bet I obliterated your plans. That's what I did."

"Shh! Not so loud." Dara looked at the people around them turning their heads. "What are you trying to say? *Quietly* this time."

"I met with Dr. Jett—well, Jett as he prefers to be called. That's right," said Sauce, "I spoke with him, told him the whole story about the guy impersonating Gladys wanting me to *investigate* him. I'm not quite the fool you thought, now am I?"

"No, Sauce, you didn't!" Dara sounded sympathetic. "You really are a mess! If you really saw him, then tell me, what does he look like?"

"How dare you call me a mess? You and your mom breaking into my house, murdering her manager then framing someone else for it—who's the real mess around here? I saw him. He's in his early fifties, soft and round with grey hair jutting out around the ears. At least now you won't be able to blindside Jett. He's nice and smart and will see you guys coming a mile away."

"Real funny, Sauce." She grimaced her disapproval.

"I'm not kidding! I met with him."

"That's not what I meant. I was talking about your sick joke about him seeing me coming. First you say he's a nice guy, then you joke about his visual impairment?"

"He's not blind. I spoke with him. He read from a textbook, for Christ's sake."

"I said visually impaired, can't see farther than a few inches without those hideous spectacles that look like binoculars."

"I tell you he's not blind."

"Of course not. *You* are! My God, Sauce. What happened to you? You used to be so perceptive and funny … and nice."

"You happened to me, remember? Don't turn this around. Jett knows all about your interest in him. Whatever you had planned for him won't work anymore. That's one less victim, one less notch on your belt."

Dara stood up and pushed her chair toward the table. "I guess that's all there is to say, then," she said, adding, "I feel so sorry for you."

Sauce watched her leave the restaurant, then flagged a waiter over and asked him to bring the bill and another double martini.

"That's the best she could do?" he thought. "Feel *sorry* for me? Sorry that they thought they'd get the best of me. That's all she feels." He paid the bill and asked the maître d' to call him a cab. He figured after the drinks he better just return in the morning to fetch his car. On the way home he asked the cabbie to stop at a liquor store.

He entered his home, reset the alarm and sat down on the sofa with his bottle. "I'm already half buzzed, might as well go all the way," he said to himself. "Farewell to you, Gladys." He took a long swig from the bottle. "And good riddance to you Dara!" he added as he guzzled some more.

CHAPTER 11

Mornings were often the most challenging part of Sauce's day. This particular morning was especially hard as Sauce resisted the urge to open his eyes. He had tossed and turned all night, alternating between hating Dara and wishing her dead, and loving Dara and wanting her in bed. He woke up many times feeling sick from the alcohol and miserable about the way he'd talked to Dara in the restaurant. He would then drift back to sleep, only to be awakened again, by unsettling dreams.

Lying awake, feeling the bright sunlight hitting his closed eyelids, he recalled one of the strangest dreams from earlier that morning. "Odd," he mused, providing his own running commentary to his multilayered thought process. "I don't usually remember my dreams in such vivid detail." It was more of a dream within a dream. At first he was at the university participating in an experiment. He thought he had volunteered but the Mackie kid was there saying, "I caught him, so I get the brains." Jett was there too and he answered, "I was hoping you'd say that since there's barely enough to feed a baby in this guy's head." They began carving him up, tossing bits and pieces playfully at Edith as she typed on her keyboard without noticing as an arm and then a foot hit her in the head.

The dream suddenly shifted. Sauce thought he had woken up and was lying in his bed, naked, covered by just a crisp, clean white sheet—that's how he became aware that it was still a dream. The sheets on his bed were lime green, certainly not crisp and, regrettably, in need of laundering. Turning his head, he saw he was not alone. A woman was lying on her side next to him. Only the top of her forehead and her thick blonde hair, resting on a pillow, were visible. He reached over and tapped her shoulder. She looked up at him and answered, "Not again. I have to get some sleep before morning." Then she closed her eyes. It was Dara. To make sure, Sauce lifted the sheet. It certainly was Dara, naked and in his bed.

These dreams seemed so real, so vivid in detail. He recalled another where he and Dara were arguing in the living room. And another where they were together in the shower, and then in bed making love. The erotic images cascading through his mind raised his blood pressure and began to arouse him, which had the painful side-effect of increasing his nausea. He turned over, buried his head in the pillow to block out the light, and moaned loudly.

"Stop feeling sorry for yourself. It's almost two in the afternoon. It's about time you got up. We have things to do."

Sauce raised himself onto his elbows and looked back towards the foot of the bed. Dara was standing with her hands on her hips, dressed in a pale blue skirt and white, short-sleeved blouse. "Get out," he said as loudly as he could, which, given his hangover, was barely above a whisper. Looking down he noticed the sheet was white.

"That's not what you said earlier," she replied with a half-smile and a flick of her hair. "Okay, so you did say that when I first arrived, but after you calmed down you seemed to enjoy having me … around." She laughed and walked out of the bedroom. "Have a shower and get dressed; breakfast will be ready in about fifteen minutes," she yelled.

Sauce rolled out of bed and landed with a thud on the floor. Perspiration poured over his face, partly from the shock of seeing Dara and realizing that his previous recollections had not been dreams, and partly from the rising nausea of his hangover. He looked up and, seeing his pants and jacket from the previous night hanging on the chair next to the bed, knew what he had to do. He crawled across the room, reached into his jacket pocket, and pulled out the paper Jett had handed to him two days ago. He scurried to the dresser, grabbed his cell phone and quickly tip-toed into the bathroom. He closed the door, turned on the shower to provide some background noise, then sat on the floor next to the toilet and dialed the number.

"Sauce, I'm so glad you called," answered the cheery voice on the other end. "How did it go last night?"

"She's here!" he answered in a breathless, exasperated, though hushed, voice. "She's been here all night!"

"You dirty devil! I didn't know you had it in you. Have you told her yet? I can just imagine how much more effective the shock was after a night of lovin' and squeezin' for her to hear that you betrayed her confidence by coming to see me. Sauce, I admit, your plan was much better than mine!"

"No, you don't understand. I did tell her last night, at the restaurant like we planned. And she stormed off just like you said she would."

"I don't follow," said Jett. "You're not making sense. Either she stormed off or she didn't."

"That's what I'm saying," answered Sauce. "She did, but now she's here, and apparently she's been here most of the night."

"Apparently? You mean you aren't sure?"

"Yeah, that's what I mean. Look, after she left I may have had a few drinks. Well, more than a few. So this morning she's here and I'm not sure, but I think we slept together; you know, *slept together*."

"You're not sure if you had sex or not? Sauce I may not be the first one to point this out but you have to face the facts. If you can't remember having sex, then you might have a drinking problem."

"You think?" snapped Sauce.

"This is no time for sarcasm. They've already committed murder! Then yesterday you came to my office to tell me they have their sights set on me next. The more I thought about it last night, the more I worried about what they plan to do to me. Yet you, the only other person who knows about this, got plastered and spent the night with one of them. What's your game, Sauce? Are you trying to get me killed?"

"No, no, of course not. I just slipped up. That's all."

"You just slipped up? With my life at stake? And what is that annoying noise in the background?"

"The shower," Sauce whispered. "I didn't want her to hear me making this call."

"You're hiding in the bathroom?" yelled Jett. "Sauce, you're not thinking. She had all night, while you were lost in a drunken stupor, to search your house and your clothes. She must have found my cell number. They're probably accessing my phone records as we speak. They'll know you called me!"

"You think they can do that?" mumbled Sauce.

"You're the private investigator! Don't you guys all have insiders at the phone companies who'll provide that kind of info?"

"Well, no," said Sauce, embarrassed that he wasn't that efficient in his occupation. "But you're right. It probably isn't that hard."

"Now, listen carefully," said Jett in a determined, authoritative tone. "We can still salvage this. We can't keep talking, so I'll only say this once and you'd better get it right. Quickly finish up in the bathroom, then go straight to her and confess that you called me. Tell her I was belligerent, furious that you told her about our meeting in my office. Say I accused you of betraying our confidence. Make some excuse about me lying to you or threatening you or something. Convince her that you don't trust me."

"I know, I could say something along the lines of you having lied to me about being blind. She brought that up last night and I didn't believe her. You're not, are you?"

"She's good. You see what I mean about them having me in their sights. Yes, I am virtually blind. I don't advertise it though, which is why it didn't come up during our conversation."

"But I saw you read from a textbook."

"Braille, of course. All of my textbooks are in Braille. You would have noticed that if we hadn't been distracted by so many interruptions from my students. The fact that Gladys knows about my impairment confirms she's been watching me for some time. You're my only hope! Don't fail me now, Sauce. Hurry and get cleaned up, and take command of this situation. You have to figure out a way to stay close to Gladys's daughter so you can warn me if she's about to strike. Follow her around, and don't let her out of your sights. Also, don't call me again! I'll get in touch with you soon to find out where we stand. And above all else, keep a clear head. You hear me! Stay off the sauce, Sauce. Goodbye!"

Sauce placed the phone on the counter next to the sink and stepped into the shower. The water just started to soak his hair when he heard the creak of the bathroom door opening. He poked his head around the curtain. There stood Dara, an apron tied around her waist and a spatula in hand.

"Are you trying to drown, or did you simply fall back asleep?" she asked.

"I'm almost done."

"Well be quick about it. Your breakfast is getting cold."

Sauce quickly lathered shampoo in his hair, covered himself with soap, and rinsed off. He hopped out of the shower, taking care to ensure Dara was out of sight, toweled off, and stepped gingerly into the bedroom. He was relieved to see he was alone. He opened the top dresser drawer, to get underwear and socks, and gasped. His clothes were gone. In the drawer was an assortment of neatly folded panties and bras of various styles and colours, and packages of nylons. He slammed the drawer shut and opened the next one: blouses. He finally found his own clothes in the third and last drawer.

He grabbed what he needed and moved to the closet to get pants and a shirt. He slid the glass closet door open to find a colour coordinated collection of dresses, skirts, and blouses on the right side, and a drastically reduced selection of his own clothes on the left. Incensed and confused, he hurriedly dressed. Before confronting Dara, he searched the bedroom for the one tool he felt he absolutely must have in his pocket to defend himself. Unable to find it in the bedroom, or the bathroom, he poked his head around the bedroom door, and seeing that Dara was occupied in the kitchen with her back to him, he sneaked into the living room. He was in the process of searching between the cushions of the couch when Dara called out from the kitchen, "You won't find it there!"

"Uh, what do you mean?" he answered, trying to sound innocent.

Dara walked into the living room. "Your memory helper, the recorder. I threw it out."

"Why would you do that? It was mine. You had no right."

"It was holding you back, so yes I did have a right," she answered. "Forget about it. Come sit down and have breakfast." She turned and walked back into the kitchen.

"Wait a minute!" He followed her into the kitchen. He was about to curse but was caught off-guard by the odours of baked bread, fried eggs and coffee. He stumbled toward the table and sat heavily, feeling ill and weak.

"See what you've done to yourself," she admonished. "Normal people would be salivating with pleasure at the feast I've prepared. Drunks, like yourself, just feel sick from the smell. Sauce, I meant it last night when I said you are a mess."

Sauce rubbed his temples, trying to gain control over his senses. He tried to shift the conversation. "Where are my clothes?"

"I needed room for my things. Your closet is pretty small, you know. Besides, I only threw out the worst of the lot, though all of your clothes went out of style years ago. Don't worry, we're going shopping after breakfast to fix that."

"What the hell are you talking about?" Sauce looked up at her in bewilderment.

Dara placed a glass of pink liquid in front of Sauce and handed him a couple of pills. "These will help with the hangover."

"What's this crap?" He pointed at the glass.

"Just fruit, blended with some vitamin supplements and milk. Drink it, and I'll bring you a cup of coffee."

Sauce didn't know which of the many questions racing through his muddled mind he should ask first. He sat in silence and downed the pills and the smoothie. Finally he settled on asking, "Why are you here?"

Dara delayed answering. She finished assembling his plate of toast, eggs and ham and served him. She then picked up two cups of coffee, put them on the table, and took a seat next to Sauce.

"Eat and I'll explain."

Dara waited for Sauce to pick up his fork and begin to eat. "It's not your fault. I realized last night that I am partly to blame."

He looked in her eyes, expecting signs of deceit and sarcasm, but saw only empathy and warmth.

"When I first called you last week, I expected the same happy, clever, and honest Sauce I met three years ago. I had no idea then what you had done to yourself."

"I've changed. What a shocker? People do that in three years."

"No, you haven't. Not really. You just stumbled. Partly because of me, partly because of your mom dying, and the timing, of course. But people die all the time, and people go in and out of relationships all the time, without becoming zombies, like you have, in the process."

"So that's how you see me now? A zombie?"

"Call it whatever you want. I know what I saw when I entered your living room last night. You were passed out, still holding a half-empty Mickey in your hand, with drool running down your chin." She paused and took a sip of her coffee.

Sauce started to feel energized by the food and medicine and attacked, "You seduced me!"

"I comforted you, cleaned you up, and put you to bed."

"You had no right! You moved in for Christ's sake."

"I had every right. You weren't like this before you met me. You were motivated, clear headed and the most honest, kindest person I had ever met. Those weeks we spent together were the best days of my life."

"Yeah right. That's not how I remember it."

"What do you remember?" She stared into his bloodshot eyes. "Oh, right. You can't remember anything. Isn't that why you started carrying around that stupid recorder? It's just one of your crutches. A digital crutch to compensate for your vodka crutch. Think about it, Sauce. Was I the first person you fell in love with? The first person you thought you wanted to share your life with? I get it. You were hurt when I broke it off."

"Don't flatter yourself," he mumbled through a mouthful of food.

"Mummy taught me that the best way to say you're sorry is to fix the wrong you've caused."

"Yeah, your *mommy* was a great role model," he interjected.

"Perhaps not, but here we are, and I'm fixing this problem. Don't look at me like that. You'll enjoy having me around."

Sauce was about to put his coffee cup to his lips but stopped to contemplate Dara's statement. "You're staying?"

"By your side, until you are back to your old self."

"I've changed."

"Superficially, yes. The old Sauce is still there. Why do you think you kept agreeing to do what I asked of you? You said you wouldn't come to the courtroom, but you did. You complained about seeing Mummy, yet you still went to her house. You're still you, despite the damage brought on by a few years of drinking and self-loathing."

"And if I ask you to gather your things and leave?"

"Yeah, right." She laughed, picking up the dishes and carrying them to the sink. She abruptly changed the subject. "As I said earlier, we have a big day ahead of us and it's already two-thirty. You haven't even shaved yet, or do you need me to do that for you too? Go on, get ready and we'll go shopping."

Sauce stood up, but then he remembered his phone call in the bathroom and sat back down. He pondered for a few seconds about how to broach the subject. "Why did you run out of the restaurant last night if you are so intent on saving me?"

Dara walked over to Sauce and stood behind him, rubbing her hands through his hair. "You didn't mean any harm. You were just confused. I was hurt that you contacted Dr. Jett, but after thinking about it, I realized it made sense. You were just trying to reach out to someone for support. So, now you have me."

"I called him, this morning, before my shower."

Dara slowly took a seat at the table. "You told him about last night? What did he say?"

"He was furious." Sauce, matched Dara's sympathetic tone, trying to sound genuine. "He … he was different than when I met him in his office. I asked him about his visual impairment, and he accused me of calling him a liar. He even threatened me. He said I betrayed his confidence by telling you about our meeting. He told me I'd better watch my back. I'm starting to think Gladys might be right about him being dangerous."

"He is, believe me," answered Dara. "I was really worried when you said you talked to him. You have no idea what he is capable of doing. You were never supposed to become one of his targets. That's why Gladys wanted you to just watch him, from a distance. You were an innocent, someone he wouldn't suspect. Now that he knows about you … Well. let's not dwell on that right now. You'll have a clearer idea of what kind of man he is after today.

First though, get cleaned up and we'll buy you some decent clothes."

CHAPTER 12

"Dara sure knows how to use a clutch," thought Sauce. He was impressed at her skill behind the wheel of the powerful Porsche Carrera, smoothly weaving around slower traffic, easing into a turn, barely touching the brakes, then accelerating through the bend. Sauce noticed that for the first time in many years he wasn't feeling any of the symptoms of car sickness he usually felt as a passenger. Dara was in control, and he didn't mind.

He tried to ask where they were going but the exchange that ensued—Dara asking "What?" then Sauce repeating himself—proved futile. He decided to sit back, watch the scenery, and wait. Sauce realized his initial assumption about shopping in San Francisco was wrong when they passed Candle Stick

Park, then the airport, and continued out of the city. It was only after passing through San Mateo that Sauce correctly surmised that Dara was heading for the posh shops clustered in the richest part of the state, the software "Mecca" of America, San Jose.

"Jett would never guess my luck," he thought. "He needed me to stay close to Dara, and here I am riding in her car going shopping, probably so she won't be embarrassed by my wardrobe when we're together. She thinks she has me whipped. Perhaps later when I get home, I'll give her a little scare by taking a walk in the neighbourhood. I could spend a couple of hours in the pub, just long enough to make her frantic. She might even decide I'm a lost cause and move out of my house. I would just have to start following her to keep Jett happy—though given how she drives, I might have to figure out how to plant a LoJack in one of her wheel wells."

Dara pulled into a private underground parking garage and parked in a spot marked 'reserved'. "I called ahead to make sure Francis was available to help us," she remarked as they walked up a dark staircase to the street level stores.

Sauce followed, noting that Dara's confident stride suggested a strong familiarity with the surroundings. "Typical woman," Sauce commented, "as long as you're shopping you're in your comfort zone."

"Typical? I never thought I'd hear that word applied to me." Dara, gave a playful laugh. "Besides, I'm not shopping. You are."

"I don't have any money for new clothes."

"That's okay. You can owe me," she stated emphatically, as they walked through the door of a men's clothing store.

"Dara, my dear, what a pleasant surprise. I was so happy to get your call."

"This must be Francis," thought Sauce watching the short, thin man give Dara a warm embrace and kiss on her cheek. Sauce didn't quite know why, but he immediately had a good feeling about him. He noticed his walk: self-assured, graceful, yet not effeminate. Francis's look was non-intimidating and non-threatening, partly due to his height—no more than five feet tall—and his svelte physique. More importantly was the kindness and warmth in his blue eyes, the fatherly impression created by the neatly trimmed graying beard and the almost heart-shaped triangular face. In addition, Francis's warm, slightly raspy, tenor voice seemed a perfect fit for the man's appearance.

Dara pointed toward Sauce with an open hand, palm up. "Francis, let me introduce my friend, Byrne."

"I am honoured. Dara is not one to use the term *friend* lightly."

Dara continued, "As you can see, he needs a complete wardrobe. I mean right down to his skivvies."

Francis scanned Sauce's appearance. "Of course. If you don't mind the pun, these are fit to be burned!"

"Funny. Let me remind you, this is all Dara's idea."

"No offence, Byrne," said Francis sternly. In deliberate toe-to-heal steps, Francis circled Sauce, casting measurements into the air as if he was giving dictation. "Six foot one, sixteen-inch collar, chest, about forty-six …"

"Forty-eight," interjected Sauce.

"We'll start with a forty-six," continued Francis unabated, "and waist, ah, don't suck in your belly. You want to be comfortable. Yes, that's better. Waist thirty-eight."

Francis walked toward a rack of suits and turning to Dara enquired, "How formal should we go, my dear?"

"Business casual, suits he can wear with or without a tie … three different styles and colours. Byrne would also like something a little more sophisticated for this evening. In that dark blue, perhaps." Dara pointed to one of the suits.

"Let me do my job," chided Francis. "That colour won't flatter Byrne's pale skin tone and brown hair. Take him out in the sun for a few days and come back and he might be able to wear that blue. No, I'd say, charcoal. It must be charcoal."

He led Sauce around the store, occasionally taking a shirt off a rack, holding it up to Sauce's face, and either adding it to the collection on his arm or putting it back. At the fitting room, he arranged the clothes in the order that Sauce was to try them on. "Start with the briefs and socks, and tell me those don't make you feel like a new man on their own. Then the pants and shirt, and show me so I can chalk in the alteration marks."

"Sure, no problem," answered Sauce.

He closed the door and proceeded to remove his clothes. Dara broke the silence, asking him, "Sauce, do you mind if I borrow your phone for a second?" Sauce slid his phone under the door, not sure whether it was a good or bad idea, but relenting since he had agreed with Jett that Dara could have already gathered all of the numbers from it earlier that morning while he was asleep.

He decided to make a joke, rather than offer resistance. "You're not going to call overseas are you?" There was no reply. "Dara, I said you aren't going to rack up my cell phone bill with long-distance calls are you?" Again there was no reply. "Dara, you there? Dara!"

"No need to shout, Byrne," said Francis on the other side of the door. "Dara stepped out for a minute."

"With my phone," complained Sauce.

"That's my Dara. Never a dull moment," commented Francis. "Come out here as soon as you try on the charcoal pants you'll need for tonight so I can mark them. My seamstress will alter them while we deal with the rest of your clothes. Oh, and here are the shoes Dara wants you to wear." He slid the shoes under the door.

Sauce put on the pants and a lavender shirt, then stood on a low foot stool in his new clothes, watching Francis place small chalk marks at various points along the seams. "I guess you've known Dara for quite a while," he prodded, motivated to learn the roots of the "my Dara" comment that Francis had made earlier.

"All her life," he volunteered, dismissively.

Sauce didn't want to appear pushy and waited a few minutes, stepping down from the stool and donning a suit jacket, which Francis attacked as methodically as he had the pants. "Did you live in San Francisco near Dara and her mom prior to moving to this part of California?"

"Dara didn't tell you anything about me before coming here, did she?" asked Francis with a soft chuckle.

"To be honest, she kind of sprung the whole shopping thing on me this morning, after, uh, breakfast."

"She always was impulsive. But also kind and generous, like her mom."

"So you're friends with Gladys?" asked Sauce.

"Brilliant woman. A friend of my wife's really. We lost touch a long time ago, but I remember her as always putting Dara's needs first. Which is all a parent can do, now isn't it?"

"I'm not sure we're talking about the same Gladys. Wasn't she always on the road doing performances? Dara wasn't even with her. Some of the recent news articles have been calling Dara a fake, because none of the reporters even heard about her until a few weeks ago."

Francis helped Sauce remove the jacket and pointed to the fitting room. "Now give me those pants and try on the grey ones." Then he continued with their previous conversation. "Gladys never really cared for the media, when it came to her family that is. She didn't want Dara to get exploited as celebrity children often are."

"It's the price of being famous; that's all."

Francis took the pants from Sauce and carried the suit to the backroom, returning a minute later. Sauce met him at the floor-length mirror, wearing a grey suit. Sauce continued talking while Francis set to work. "So you don't think Gladys's fame and fortune affected Dara's upbringing."

"On the contrary, of course it did. Dara hardly ever saw her mother for the first few years. My wife was as close a friend as Gladys ever had, so she offered to raise Dara, along with our own two daughters, you know, to protect the poor girl. Dara stayed with us, even took some of my dance classes—I teach at the community center. But you know, kids get older, live their own lives. It must be four or five years since we saw Dara around here."

"And I missed you terribly," interrupted Dara, sneaking up behind Francis.

Sauce looked up to see Dara in a bright blue evening gown. "Wow, you look … well, I mean I didn't notice the quick change phone booth outside."

"Does that mean you think I'm super?"

"No, just a thief." He saw that both Francis and Dara looked a little perturbed at his accusation, so he abruptly clarified, "You stole my phone!"

"Oh, that," said Dara with a smirk, "I already returned it. I went to the UPS store and had it couriered back to your house."

"Now why would you do that?" asked Francis. "The man may need his phone."

"Not today he doesn't. I intend to monopolize one-hundred percent of his attention." She laughed, turned her back to the men, and started to look at ties.

Francis threw his arms in the air to suggest they had lost the argument. "Dara, I was just telling Byrne about the good old days." Francis motioned for Sauce to get back into the fitting room for the next outfit.

"Yes," said Sauce, "I'm learning all your secrets."

"What secrets? Just because the media is kept in the dark doesn't mean my life is any more secretive than yours."

Sauce proceeded to change as Francis talked. "As I was saying to your friend, we hadn't heard from you for years. I was so happy when you called a few weeks ago to catch up."

Sauce was turning over recent events in his mind and made a connection: "Was that when Dara bought the suit Gladys wore in court?"

"Clever boy!" said Dara with a huge smile. "Considering your progress when only a few hours sober, imagine what puzzles you'll be able to solve after a few days!"

Sauce ignored her comment, and hoping to deflect the suspicions of his tailor he quickly asked, "Tell me Francis, do you and your wife accept this guy's story about being Gladys?"

Francis paused, then said, "I believe most people are honest until proven otherwise. So the best answer I can give to your question is that this man has never lied to me before. And there's Dara. She has never lied to me, either. Has she ever lied to you?"

"At least once. Just yesterday she said I was a mess!" Sauce came out of the fitting room with a big smile, and with a dramatic swing of his arms asked, "Do I look like a mess?" He liked Francis and hoped his exuberance would prevent a confrontation. He reasoned that Dara had asked Francis to support her story, and as an old friend, and surrogate parent, he obliged.

Sauce and Dara finished their business with Francis and returned to her car. "Aren't we the most beautiful couple in the city, now?" asked Dara with a laugh as she started the car.

"All dressed up and nowhere to go," shouted Sauce over the loud roar of the engine as Dara reversed.

"Sit back and be patient. We don't have too far to drive." She flashed him a devilish grin.

As they zipped through the streets of San Jose, Sauce decided to try another question. "So how did he do it, the blood test, I mean?"

"You're asking that question now?" Dara yelled back. "Why didn't you ask Mummy that when you met with her?"

"You did say sobriety is sharpening my senses. Anyway, I get that the fingerprints could have been substituted at any time, but the blood test would surely have revealed the Y-chromosome of a male."

"You should really suspend disbelief for the rest of the day, Sauce. I promise, you will get a lot of answers where we are going. And most likely have a lot more questions as well." She flashed the kind of smile that worried Sauce. He speculated that he may not like the forthcoming answers.

Dara pulled into the parkade of the Santa Clara Valley Medical Center in the heart of San Jose, slowed into a stall, and turned off the engine. "We walk from here," she quipped. She motioned to the recently purchased packages and added, "Take those with you."

As they walked into the hospital Sauce asked, "Was the real reason you got rid of my phone because of hospital restrictions on cell phone use?"

"No," she answered straight-faced. "It was to prevent anyone from following us by exploiting your phone."

"Oh, I see. I'm being followed, am I? Jett again, I assume."

"Dr. Jett isn't working alone, Sauce. But yes, he does have your cell number. A phone can also be used as a tracking device by someone with the right connections. But I was more worried about him calling you and asking where you were." Sauce caught a brief smirk on her face as she said this, but remained silent.

They entered a service elevator, and Dara placed a key into the control panel. A few seconds later, the elevator doors opened at roof level. Sauce could hear the loud whir of a helicopter's propellers and correctly surmised they were about to be airborne.

"I don't like to fly," yelled Sauce over the noise. Dara ignored him and kept walking toward their transportation. Sauce followed obediently. An attendant held the door open as Dara climbed into the rear passenger compartment. Sauce looked in and mouthed the words, "You've got to be kidding!"

Dara leaned toward his ear and shouted, "If we had time I'd drive. I hate flying, too. Especially commercial airlines: you have to place your trust in too many strangers at one time. I avoid them whenever I can. Sometimes we have no choice. Besides, you'll love the view of the countryside from above. Come on, Mummy hand-picked the pilot. We'll be safe."

Sauce tried to mentally prepare himself for his first helicopter ride as he climbed in next to Dara and hurried to connect his seatbelt. He put his head back and closed his eyes as his body felt the craft rise from the hospital's helipad and tip forward as they made their way skyward. Sauce felt more nauseous than he usually did on mornings after his alcoholic binges, which lately had been every morning.

"I'm gonna be sick."

"No, you're not!" Dara shouted back at him, grabbing one of his hands in her own. "Open your eyes so your brain can orient to the movement of the helicopter. Breathe deeply. That's right. Now look at the farms down there. Isn't California beautiful from up here?"

Sauce opened his eyes and immediately deduced that since it was early evening, and the sun was on his left, that they were heading north. Dara was right; he was starting to feel better. He looked at Dara and quipped, "Are you smuggling me into Canada?"

"I wish I'd thought of that. What a *capital* idea!"

"Oh, I see," Sauce answered in her ear, "Sacramento." He said this last word with a note of disappointment.

"Don't tell me you're not impressed. Have you ever been there?"

"Once, with my mom on one of our summer holiday trips. She wanted me to see the government buildings. She told me if I didn't mess things up in law school, I might be able to work there one day."

Dara leaned toward Sauce and kissed his cheek. She looked at him sympathetically for a moment then smiled. "You might be able to make your mom proud then," she said. "When you meet the governor, why don't you ask him for a job?"

"The governor?" asked a startled Sauce.

"Yeah. We're having dinner with him and his wife this evening."

CHAPTER 13

The helicopter landed on the lawn of a large estate, northwest of the city, adjacent to the Sacramento River. As they were landing, Sauce noticed a few children playing near the large oval pool behind the house, some women in beautiful gowns standing on the nearby grass, a group of men—presumably the husbands—near the sprawling, rancher-style house, and many thick-necked men in black suits—the security detail—around the perimeter of the property.

"Leave the bags in the helicopter," Dara told Sauce as they exited. Two of the men in black had been standing by the landing pad to receive guests. They led Dara and Sauce toward a canvas hut, the makeshift security office, where a list was checked and clearance for their entry into the party was confirmed.

Sauce nudged Dara's arm, pointing out a frenzied brunette running across the grass towards them. Dara started walking in her direction, with Sauce following closely behind.

"Miss Stockard, finally! Please tell me you have good news. Tell me she's not in danger."

"She's fine, Mrs. Sanchez," answered Dara. "As we explained before, the future can change. Right now, though, she's safe."

She embraced Dara for a few seconds. "I didn't sleep a wink last night. Neither of us could. Onofrio stayed in her room at the foot of her bed. Then we heard that you came alone … I thought you were bringing her, this time."

Sauce felt left out of the conversation and the comment about Dara arriving alone didn't help. He cleared his throat loudly, to indicate his discomfort.

"Don't worry. She'll be here in time for dinner. Oh, and this is the man I told you about, Mr. Byrne Aase. Byrne, this is Renata Sanchez, wife of—"

"The governor," he interrupted, happy to join in the conversation. "I recognize you from the television. Pleased to meet you." He put his hand out and received a warm hug and kiss on the cheek instead of the expected handshake.

"Thank you for helping Miss Stockard and Gladys with our troubles. Please, come in and meet our guests. I'll go tell Onofrio you are here."

"We'd love to," said Dara, wrapping her arm around Sauce's and guiding them in the direction of the other guests.

"Doesn't she know that Gladys can take care of herself? Why is she so worried?" asked Sauce.

"She was asking about her daughter, Annabelle, not Gladys." Dara pointed to the four children playing next to the pool. "See the little girl in the yellow bathing suit? That's her."

Sauce stopped walking and looked Dara in the eye. "Wait a minute. That doesn't make any sense. If she's right there, why would Gov. Ono's wife ask you if she's safe? She can see for herself. And why would she be expecting you to be bringing her?"

"No. You're all mixed up! Yes, she is worried about Annabelle, but she wasn't expecting her to arrive with us. I guess she assumed Mummy and I would be arriving together."

"Gladys is coming here?"

"Later, after most of the guests have left. *Gov Ono*—if you use that disrespectful name around him he'll knock your head off—asked Mummy to come, and she really likes the man. She's even proud to have voted for him; how many people are actually proud of the politicians they put into office two years later? So, she'll be here."

Sauce remained confused, though he hesitated to ask more questions until he gathered more information on his own. Dara's answers merely suggested more questions. Sauce wanted answers and figured he was on his own to find them. They continued walking toward the guests and were approached by a young woman in tan pants and a white dress shirt with a gold nametag that read "Katherine" pinned to the shirt pocket. "Can I bring you anything from the bar?" she asked.

"Double vodka martini for me," answered Sauce. Through his peripheral vision he could tell Dara was staring at him, so he corrected his order, "Uh, make that a single martini."

Dara intervened. "Honey I changed my mind on the drink," she said softly to Sauce, loud enough for the waitress to hear. She pulled him away from the temptation. As they walked toward the pool she whispered in his ear, "No more games, Sauce. I need you to listen to everything and think clearly about what you learn tonight. Trust me, you won't be disappointed."

He was about to say, "It's only one drink," when Dara changed the subject. "See those children." She motioned to the same four children she had pointed out earlier. "You know the pretty blonde girl now. The other three, Karla, Iona, and Valerie belong to members of the state legislature. I want you to remember their names. Can you do that?"

"Sure, Karla, Iona, and Valerie. No problem," answered Sauce.

"And Annabelle, her name goes first. Also, there are two other names that come before hers, Kiefer and Ursa."

Sauce counted the names out on his fingers, "So K, U, A, K, I, and V, like an anagram."

"A puzzle, of sorts," said Dara. "At least that's what we thought. I'll explain all about it at dinner. For now, just remember the names."

"All part of the mystery of Good Gladys, I guess," said a smug Sauce. "I should have expected some kind of demonstration. That's what it is, isn't it? Gladys is working these people. It makes sense. They have money, and Gladys is the expert at separating people from their money."

Dara smiled at him. "I'm glad you are thinking clearly. But please, as I said, listen and learn. Especially during dinner."

"And if I happen to say something that spoils your mom's plans?"

"You won't. I trust you." She kissed him softly on the cheek.

Sauce was confident that he was being played. He looked over at the waitress, dutifully distributing alcohol to the other guests. "I suppose Dara was right about that," he thought. "The last thing I need is a muddled brain when Gladys arrives. Besides, as soon as Dara gets me back home, I can slip out for a walk to the store for that drink. Given the circumstances, I can hold out for a few more hours."

They walked a few more steps when Dara leaned toward Sauce's ear. "How about you mingle a bit? I have to use the washroom; I won't be long."

Sauce looked at the other adults. He watched their conversational ease and noted their manicured nails. Despite being dressed appropriately, he knew he didn't belong. "Mingle? I don't think so," thought Sauce. Instead, he wandered closer to the children who were splashing in a shallow part of the pool.

"Feel like that drink now?" said a voice behind him. He turned to see Katherine the waitress. She had a pleasant smile and stood arrow straight with one hand behind her back and the other holding a tray. In the center of the tray was a single, tall glass of bright pink bubbling soda with a long purple curly straw extending from it.

"Aren't *you* the devil incarnate? Trying to get me in trouble or something?" joked Sauce.

"It is a party. Some people don't get that." She looked in the direction of the house. "I'm so bored; most of the guests don't drink! They're basically paying me to walk around and do nothing," she said loudly.

"Sounds like the perfect job for a young person like yourself." She was no more than twenty and Sauce figured she needed the job to pay for school. "Have you been working for the governor for long?"

"A few years. Only part time, of course, while I go to school. In fact, my shift is almost over; I only got four hours today, mostly to help set up. I'm not complaining. I don't mind taking orders. Like now," she said pointing to the governor, who was animatedly talking with a group of statesmen near the house, "he asked me to bring this to his daughter. Doesn't want her to dehydrate in this heat, I guess."

Sauce had been too caught up in the novelty of the situation to notice the weather, but now that she mentioned it, he started to feel himself become sweaty and uncomfortable in his new clothes.

"Well good on you for working your way through school," complimented Sauce.

"Not that I have a choice." She scowled. "My dad certainly can't afford my schooling on the little he scares out of tourists with those two branches on Fisherman's Wharf."

"Branches?" said Sauce enthusiastically. "You mean that's your dad hiding behind the fake bush, jumping out as people walk by, scaring them to death. That's brilliant! He's famous. I can't believe the San Francisco Bushman is really your dad."

"Don't," she said abruptly, with a straight face. Her expression changed as she laughed softly. "I'm just playing around. My dad's not the Bushman. I'm sorry for preying on your gullibility. I know it was kind of in bad taste—I just figured you looked like the kind of guy who could take a joke."

Sauce felt a weight lift from his shoulders. He wasn't offended at the ruse; he appreciated it. Sauce felt more at ease; the joke helped him to forget his awkwardness. "No harm done. You know, I think I would like that drink now," he added, looking in the direction of the house and seeing Dara was still out of sight. Recognizing that his window of opportunity was diminishing he whispered, "You'll have to be quick though before my, um, date returns."

"No problem," she answered with a warm smile. "Just let me deliver this to little Annabelle."

Suddenly eager to procure his drink, Sauce offered, "Let me do that" and reached for the glass. The waitress jolted to the side to prevent Sauce from touching the glass. Her sudden movement caused Sauce to slightly miss, knocking the glass from the tray. It shattered on the ground.

The waitress's face turned crimson as she screamed, "You fucking asshole! Look what you've done!"

The smashing of the glass, combined with the shouting of obscenities scared one of the young girls into releasing a deafening scream. Sauce turned in the direction of the scream and before he could apologize or explain, he was tackled to the ground by a security guard. In seconds they were surrounded by security guards and party guests.

Lying on the ground with a guard on top of him, he looked to his side and saw that the waitress was in a similar position: arms pinned behind her, with a guard pressing his knee into her back. Sauce looked to the other side and saw the children being rounded up by their mothers and led toward the house. He could also see Dara running from the house to the scene of the crime.

"It's just a broken glass. That's all," yelled Sauce in defense of himself and the waitress.

Dara knelt next to Sauce and whispered in his ear, "Keep quiet, you fool. Don't say a word."

"We didn't do anything wrong." Sauce noticed the waitress had not said a word after her initial outburst, and he felt ashamed that she was probably going to get blamed for his mistake. "It's all my fault. She was just following the governor's orders, bringing a drink to his daughter. I'm the clumsy idiot who knocked it off her tray."

The governor stood over Sauce and the waitress and shouted, "I didn't give any such order to her!"

Sauce turned to the waitress with a look of confusion. She just lay there for a few seconds silently, then blurted out, "It was *her* fault." Sauce followed her gaze and saw she was looking directly at Dara. "She told me to do it. She said if I didn't give the drink to Annabelle, then Gladys was going to do the same thing to me that she did to the security guard in prison. I'm innocent! It's all her."

Sauce was shocked by the accusation. Adding to his confused state was the governor's immediate response. He ordered the guards to take the waitress into custody and move her to the house for questioning before the police arrived. He then told them to release Sauce.

He grabbed Sauce's hand and said warmly, "I don't know what to say. You saved my little girl. I'm sure when we test that glass we'll find some lethal concoction. You … you saved our little girl." Tears were welling in his eyes. He wrapped his arms around Sauce and shook him vigorously. Sauce was even more surprised when the governor turned to

Dara and said, "We owe you and your mother our lives. Thank you!"

Sauce stayed silent and watched as the waitress was escorted toward the house by two guards. Dara put her arm in his and helped him to his feet. She kissed his cheek. "Byrne, I think you should be there when they question her. I'll come join you in a little while. First, the governor and I will go see how Renata is doing; she must be frantic." She gave him a nudge toward the house. "Go on. The guards will tell you where they took her."

Sauce was in no shape to argue. The whole situation seemed absurd to him. Nevertheless, he listened to Dara and walked to the house. He asked the guard at the entrance about the location of the waitress and was shown to a sitting room. She was seated in an armless chair and a guard was standing above her, assailing her with questions.

"Once again, Miss Bellows, who sent you?"

"I already told you! It was that woman."

"You're only hurting yourself by not cooperating. Trust me, no one is listening to your lies. Give us a name!"

"You fools! I've told you everything, yet you are letting her roam this house freely. She's going to strike again."

"I told you … " The guard was about to continue when another guard interrupted the interrogation from the hallway.

"Sir, we've found it." Sauce moved aside from the entrance to get out of the way of the guard who ran into the room.

"It was at the bottom of the kitchen garbage receptacle." His gloved hand was holding a small amber coloured bottle with a dark brown cork stopper. "There's still some liquid in the bottom," he continued, handing a latex glove to the guard in charge, followed by the bottle.

"Well, miss, what do you have to say about this?" he asked.

"I've never seen it before," she answered curtly.

"I bet we'll find your prints all over it, won't we? Come on. You may as well tell us who gave this to you. We know you aren't acting alone. Tell us now and the courts will be lenient."

She didn't say another word. Despite the barrage of repeated questions and accusations, she simply stared at the ground. After about fifteen minutes, Dara came to the door and got Sauce's attention with a soft, "Psst!"

"Well?" she asked when he had joined her in the hall.

"I'm not sure what they hope to accomplish in there." Sauce thought for a moment about the situation, his head spinning with the possibilities, though the most likely one was that the waitress had been truthful. "She insists that you sent her with the drink."

"And you believe her?" challenged Dara.

"I don't know why she would lie about that. I mean, she's just a kid."

"Don't say another word," said Dara, softly. Her tone added to Sauce's surprise. He'd expected expressing his belief in the waitress's story would provoke anger, or defensiveness. Dara, however, was stoic and calm.

"I'm not going to tell you you're wrong. You're old enough to draw your own conclusions. Please, though, don't say anything to upset our hosts. Trust me, Sauce, you're the only one who believes her story. So be very careful what you say during dinner. This family has been through enough today. I know that when you hear the facts, your opinion will change." She put her arm in his and started to lead them down the hall. "For the record, though, I am really proud of you. You saved a little girl's life today."

"That's another thing. The governor was acting like I'm some sort of hero. I just bumped into the glass. It was an accident."

"Things happen for a reason, Sauce. You were in the right place at the right time, and a little girl is alive and safe. Those are the facts that matter, nothing else."

Sauce stopped before exiting the house, looked into Dara's eyes and challenged, "And what about the waitress. Which facts will matter for her?"

"We know her facts. We didn't before, I mean, but the facts are pretty clear now. She has been employed by the governor for four years and had developed a lot of trust over that time. We figured there was someone among the house staff who was feeding Jett information, but she was far down on the suspect list."

"Jett? You have him pegged for this?"

"We know this is his work. The poison in that drink was probably something special and slow acting that he created. The forensic specialist will probably have a hell of a time figuring out what's in it. Nevertheless, we do know Annabelle wasn't supposed to die until tomorrow morning, so the poison wasn't supposed to affect her immediately. The waitress would have escaped, and we may not have even connected her to the crime if it wasn't for you."

"How do you know all that? It seems awfully suspicious that you would concoct such wild assumptions."

"Yes well it *would* seem that way to you." She continued to lead him onto the patio. "Mummy will be here soon and all of this will become a lot clearer. Come on." She lead him toward a row of deck chairs. "Right now, we should leave the family alone to calm down."

Sauce looked out at the patio and the lawn, and immediately noticed that except for the security guards scattered around the periphery of the property, they were alone.

"Where did everyone go?" asked Sauce.

"The governor asked everyone to leave. The party was ruined, so everyone agreed to reschedule it for another day. It will be just him, his wife, you, me, and Mummy for dinner."

Dara's eyes were drawn to the incessant trembling of Sauce's hands. She held one of his hands up in the air. "Getting anxious? I guess it has been quite a day for you to go without your crutch. Come here and lie down." Sauce didn't resist, feeling weak kneed, partly from the tension and partly from the absence of alcohol. He found that Dara pointing out his tremors increased his awareness of his fragile nerves. He lay back on the deck chair and closed his eyes.

"That's right. You relax here and I'll get you a drink … of water."

"Cruel." Sauce scoffed as Dara walked away. He kept his eyes closed and tried to drown out his ache for booze by focusing on the information provided by his senses. He could hear voices in the distance, though the words were indiscernible. He also heard a car departing nearby and assumed the waitress was being transported to the police station. He could feel a warm breeze and smelled a familiar scent in the air. A song entered his head and he assumed that it was triggered by the "warm smell of colitas." He drifted between consciousness and unconsciousness as the song played in his mind, adding to his already confused state.

CHAPTER 14

Sauce woke with a jump, falling out of the lawn chair onto the hard red brick of the patio. He initially thought he was dreaming that he was back in the helicopter, flying over central California. As the noise got louder, the dream changed into a chase scene, and the copter was about to run him down in the open desert. As Gladys's ride passed over Sauce, the wild wind from the turbine shook his chair violently. Sauce looked behind him to see the helicopter landing and wondered if this was going to be the real Gladys. Seeing the governor and his wife run out to meet the arriving guest, he jumped to the wrong conclusion.

Returning from the landing area was the governor and his wife with the man who claimed to be Gladys between them.

"Get up Sauce!" said Dara, offering a hand to him. "It's impolite to greet new arrivals while lying on the ground." Sauce reached for her hand, and his eyes widened at the sight of a glass of white wine in her other hand.

"Is that for me?" he asked, hoping the answer was yes.

"It's mine. I didn't know if you were awake yet. I guess not even you could sleep through that noise."

"No kidding! The place was shaking so much I thought it was going to land right on top of me" Sauce brushed the dirt from his suit and attempted to smooth some of the wrinkles in his pants. "How long was I out? A couple of hours?"

"You didn't miss anything," offered Dara. "Of course I could have used the company this afternoon after everyone left. But you were so tired. I brought your water and saw you were sawing logs; you looked so peaceful. I hope you feel better now. You look refreshed."

"Thanks. I feel rested. Still want that drink, if you want to know."

"I'm not sure if that's a good idea. You should ask Mummy if she thinks it's okay to have one."

Sauce looked at Dara for a smile or smirk but her face was expressionless. He pointed in front of him and retorted, "If only she was here, instead of him!" His voice was loud enough to carry over the lawn to the approaching threesome.

"You see Governor," said Gladys loudly. "Your hero has a uniquely open, honest and skeptical mind. He isn't like most people you encounter: yes men, takers, political backstabbers. They are closed to the needs of others and serve themselves unwaveringly. Mr. Aase is a real man, his own man."

"I have to admit, I was a little nervous when you told me you were sending a complete stranger with your daughter. Especially considering you wouldn't let us do a background check on him—and with our daughter's life on the line." The trio reached Dara and Sauce, but the governor finished his thought before exchanging pleasantries. "I don't consider myself to be the sort who blindly trusts his advisors. I made an exception for you, but I was still very uneasy about it. I even assigned two guards to focus all their attention on Byrne this afternoon. As usual, however, you had everything under control. You told me the other day that by the end of this evening I would be willing to put my life in Byrne's hands, and by God you were right."

Renata had her arm in Gladys's, and she leaned over and gave him a long kiss on the cheek. "Our daughter is alive because of you. I can't believe this nightmare is finally over."

"I wouldn't be here if this situation was over." Gladys looked sternly at Sauce. "And neither would you." She paused, then beamed a smile at the governor's wife. "Please, life is too short not to celebrate our successes. I believe dinner is ready, is it not?"

Renata answered enthusiastically, "Yes! Everything is set in the dining room." She led the procession, still holding Gladys's arm, and the others followed closely behind. Sauce stayed silent, feeling bewildered at the esteem bestowed on the Gladys imposter by their hosts.

Seated at the table, waiting for the first course to arrive, Sauce tuned out the small talk about the weather and the pleasant flight to Sacramento and tried to make sense of the situation he was in. He detested taking credit for something he hadn't done, so being called a hero when he knew he had not done anything remotely heroic ached as strongly as his desire for some of the wine that had been dispensed at each table setting except his own. He looked at the water glass in front of him, which seemed like a beacon advertising his recent overindulgences—even the house staff must have been told that he was a lush. But then who treated an alcoholic like an honoured guest, especially when you suspected an attempt had just been made on your young daughter's life?

He also couldn't fathom why no one gave any credence, not even for a second, to the accusations made against Dara and Gladys. Dara was right; Sauce *was* the only one who believed the waitress. Sauce wondered if this was part of Gladys's gift, the reason why she had become so successful. Somehow, she could make some people believe pretty much anything.

They even acted like this man sitting across from Sauce was, in actuality, Good Gladys. He watched the body language of the governor and his wife who treated Gladys like a real woman trapped in a man's body. Sauce felt the hairs on his arms tingle as Renata complimented Gladys on her ability to wear a suit, and not look too feminine while walking. She added that she was impressed with Gladys's recent improvement at shaving so she was able to get away with only a couple of nicks here and there, given how little practice she has had. Gladys, in return, pointed out that she has been treated with much more instant respect from both men and women than she ever had before her transformation. She suggested to the governor that he should be more appreciative of his female colleagues, who have had a much more difficult time gaining voter acceptance than their male competition.

The last straw for Sauce was Dara's comments about how the last few weeks had made her feel like she finally had a dad, as well as a mom. She said Gladys's transformation had awakened her to some of the things she may have missed out on growing up without a father. This comment touched too close for Sauce to ignore. After all, he had just learned that Dara grew up with Francis and his family, so in essence, she always had a dad, unlike Sauce whose dad left his mom when he was just one. She had no idea what it was like to have only a mother: a mean, controlling mother.

He decided to address this ongoing injustice. He ignored Dara's earlier instructions to be considerate, shouting, "Damn it! I have heard enough!"

At first the table became silent. Everyone looked at Sauce, with blank expressions. The governor and his wife began to quietly chuckle, and the corners of their mouths started to rise. Then Dara shattered the tension with a loud laugh, and the others followed immediately. Even some of the kitchen staff could be heard laughing in the other room.

"Another fabulous prediction," chortled the governor. "Gladys, you continue to amaze us!"

Renata looked at Dara and said, "I admit, I was skeptical when you said he wasn't privy to any of our history together. How could he act so bravely, as he did earlier, and not have known, I thought?" She looked sympathetically at Sauce. "Please, Mr. Aase, don't look so hurt by our laughing. Believe me, we aren't making fun of you. We are just a little giddy about today's success, all because of Gladys. And then to have her latest prediction come true just reminds us that we are so fortunate to have her on our side."

Sauce was stunned to be silenced by their laughter. He was prepared to continue expressing his anger, but Dara stopped him. "I'll explain, Sauce." She looked at the governor and said, "All of his friends call him Sauce." She put her hand on Sauce's and continued, "Gladys told the governor just after she landed that before the first course was served for dinner, you would yell out an obscenity at the table."

Sauce couldn't contain himself any longer, he stood up, grabbed Dara's wine glass, and gulped down it's contents. Placing his hands on the table and glaring at the governor he shouted, "If I slap a man, you can be damned sure he'll react violently in return. It's a damn parlor trick. I can't believe an educated man like yourself is buying into all of this *predicting the future* nonsense. Look at him." He pointed at Gladys. "He's not Gladys. He's a man, for Christ's sake. A very clever manipulator and that's all."

"No *she's* not!" returned Renata.

"Really?" continued Sauce. "How can you be so positive, so goddamn sure of yourself that this guy and Dara aren't making fools of the two of you?"

"We were there," said the governor, calmly. "We saw Gladys transform. I was sitting this close to her when Gladys dissolved away, right before my eyes, and rematerialized just as you see her now."

"Please Sauce," said Dara, placing a placating hand over Sauce's once again, "sit down. I told you everything would be explained tonight, and it will be. We want you to join in our confidence. So don't worry; we understand that you're confused. Only a fool wouldn't be, and you're here because you're no fool."

Renata called out, "It's alright, Martha. You can serve the first course now."

As Sauce slowly sat down and adjusted his chair, Dara leaned toward his ear and softly chastised, "You shouldn't have taken my wine. Though I suppose I am partly to blame for leaving it within your reach." Sauce stared at her for a moment, incensed that she would focus on that particular aspect of his recent behaviour.

Without delay, however, Gladys turned to Sauce and stated, "If you'll allow me to monopolize the conversation while you eat, it would be my pleasure to explain. I think I should start at the moment when I first became aware of the danger facing Onofrio and Renata, which was about two months ago, while I was on tour doing a four-night set of shows in Los Angeles."

Sauce immediately thought of Jett and his attendance at one of those shows and changed his mind about interrupting Gladys. He started to eat the salad which had been placed in front of him and listened carefully, an activity that seemed much easier now that he was beginning to feel the effects of the alcohol coursing through his veins, settling his nerves.

"My gift often brings knowledge to me that is unpleasant, even criminal. I have been fortunate on many occasions, too many I am unhappy to say, to become aware of crimes about to be committed: hateful, murderous intentions on the part of members of my audiences. Fortunate may seem like an odd word to use, since fortune is what we make of our situation, rather than something we are destined to acquire. So when I say that I was fortunate, I mean that whenever I felt I could make a difference in this world, I would act to prevent harm. I have saved many lives and stopped numerous destructive acts from occurring. I am not claiming to be a saint. No, if I was only more concerned for others, than for my own safety, and well, for my career, I would have been able to help many more people than I have."

Sauce couldn't help but utter an audible contemptuous grunt to this statement. The governor responded with an uncharacteristic chortle, which sent a piece of lettuce flying from his mouth onto the center of the table. "Sorry, but that was kinda how I reacted when I first met Gladys!"

Gladys smiled and continued, "I am well aware that you have a low opinion of my profession, Sauce. And yes, Onofrio shared your sentiments and told me, basically, to get lost, at our first meeting when I offered to help save his daughter."

"You quickly made a believer out of me after that night in your house," said the governor.

"Well, we are jumping ahead in the story a little. Let me go back to the night of my last L.A. show." Gladys paused to take a bite of her salad, then cleansed her palate with a sip of wine before continuing. "You've never seen me perform, have you?" she asked, looking at Sauce.

"No, of course not."

"Then I should explain, briefly, how my gift works. You see, the audience has an expectation when they come to see me that I will, let's say, cut to the chase and demonstrate my unique talent. You know about that, I hope."

"You mean your supposed ability to tell anyone when they are going to die."

"Not *anyone*, Sauce. I don't have that kind of control. No one does. The fact is, I don't know when or if that information will be sent to me."

"From beyond, you mean," said Sauce, rolling his eyes.

"Beyond, from spirits, from people who have passed on, yes, that's right. Oh you don't have to hide your skepticism. Skepticism is positive, it's healthy. And I have heard it all before, and everyone at this table has had similar feelings. Yes, that's right, even me. And especially Dara. Until a few years ago, even she didn't know that my gift was real. So enjoy your meal and don't feel like I'm interpreting your silence as anything other than an expression of your hunger. I certainly won't assume that you believe. So please, eat."

She took another bite of her salad. "Renata this is really good. I especially like the smoky after-taste from the roasted endive." She took another sip of wine before continuing. "Most of my shows are a lead-in to the main event, which as I said, I can't control and often can't even provide during a show. I explain this at the beginning of every performance, and of course, during the many interviews prior to a tour.

"So that was how the show began in L.A. I gave my usual disclaimer and assured everyone, that if they concentrated on wishing me well in my performance, peace and love and all the usual good feelings that assure the spirits my intentions are pure, then I might be able to make a connection for some people in the audience.

"My preamble always produces some information. Often I will just look into the eyes of someone in the audience and know that they are being sent a message from a lost soul, a loved one usually, sometimes a distant relative or even a total stranger with advice for the future. On even rarer occasions, I receive a message I just know was sent for me. A call to arms, you could say. For example, in Italy once, I was told that the man I was looking at was planning to kill his adulterous wife. That was really early in my career, oh about fifteen years ago. It really rocked me, though I knew I couldn't ignore what I had learned. I contacted the local authorities, and they were much like yourself, oblivious. They laughed at me. A week later, they called me to say I was a 'person of interest' in the murder of the very same woman I had warned them about.

"Needless to say, I was found to be blameless. In fact, I have been vindicated in a way, as I have worked with law officials in at least a dozen countries, helping to prevent many crimes. You haven't read about this side of Good Gladys, of course. The papers focus on crimes that were committed, rather than those that were prevented. After all, people are much more interested in the bad guy. I bet there are a lot more pets named Voldemort and Vader than Potter or Skywalker!"

"That's funny," interrupted Renata. "Just the other day I met a woman who called her dog Cujo!"

"My point exactly," said Gladys. "Not that I want to have pets named after me," she added with a sly smile. "Getting back to my main point, at the L.A. show I received some information I couldn't ignore. I knew I had to act on it without delay. It was near the midpoint of my show and I had just begun asking people to come up on stage so I could hold one of their hands—that often yields the best results. As my stage crew was busy setting up a queue at each side of the stage, I continued to look into the eyes of the people who remained seated, just in case I was able to receive a personal message for one of them. For some reason, my eyes kept being drawn back to a seat in the lower balcony. There sat a modestly dressed man with a thin goatee and dark glasses. I could tell right away that he was blind and felt a deep connection to his spirit. I felt fear, but also intense anger, the kind I have learned to associate with an ability to hurt others.

"Just as I was about to abandon him and focus on the people approaching the stage, it happened like a flash. I can still see the images so clearly in my mind. There was a stream of letters, flashing one after another. The first was a K, then a U. As I often do in these situations, I requested that whoever was sending this information to me provide more detail, you know, more than just a single letter. I felt a darkness like you cannot imagine. Then the letters started to flash before my eyes again: K, U, A, K, I, V. I felt like death was all around me and knew those letters were meant for me and not for the man I was staring at. I concentrated and eventually was rewarded with a list of names: Kiefer, Ursa, Annabelle, Karla, Iona and Valerie."

She paused as both the governor and his wife stopped eating and grasped each other's hand at the mention of the list. Gladys reached over and put her hand over the governor's. "It's all right. We've won today, so we know we can beat him."

Sauce watched silently, recognizing that the distress he was witnessing was real, even if the story was not.

"Though that was all the information I was provided, I knew I had to do something with that list. After the show, I searched the names on the internet to see if a connection could be found. The first name kind of threw me off, since I got thousands of search results for that famous Canadian actor. I decided to focus on the second name, Ursa so I typed 'Ursa California Dead' into the search window. There it was on the screen, the answer I needed. Kiefer and Ursa were already dead, Ursa having been killed the day before the show and Kiefer just a few weeks before that. I searched for famous Annabelles in California and the third result was a photo of the governor, his wife and their baby daughter at a campaign fundraising dinner I had attended a few years back. This was no coincidence! I instantly knew their little girl was the next one to die, and the blind man who attended my show was the killer.

"The next day I contacted the FBI and told them I needed to warn the governor that his daughter was in danger. I was shocked to learn that the governor had already received a letter threatening his daughter's life. In fact, it stated that as of tomorrow morning, she would be dead. So you see why Renata and Onofrio are so happy. After all they've been through these last few weeks, we succeeded in preventing that promise from coming true. And you see, Sauce, it didn't even matter if you believed in me, or even knew why we contacted you in the first place. We saved Annabelle, and we couldn't have done it without you."

CHAPTER 15

Sauce shook his head, quietly chuckled and continued eating.

"You don't believe a word she said, do you?" suggested the governor.

Sauce finished his mouthful of food before answering. "I can tell that you do. It's obvious Gladys has convinced you that everything she says is true and honest. That's her business. She wouldn't be 'Good Gladys the famous psychic' without her believers." Sauce could see the anger in the governor's eyes and quickly added, "I don't mean to offend you, but this is an old story that's been told a million times. Even Conan Doyle—a brilliant mind who created a world of crime and detection that continues to enthrall readers years after his death—defended the mystics of his day, even after each and every one was continuously proven to be a fraud and a con artist."

As the salad plates were removed from the table and the main course was placed in front of the diners, Sauce continued to relate his grounds for disbelief. "When I was an undergraduate, there were many students who bought into this nonsense. I did a little investigating back then and came across a very enlightening book by the great magician Houdini. He spent years of his life and thousands of dollars scrutinizing every claim of paranormal abilities that he could find during his lifetime and wrote about many of these investigations. He genuinely wanted to find evidence of an afterlife, but couldn't. In fact, he was able to prove, yes prove, that every single claim of psychical ability was a ruse, designed to fool people for financial gain. Nevertheless, he ended the book with the realization that all of the evidence he gathered wouldn't diminish the success of the next charlatan. He wrote that despite the irrefutable evidence, people will still believe and psychics will still succeed in creating new methods to deceive a willing public. This whole situation involving your daughter is just a new technique Gladys has invented to sustain her career."

"But the letter, and the attempt on our daughter's life?" asked Renata.

Sauce looked at Gladys with contempt and answered, "What attempt on her life? Look, I don't claim to be as smart as these people. Gladys has been running this psychic scam for many years. I'm sure she will be able to counter whatever explanation I offer with more words and lies."

"Come on," challenged Dara. "Don't cop out! Give it your best shot. How did Mummy create this situation?"

"All right," said Sauce. "First of all, I'm sure she had most of this planned well in advance. She probably scoured the papers before arriving in California for those shows and learned of two kids who died under mysterious circumstances; people are always dying, so that part of her scheme was trivially easy. I figure Gladys and her entourage of criminals, are quite adept at research; advances in technology, like internet search engines, have been a boon for your kind, haven't they?" he asked, looking at Gladys.

"Please, don't stop," said Gladys. "I'm quite enjoying this."

"Sure you are," snapped Sauce. "So, you found a couple of kids who died and remembered seeing the governor at that fundraiser years ago with his baby. You hatched a plan to take advantage of a parent's number one fear. Oh, yes, for the plan to work, you needed a villain. A blind professor attends one of your shows and you decide he will fit the role nicely. He does have a villainous look, doesn't he? A professor with a pointy beard. How perfect! Oh, what else?" Sauce paused and thought about the planning that must have been done in advance. "Ah, the letter. Gladys sends a threatening letter to you and your wife, then contacts the FBI claiming to have knowledge matching the contents of that letter. You see, everything can be explained away."

"Not everything," said the governor. "Katherine, our student waitress, just tried to kill my little girl!" He pounded his fist on the table at the word 'kill'.

"I don't mean to sound insensitive, but we don't know that. She claims that Dara gave her the drink … Dara who was in your house and could have planted the vial found in the garbage can. I wouldn't doubt that the chemical analyses of the drinking glass chards and the vial come up empty. She'll tell you that a professor of chemistry could easily develop a poison that is undetectable or unknown. But without any real evidence, you should consider that perhaps your daughter was never in any real danger from the beginning."

"Gladys, would you allow me to provide the rebuttal?" asked the governor.

"Certainly," she answered, smiling at Sauce.

The governor stood up and calmly walked around the table to Sauce's side. He leaned down and presented his cell phone. "Here is a text message I received just before Gladys arrived. Read it aloud, if you will."

Sauce looked at the screen and read, "Three mice tested with each sample. All died in less than an hour."

"No doubt about it: poison. Slow acting, since it took about an hour to have an effect on the little mice." He walked back to his seat then continued, "The waitress has since confessed. In fact, she has changed her story a half dozen times since arriving at the police station. Unfortunately, we aren't going to be able to use any of that testimony. Partly because she kept contradicting herself, but most importantly, because she is dead. Whoever provided the dose for my daughter, also slipped her some before she started her shift, presumably so she wouldn't be able to testify after the deadly deed. You must concede, *Sauce,* that there is at least a modicum of truth in what Dara and Gladys have been telling us."

"Yes, I guess I was wrong about that. I beg your pardon, but—"

"There are no buts about it," snapped the governor. "We were threatened in a letter, told that our daughter would die. Gladys then came to us and said she could help us, and she did exactly as she said she would do. We didn't believe her at first. Like you, we thought it was all a scam. Then we visited her house and saw with our own eyes things we would never have imagined. So yes, this person seated at our table is Gladys!"

Sauce moved his fork back and forth across his plate for a few moments as he considered his response, turning the neat assortment of vegetables, and sliced grilled steak into a stew. He immediately saw errors in the governor's reasoning, but didn't want his rebuttal to come off as a statement about the governor's intelligence. Positioning his utensils at ten and five o'clock on the plate, as his mother had told him to do to signify completion of a meal, he breathed in deeply, wiped his mouth with his napkin, and spoke, clearly and slowly.

"The waitress changed her story, though, I assume you would have told me if she implicated Dr. Jett during her ramblings."

"No, she did not mention him," answered the governor.

"No, I didn't think so. As far as the police can tell then, the changes to her story could simply have been a side effect of her worsening condition: mental delusions brought on by the poison in her system."

"Not likely. It precisely coincided with the contradictory evidence presented by the detectives."

"Ah, but as her mental state destabilized, she may have offered alternative answers as a confused reaction to the interrogators tenacious disbelief in her earlier testimony. You see, the truth of her initial accusation may not have changed; she changed. The poison did that."

"You are not in possession of enough facts to make that assumption," interrupted Renata. "We know Dara is innocent."

"How can you be so sure?" asked Sauce.

"From the moment Dara entered the house this afternoon, she was with me," replied Renata. "Yes, that's right. I was with her every moment. She did not enter the kitchen; she did not speak with Katherine. Not a single word or even a glance was exchanged between them. It was this piece of evidence, provided by the police to the waitress, that prompted her to change her story."

Sauce was unfettered by this revelation. "That makes the waitress's confession even more puzzling. Why change the story at all, if not to implicate the person truly responsible?"

"I thought *you* were the investigator," said Gladys. "Perhaps you could help us find that answer."

"I suspect if I start to look into this, you won't be happy with what I find," answered Sauce gruffly. "The first thing I would look into is why your manager was killed. First him, then the guard in jail, and now the waitress; it seems bodies are falling all around you."

Martha approached the table to remove plates. Gladys sat back and waited for the table to be cleared and dessert to be served then restarted the conversation. "How would you go about it? The investigation. Where would you look first?"

"Seriously? If I told you that you wouldn't need Dara to move into my house and attach herself to my side like a remora."

"You are hardly a shark, Sauce," laughed Dara.

"Nevertheless, if I was to make a go of this, I would need space. She would have to leave my home."

"Or we could find a compromise position," answered Gladys. "Onofrio, could you spare one of your most trusted security men to ride along with Byrne during the day?"

"You know, Gladys, that is a brilliant idea," answered the governor enthusiastically. "He could ensure that Jett doesn't harm our hero and provide me with daily reports on their progress. And I know just the man. Yes, I will arrange that right after dinner."

"Wait a minute!" asserted Sauce. "I don't need a babysitter. I meant that you would leave me alone to investigate my way."

"You said you wanted Dara to leave you alone. Well, concede to have another professional working with you during the day and you will be free from Dara during the day! At night, however, Dara will still be with you, to protect you from yourself, more than anything, I imagine."

"And what if I just hide away in a cheap motel somewhere instead. I could slip away in the middle of the night and—"

Dara laughed. "No you couldn't!"

Sauce was stumped by the certainty in her voice. He thought about the number of times she had been able to outwit him already in the past week alone and conceded she was probably right. He considered his options and saw no way out. After a minute of contemplation, he proposed a compromise of his own. "I see I am not going to get my way here. So how about this? I agree to work with your man, but I run the investigation, not him. He follows my orders."

"Done," chirped the governor.

"But I'm not done yet," continued Sauce. "In addition, you have to tell me one other thing. Why do you keep insisting this man is the real Good

Gladys? What happened in Gladys's house that has you so convinced he is not merely a charlatan?"

"Can I?" asked Gladys, looking first at the governor, who nodded his approval, then at Sauce, who mumbled a reluctant, "Go ahead."

CHAPTER 16

"The governor already told you he didn't believe me at first. In fact, like you, he didn't have a very positive opinion of me or my gift," began Gladys.

"I believed," said Renata. "Many years ago, I saw you on television. You had accurately predicted the day a woman's mother was going to die. It was one of the most powerful and emotional demonstrations of psychic ability I have ever seen. The woman recounted how she had not spoken to her mom in years; she acted on your prediction and was able to make up and apologize, one day before her mother passed on. The whole studio audience was in tears."

"Yes, that was my first appearance on the Amber Ellis Show, I think. My gift was just starting to come into full fruition, and I was so happy to have been able to help that family."

"Oh, please!" smirked Sauce.

"Precisely! That was the governor's response when I first told him over the phone about the list," continued Gladys. "I knew his daughter was going to die if I couldn't convince him I was telling the truth. As we said, the governor told me to get lost. So I asked Cole for suggestions, but he was more concerned about how to make money from this situation. As a manager I suppose that was what he was paid to do, to look out for my financial interests. He suggested a public display, a grand show of some kind, with the governor in the audience. I told him, though, that this one had to be kept private: there were all those kids on that list who had to be protected, after all. We disagreed for a little bit, and I think, had he lived, we would probably have gone our separate ways over this. I believe it was his insistence that he should profit from this situation that eventually led to his death.

Sauce was about to interject when Gladys insisted, "Don't interrupt, please." She looked at Renata and continued her story. "It was my argument with Cole that got me thinking I needed someone else on my side to succeed with the governor. And who better, than his wife." Gladys reached over and squeezed Renata's hand.

"I suggested the séance!" volunteered Renata, her face showing intense regret. "It's my fault you are like this." Tears welled up in her eyes.

"Nonsense," consoled Gladys. "I told you, this is my punishment for a long life of abusing my gift. I had a lifetime to correct my mistakes, a lifetime to avoid this fate. Imagine how terrified the world would have been if it had happened during a live television show or before thousands at a stadium performance. So you see, it was better this way."

Gladys quickly kept talking. "Dara met with Renata and convinced her of my sincerity. Renata proposed that I attempt to contact either Kiefer or Ursa in the presence of her husband. She thought a genuine demonstration of my abilities might help him to see the light. At first I thought the idea was preposterous, but well you know the expression, 'the spirit is willing, though the flesh is weak.' My reluctance was simply earthly fear. During a moment of quiet reflection later that night, the spirits insisted I do as Renata suggested. I still thought the idea was silly and doomed to failure, but a nagging voice kept telling me to go through with it. I called Renata the next day, to enlist her assistance. You see, I can't just connect with those who have passed whenever I want. It's not like calling someone over the telephone. Establishing an ethereal connection is a rare and unusual event, not one you can predict and plan. My experience at these things told me the probability of success would increase if we request communication in the presence of the loved ones of the deceased.

"Renata contacted those who had been closest to Kiefer and Ursa. So it happened on the evening of the next full moon. Onofrio, Renata, Senator Prouit and his wife, and Senator Braush and his wife entered my home. Cole agreed to act as the host, rather reluctantly as he held to his conviction that a public display was more in our interests. Nevertheless, I convinced him to help by threatening to manage my own affairs and cut off his lucrative income—to be honest, I silently intended on doing this in the near future anyhow.

"As I was saying, Cole greeted my guests—"

"Why didn't Dara greet the guest?" asked Sauce, interrupting Gladys.

"You know me," answered Dara. "I love to travel."

"Please, Sauce. You asked to hear this," chided Gladys. "So there we were," she continued, her voice a little louder, as if to warn against further interruptions. "The guests were seated around my dining room table, the lights dimmed to calm the nerves, incense burning to show respect for the dead. I was already seated at the head of the table in quiet prayer. Cole had instructed everyone to respect the silence of the room, as I had been in a trance-state for hours already, a necessity that is always overlooked in movie portrayals of such events. Cole also told the wives of the two senators that as soon as they were seated, they were to use the pen and paper on the table, and write the name of the spirit to be contacted. These papers were to be folded three times and burned in a little bronze cistern in the center of the table. Once that had been done, with the air heavy from the smoke, we all joined hands. My hands were held by the governor on one side and Renata on the other side.

"As soon as the circle was completed, I felt an intense warmth. It was like fire had filled the room. I screamed out in agony. I knew we were in the presence of the most powerful force I had ever felt. Then I was gone, out of the room. For me, it felt like hours. When I returned to the room, I opened my eyes and saw that the senators' wives had both become overwhelmed by what they had witnessed and collapsed. I was still holding the governor's hand on one side, and Renata's hand on the other. They were trembling. I looked at my hands and saw that they had changed. My beautiful manicured nails with glistening aqua coloured polish had become plain, unadorned man's nails. My fingers were male. Cole jumped from his seat at the other end of the table and turned on the lights. Everyone stared at me, because I had been transformed to this person you see before you now."

Sauce noticed that the governor and his wife looked at Gladys with renewed awe. Sauce was unimpressed, though. He looked sternly at Gladys and asked, "Where do you get this stuff? The incense, the smoke, the ambiance—all standard hocus-pocus of your ilk. But the woman to man transformation, that's genius. That has to be a first. I'm sure when you get a chance to write this up, the book will sell millions. And you just left our esteemed hosts sitting there in the dining room after you disappeared for hours?"

"She was only gone for seconds," corrected the governor. "Yet neither Renata nor I noticed her hand leave our grasp. It was almost instantaneous, really."

"It only seemed like hours to me," added Gladys.

"Not to encourage your fantasies, but I have to ask: where did you go for those hours?"

The governor and his wife stared longingly at Gladys. Gladys shook her head and replied, "That is something I have not discussed, not even with Onofrio and Renata. Seeing the shock on everyone's faces that night, I pretended to faint. Cole, mercifully, ushered the guests out of my house. You have no idea the state I was in. I was, well am, a man. You've had your whole life to get used to it, but for me the change was an assault on my whole being. The hormone changes, the change to my center of gravity, I didn't know what to do with myself. Fortunately, I had Cole and Dara to help me get accustomed. Cole taught me how to shave—I tried one of those infernal electric things, but it left an awful rash. Dara helped with clothes, posture, and other things so I could go out in public without drawing attention.

"The worst part was Cole badgering me during the weeks of my adjustment to arrange interviews and press releases. He wanted to make money from this. But I told him I was being punished for profiting from my gift. He didn't care about eternal retribution; he got angry at my resistance and wouldn't return my calls. That's why I went to his office that fateful day. I wanted to make sure he wasn't defying my orders for privacy. When I entered his office, though, he was already dead."

Sauce wasn't giving up on his earlier question, "If I promise not to be shocked, will you answer my question? Where did you go during those hours?"

"As I said I have kept that to myself. But I am going to tell the whole story. Remember when you visited me at my house and I told you I had consented to an interview with Amber Ellis?"

"I know it didn't happen."

"True. The network refused to allow it. They needed time to set up the infrastructure for the telecast. The show, of course, has always used the 'audience interactive system' or AIS. As Amber conducts her interviews the studio audience and viewers at home can show their 'real-time' approval of the guest by texting in a plus or minus sign. Viewers see the results on a continuous display they call the Fan Approval Meter. The AIS charges three dollars per text, freeing the show from pausing too often for commercials. The network expected a windfall from my interview and needed an extra week to shore up the system to accommodate the large number of texts."

"And *you* didn't want to profit from this tragedy?" Sauce shook his head and smirked.

"I won't get one penny from the interview," she answered defensively. "Anyway, I feel like the time has come for me to tell the world what happened to me, but not for personal benefit, for Annabelle and the other children left on the list. The spirits insist it will save their lives."

"The spirits insist, do they?" said Sauce. "I thought the séance was a bust. Or did you actually talk to those kids during the hours you were *missing*?"

"What kids?" asked Renata.

Sauce was taken aback at both the question and the inquisitive faces that stared at him from all sides of the table. "You know, *the kids*! Kiefer! Ursa! What's the matter with everyone? Weren't they the whole reason for the séance in the first place?"

The governor, his wife, Dara, and Gladys erupted in laughter. Sauce's face became hot and red from anger, tinged with embarrassment, though he couldn't fathom why he should feel embarrassed. He yelled, "Was this whole evening a bloody joke?"

"No," said Dara softly, "sorry about that. It's just that we forgot you weren't aware. Mummy forgot to mention that the first two names on the list weren't the names of kids. They are the names of Senator Prouit and Senator Braush's prized dogs."

"You held a séance so you could connect with pets?"

"I told you that I had thought the whole idea was silly," remarked Gladys.

Sauce was in a daze for the remainder of the evening. He felt like a foreigner in a country where the natives spoke a different language, obeyed odd social mores and followed logic that Sauce couldn't comprehend. He vaguely recalled the governor thanking him as he left the estate, the dots of light beneath him as he flew southward over California and the drive along the busy freeway into San

Francisco. All the while he mumbled answers to questions, receiving unusual facial expressions in return. He knew Dara had helped him out of his clothes and into bed. He then drifted for hours in and out of consciousness as his brain attempted to sort out the details of the evening. Then, finally after several hours of restlessness, he fell into a deep, penetrating, cathartic, sleep.

At six the next morning he awoke, refreshed and full of energy and ideas for the day. He looked at the side of the bed next to him and saw that Dara was still sound asleep. He slid quietly out of bed, into the bathroom to splash his face, brush his teeth, and shave. Seeing that Dara was still sleeping, he grabbed some of the new clothes that now occupied his closet, dressed in the living room, grabbed his keys and cell phone, and softly closed and locked his front door as he stepped outside.

"Shit!" he thought to himself looking out at the road. "My car is still at the damn restaurant." He started to walk down the road and pulled out his phone to call a cab. Struck with inspiration he selected the number for his friend Officer Hammi instead.

"What? Who is this?" came the sleepy reply.

"Don't you check your call display before answering?" snapped Sauce.

"Sauce, that you? What the hell you doing calling me at this hour?"

"I thought you were on mornings," answered Sauce.

"I get days off, you know."

"Sorry, but I need a favour." H added in a whisper, "It involves the governor."

"Really? No. I would have heard if Gov. Ono had been involved in a car crash."

"This isn't an insurance thing. Did you hear about the attempted poisoning at his home yesterday?"

Suddenly Hammi sounded intrigued. "Yeah, I heard rumors that something like that went down."

"I was there. I kinda stopped it from happening. The poisoning I mean. Do you have any friends up there in Sacramento, on the force?"

"You were there?" Hammi was waking up trying to make sense of Sauce's predicament.

"Never mind that. I'll tell you all about it later. The governor asked me to find out what happened, you know, get more info on why the girl did it. Can you ask one of your friends about the waitress? You know, find out what happened to her, get some personal details if possible. This is, uh, important."

"Did he hire you, or is this more of a personal thing?"

"Let's just say I am involved and need to find out as much as I can. Look Hammi, you know me. I don't stick my neck out if I don't have to. Believe me, I'd rather avoid the whole thing, but I can't. Can you help me?"

"I can make a couple of phone calls, sure."

"Great. Can we meet for breakfast? Say in about an hour."

"You want me to call now?"

"Like I said, it's really crucial that I get some information. I don't want to say too much over the phone, but this could be a life or death situation."

"Yeah, all right. But let's make it ten. How about that place on Lombard where we ate last time?"

"Sure, thanks," said Sauce, disconnecting the call. He continued to walk and was about to call a cab when a black Toyota sedan pulled up next to him. Sauce looked into the vehicle as the window lowered.

"Byrne, right? Byrne Aase?" asked the voice inside the car.

Sauce approached the vehicle and looked at the grey-haired, wrinkled-faced, pudgy Latino man wearing a dark two-piece suit, crisp white shirt and black tie seated in the driver's seat. Sauce immediately thought the man was a cop.

"Are you looking for me, officer?"

"I'm not the police. I'm retired actually. Just doing a favour for Onofrio. Beto Torres. You can call me BT. I was told you would be expecting me."

Recalling the governor's deal to free him from Dara's vigilance, Sauce opened the passenger door and entered the car. "Call me Sauce."

"Right," the old man answered, coldly, hitting the accelerator. "I was briefed."

"So the governor told you about the letters, the waitress—about Gladys?"

"I read copies of the letters on the flight here from Washington. We spoke on the phone about the other stuff."

"Then you probably know more than me. I didn't get past the séance. Did he tell you about that?"

"As I said, I've been briefed."

"I'd like to see those letters," commented Sauce.

"Later," snapped BT, turning abruptly, without adding an explanation.

Sauce decided to accept the delay and attempted to learn more about his new partner. "So, Washington. Why he did he call you, or are you not allowed to say?"

"I'm told you can be trusted." He pulled out a cigarillo from his pocket. "You don't mind?"

"They're you're lungs," answered Sauce.

"I'm an old family friend." He snapped open the top of a silver lighter, ignited the flame, and inhaled deeply. "Annabelle's godfather too. So you see I have a personal interest in getting to the bottom of this situation."

"Why Washington?"

"I was Secret Service in my younger days. Onofrio's father is old money, had several events in common with the president. As a fellow Latino, we kind of connected back in the day. Lately I handle special jobs, the kind of events when an extra pair of eyes on the president are needed. Nothing fancy, but it keeps my hands in the game, you know?"

"Sure. I guess that makes you secret, Secret Service," remarked Sauce. Noticing that BT didn't react to his attempt at humour, he resumed the conversation. "So what do you make of Gladys then?"

"Fraud, of course. Onofrio believes in that guy, and I don't mess with another man's beliefs. As I see it, you and I have to find out if the fraud is worth investigating, or if this Jett is really our man. I was told you met him. What's your take?"

"Jett? He seems to be the only rational person involved in all of this, if he even is involved." Sauce relaxed, content that his newly imposed companion had a similar view of Gladys.

"In my experience, the one piece of a puzzle that doesn't fit is often the one to watch out for most. I guess we'll get to him later."

Sauce noticed they were slowing down at a parkade. "Where are you taking us, anyway?"

"I thought you'd want to start at the scene of the crime, Cole Beckley's office. He was the first victim, right?"

"First human victim," added Sauce.

"Right. The pets. Heard about them. Did you know they were poisoned? Not the kind of coincidence we should dismiss."

"Can you pick a lock?" asked Sauce. "I don't have any keys. Are we even allowed here?"

"Carte Blanche, I was told. Onofrio says go wherever the investigation leads. So we'll break the door in if we have to."

Sauce thought to himself, "I like this guy!" but said instead, "We have a few hours, but we have to meet someone at ten."

"Right," said BT.

CHAPTER 17

At the entrance to Beckley's office BT didn't hesitate to rip down the police tape and insert a thin metal rod into the lock. Sauce put his hand on BT's to stop him. "Do you think there's an alarm?"

"There is," he answered, continuing unabated, opening the door within a few seconds. "It's silent. Onofrio said he'd alert the monitoring station to disregard the signal."

Sauce wondered if the governor made a similar call when Dara bypassed his home security. He was impressed with BT's skill with the lock, though, recognizing that he may be able to learn a few tricks while they worked together. "Could you teach me that?"

"Shh," BT quietly instructed. He walked around the room, looking under the desk and feeling around picture frames. Finally, he gave an "Aha!" look at Sauce as he pulled a small device that had been hidden behind the top section of the window blinds. He placed it on the desk and smashed it with a stapler. "A bug," he mouthed silently, adding softly, "There's probably more than one."

Sauce took the warning and kept quiet. The two men searched through the drawers of the desk and the filing cabinet, finding nothing of interest. Sauce noticed the false ceiling and climbed onto the desk. He lifted a ceiling tile and move his head through the opening. Sauce motioned that he had seen something that was out of reach. He stepped down and the two men moved the desk over a few feet. Sauce climbed up again and lifted a second ceiling tile. He reached a hand through the opening and pulled out a leather bound ledger. He was about to move the desk back, but BT stopped him and motioned for them to leave.

Back in the front seat of the car, Sauce and BT placed the ledger between them and perused the contents. "It's alphabetized, sorted by city. Each city is followed by a row of names," commented Sauce as he took in the details, thinking aloud. "There must be hundreds of cities in here. Each one with dozens of names and phone numbers."

"Let's turn to Washington—see if I recognize any of these people," instructed BT. Running a finger down the list, he stopped near the middle. "This one seems familiar. Yeah, I know I've heard of him. Calliope's not a common name. I can't recall where, but he might be on one of our databases. Here, take the book and look up San Francisco. See if you recognize any of Beckley's local associates." BT passed the book to Sauce then reached over to the backseat, retrieving a laptop, with a cell phone dongle sticking out of the side.

"Do you think he was hiding this from the person who killed him?"

"It's a remote possibility that one of the people listed in here killed him trying to get this book. Not probable, mind you, merely one of the possibilities we'll have to consider. I would be more convinced if Beckley's office had been tossed, but it wasn't. It's more likely that Beckley always kept it hidden, as a general precaution."

BT opened the computer and quickly accessed a federal database. He entered the name Calliope and the accompanying phone number into the search window. He turned the screen so Sauce could see the resulting photo and description that came up immediately. "Hmm, deceased," voiced BT, softly.

"Yeah, looks like a dead end," joked Sauce, looking at the screen. "Two years ago, it says." Sauce looked at the photo and noted the assortment of tattoos on his face and multiple piercings over his eyes and in his ears. "Looks like a freak. What do you think?"

"Interesting," BT mused. "Long rap sheet. Petty crime, theft mostly. Carnival conjurer. Perhaps one of Gladys's competition."

"Here's a name I recognize," blurted Sauce, pointing to an entry in the list of names under San Francisco. "Kaos! He was kind of famous for awhile. He created one of the sculptures in Golden Gate Park, I think. An artist."

BT entered the name in the database, and the information that appeared matched Sauce's recollection. "Still alive. Well, that's promising," said BT, giving a slight smile. "No criminal record. Lives in the city." He pointed to the clock. "Do we have time before our meeting to pay this artist a visit?"

Sauce looked at the address displayed on the screen. "It's only a few blocks from here. Sure, let's go. We might get lucky."

Sauce gave turn-by-turn directions until they pulled up to the dual sliding metal doors of a dilapidated, corrugated metal, dome-style warehouse. The two men approached the side of the building and found the main door locked.

"Shall we knock?" asked Sauce.

"Nah," answered BT, "he may assume the worst and run." He slammed his foot against the door, smashing the frame and sending the door swinging inward. "Let's surprise him."

They entered the building and immediately heard a loud clanging of metal on metal, coming from a nearby room. They walked along a hallway, slowly approaching the source of the noise. There were several closed doors on the right and left sides of the hallway. Sauce and BT opened each door as they came to it and cautiously scanned the interior of the rooms for occupants. Each room was dusty and dark, lit only by dirt and moss-encrusted skylights high above. Sauce saw that the first room contained an assortment of metal scraps: wire, rusted automotive parts, rusted and bent playground scraps, and many sheets of corrugated aluminum. The second room contained lumber, wood scraps, huge sections of untreated, bark-covered tree trunks, and a variety of wooden window frames, household doors, and previously used siding; the air was thick with thc smcll of ccdar and pinc.

Peering into the third room, Sauce motioned for BT to accompany him inside. They entered and Sauce closed the door. "Look at that," he whispered, just loud enough to be heard above the clanging that continued to fill the warehouse from somewhere farther down the hall. "I've seen that glass somewhere before." He pointed to a bright blue jagged pane of frosted glass resting against the wall. He pulled on the top of the glass tipping it toward him, and saw a second, smaller, bright green pane behind it. He walked around the room, examining a collection of stained glass designs in various states of disrepair.

Pinned to the far wall was a large, outdated map of the world. "That's it!" Sauce exclaimed. BT closed the gap separating them and followed Sauce's gaze towards the wall map.

"I *knew* the blue and green glass looked familiar. They were used to construct a huge globe. I saw it in Gladys's library. It's massive, made of metal and glass. Kaos made it. I am positive it's his handiwork."

"Then we know why Beckley had his name in that book," said BT. "Let's find the guy and see if that's the only reason."

The two men continued down the hallway, taking a cursory look into the rest of the rooms to ensure that each was unoccupied. Finally, they found the source of the noise. A large, blue overall clad man was pounding away on an automobile-sized, silver, oval disk that was suspended off the ground by a custom, wood-framed, apparatus.

BT silently approached the man and with deft swiftness, intercepted the man's raised hand, removing the heavy mallet from his grasp.

"Hey!" Kaos yelled, shocked as his empty hand flung forward, without the resistance provided by the hammer. He turned toward Sauce and BT and erupted in anger. "Get out! This is my work day. No interviews! No interruptions!"

"Shut up!" yelled BT, holding the hammer in the air.

Kaos immediately assumed a defensive stance, leaning against the piece he had been working on with his arms crossed in front of his face. Sauce jumped to his defense. "All right!" He put a hand up to prevent any violence. "We're not here to hurt you."

"What do you want?" asked Kaos, brushing sweat from his brow into his long grey hair. The top of his head was glistening and bald, though like a monk from the dark ages, long hair descended from a ring of growth around the periphery of his skull. His long hooked nose held onto a pearl of moisture, suspended in anticipation of a final, fateful pull by gravity.

"What's your name?" snapped BT.

"You break in here, threaten me with my own hammer, yet you don't even know who I am?" shouted Kaos.

"Answer the question," replied Sauce sternly, hoping his new partner was posturing.

"Kaos."

"Then we have the right place," said BT, lowering the hammer. He started to walk around the metal disk, tapping it lightly at regular intervals. "My friend and I would appreciate your assistance. Answer our questions, and we'll leave you to continue with your grade school art project."

"Grade school! How dare you?" answered Kaos. "This is a commission piece for the Air Force base in San Diego. Have you any idea what it's worth?"

"Sure," answered BT. "I don't care. I'm interested in something you did in glass. Like these pieces over here." BT walked across the room to a ten-foot by ten-foot triptych of stained glass panels showing the Stations of the Cross. He stared at the panels for a few seconds, aimlessly swinging the hammer forward and backward.

Sauce could see the effect BT's behaviour was having on the sculptor, who was beginning to shake from the anxiety. He quickly posed the question, "What can you tell us about the glass globe?"

"The globe? You've seen my globe? Where?" Kaos inquired.

"Just answer the question," shouted BT, shaking the hammer menacingly in the air.

"Yeah, I made a glass globe. But that was about five years ago, maybe four. A commissioned piece, but I never got the final payment. It was stolen just before I could deliver it."

"Who commissioned it?" asked Sauce.

Kaos stood straight and demanded, "Why should I tell you? Some of my clients trust me to keep their identities secure."

BT walked slowly toward the sculptor, still swinging the hammer. "So, there's nothing we could say that would persuade you to give us a name?"

Kaos started to shake with fear, but held to his convictions. "For all I know, you could have been sent by a past client to test my resolve."

BT smiled and raised the hammer. "I know of a better test of your resolve." He slowly turned to face the triptych. "How good do you think my aim is? Let's see, Christ's face is about, oh twenty yards away. I think I can get this hammer cleanly through his jaw without touching the crown of thorns." He drew his arm above his head and backward, preparing to launch the hammer.

"Styles!" yelled Kaos. "He said his name was Styles. That's it, no first name. He paid fifty percent in advance, twenty-five thousand dollars, directly deposited into my bank account. I was kind of freaked out, because I didn't even tell him where. He just knew my bank and account number. The money was there the day he called to ask me to build it. I didn't think someone who would pay that much in advance would be the type of person to renege on the balance. That's all I know!"

BT lowered the hammer and turned to face Kaos again. "Did this Styles give you any specific instructions or did he just leave it up to you to create anything you wanted?"

"Uh, no. The plans were here the next day, when I arrived at the workshop, just as he told me they would be."

BT looked at Sauce. "I knew he hadn't told us everything." Looking again at Kaos, BT ordered, "Get them."

"I can't. On the phone Styles had told me to keep them in my safe when I was away from the workshop and to not let anyone else see them. But they were stolen from my safe on the same day the globe disappeared."

"Really? Curious," commented BT. "Did you report the theft?"

"No. I waited for Styles to contact me, but he never did. I was afraid, you know? Someone who can break into a safe without leaving a trace and steal a huge, five-and-half-foot diameter globe in the middle of the night is not the kind of person I want to mess with. I figured I was lucky to be done with Styles and chose to forget the whole thing."

"Why would anyone care to hide those plans? What was so unique about the design of that globe?"

"Oh, if Styles found out I talked about it … This is going to end up with me getting killed, isn't it?" shrieked Kaos.

"If it's any comfort," interrupted Sauce, "Styles is dead."

Kaos looked at BT with a renewed sense of immediate fear that he was staring at Styles' killer. He started talking in quick short sentences. "It's all glass on the outside. Supported by seventy-two equal-length curved rods inside. The whole thing is virtually seamless. The top and bottom sections were built separately. They are joined with an internal combination-type locking mechanism. The top turns on the bottom. The first time it's used, it sets the lock. Whoever has it, can turn the top once clockwise, then counterclockwise to the same positions they initially set. Unlocking it allows the top to raise up on a pair of hydraulic posts—I took them from an old Honda Civic hatchback. Opening the top also releases a heavily reinforced metal box. Inside that is a cushioned two by two by two chamber. So the whole thing is a kind of safe."

BT approached Kaos, grabbed one of his hands and smacked the hammer into his palm. "We're done here, for now," BT stated coldly. "Just one other thing, though. This safe you built, is there a back door to bypass the combination?" He stared into Kaos's tear-filled eyes.

"No. No way! I wouldn't do that. Of course, not." Kaos shook his head to support his claim of innocence.

"Let's go," said BT to Sauce. They returned to their car. As BT shut his door he mumbled, "He's lying. If we need to force our way into that globe, then we'll have to pay Kaos another visit."

"A glass safe, that's pretty clever," commented Sauce.

"Beckley was quite the character. Or it might have been all Gladys. Either way, the trick was well conceived. Sauce, I'm impressed that you made the connection between the coloured glass and the globe."

"You wouldn't have actually destroyed those beautiful glass panels would you?"

"We needed him to open up," said BT, without emotion. "If we had more time I could have tortured the information out of him. But you did say we have an appointment to make."

Sauce chuckled awkwardly, not sure if BT was joking or not.

He pulled the ledger from under his seat and flipped the pages. "There are a ton of names in here. Imagine what we could learn if we had the time to check each of these out. We've only identified two of them and already have learned a lot."

"Unfortunately, we have no idea how useful this info really is," countered BT. "The first guy is dead, and the safe may contain nothing to help us. We could waste a lot of time checking out each and every name. What we need is to convince someone else to do that for us."

"You mean like my friend Hammi, who we're meeting for breakfast? He's a cop. We may be able to convince him to enter the names in the police database. He might uncover something useful."

"A cop, you say?" BT quickly pulled a U-turn, then a hard right into a strip mall. He stopped in front of a realtor's office and turned off the engine. "We can't give up the ledger to a cop. We'll never see it again. We need to copy the San Francisco pages. Realtors always have copy machines."

He grabbed the ledger, opened his door and stepped out, followed closely by Sauce. "You can't just walk into someone's office and use their equipment!" warned Sauce.

"Really? Watch me!" BT entered the office and approached the receptionist. "Good morning, ma'am." He pulled out his government identification, flashing it briefly. "Special Agent Torres. We've tracked a serial rapist to this part of the city and are warning all women in the area to take extra precautions getting into their vehicles. Check back seats before entering, don't walk alone after dark, that kind of thing, you understand?"

The receptionist was noticeably alarmed. "Oh, my. Thank you."

"The man is highly dangerous and very likely to reoffend. Of course we are trying to inform the public as quickly as possible. You could be a great help to us; you may even save some young girl's life."

"I'd be happy to do whatever I can. Sure."

"We need to post flyers in the neighbourhood. Many women who live in this area are not home and we'd like to leave them a printed warning and contact information. Would you allow us to use your photocopier?"

"Oh, of course. It's right over here." She led them to the nearby copy room. "Let me set it up for you."

"No need ma'am," continued BT in his authoritative voice. "We've taken enough of your time, thanks. We'll just print a few copies and be on our way."

"Okay," she said, then walked back to her desk.

BT copied the ledger pages for the four largest southern Californian cities, folded the printouts in thirds, and stuffed them into the inside breast pocket of his jacket. As they were leaving the receptionist called, "Thank you for letting me know. I'll be sure to warn everyone I meet."

"Yes, ma'am," answered BT as he was leaving. "It's people like you who make our jobs protecting the pubic much easier."

Back in the car BT looked at Sauce with a wry smile. "Have you ever seen someone more happy to help the authorities?" He chuckled, obviously pleased with himself. "Now which way to the restaurant?"

CHAPTER 18

Sauce and BT entered the restaurant, located Hammi seated in the booth farthest from the entrance, and exchanged names. "You'll never guess who was at my house this morning," were the words that began Hammi's preamble about his morning adventure, which started only fifteen minutes after Sauce's call awakened him that morning.

Sauce searched his memory for past common associates but couldn't come up with a suitable guess for the person that both Hammi and he knew who would prompt the excitement evident in Hammi's voice.

"Gladys's daughter, Dara Stockard!" announced Hammi with unbridled enthusiasm. Sauce looked at BT with a confused expression. He searched for an appropriate response and opted for, "You have to meet this woman," directed at BT.

"I presume this visit was unscheduled?" questioned BT.

"Unscheduled? What gives Sauce?" asked Hammi about the person seated across from him who seemed to be uninformed about recent events in the city.

"He's not from around here," explained Sauce. "BT is new to this whole business. He wasn't in town for all the excitement surrounding the trial."

"Well, let me tell you, it's not everyday a celebrity like that visits my home. My wife answered the door and showed her in, then came running into the bedroom, screaming at me to get dressed. She then woke the kids and got them busy tidying up, fussing about newspapers lying in the hall and dishes on the counter. I have never seen her like that."

"All right, Hammi. We get it," interrupted Sauce. "She caught you off guard. Been there."

"You don't get it," corrected Hammi. "I've been a beat cop for most of my life. My kids rarely mention what I do to their friends; they're embarrassed more than anything. My wife barely tolerates me most of the time. Miss Stockard … in my home … to see me! I'm reborn. My wife actually kissed me before I left to come here. My kids couldn't wait to text their friends."

Sauce's head sank into his hands. He tried to suppress his annoyance and reminded Hammi, "Didn't you think her visit was a tad coincidental? I call you to meet me for breakfast and moments later she's at your doorstep. What happened to those keen cop instincts?"

BT gave a little chuckle, which drew a questioning glance from Sauce. "She's resourceful, that one. Your phone is compromised, obviously. Unless you want her to know our every move, I suggest we stop and buy you a new one after breakfast. You'd better take the battery out of the phone right now, so you don't forget."

"Get that stupid grin off your face," growled Sauce to an elated Hammi. "For Christ's sake, she moved into my house in the middle of the night, while I was sleeping!"

Hammi twirled his moustache and smiled. "That's *your* problem, Sauce, not mine."

"Just tell us what she wanted!" demanded Sauce, loudly.

The waitress approaching the table, changed directions after Sauce's outburst. BT looked longingly at the coffee pot in the waitress's hand and hurriedly got up from the table to follow her. She came back and took the three men's orders, poured coffee for each, then disappeared into the kitchen.

"She is gorgeous," began Hammi after taking a sip of his coffee. "The way she walks and talks … like a movie star. And smart. She knew Eloise's name, and Roland and Emilio, my teens. They sat at the table and she told them that her best friend—she was talking about you, Sauce—was good friends with their father, me! She said you had told her all about us."

"I never mentioned you," interjected Sauce.

"You must have told her at some point. You probably don't remember. She said you've been having a tough go, lately. Too much booze, not enough sleep."

"My God, she's relentless," complained Sauce.

"You're lucky! She really cares about you. Shit, my wife wouldn't try to help me if I went on a three-year bender like you. She'd just pack up the kids and sue my ass off."

"Really lucky!"

"Is any of that true?" asked BT.

"Why the hell do you think you're here?" asked Sauce. "I thought you said you'd been briefed."

BT sat silently, looking intensely at Hammi.

"Oh, you can talk around him," said Sauce noticing BT's resistance to volunteer information.

BT cleared his throat. "The governor said you were in danger and needed to be kept safe while you investigated the attempt on his daughter's life. He praised you very highly, said he believes in you; that's not something he does lightly. And I don't mess with a man's beliefs."

Sauce felt a lump in his throat. "Oh, I wasn't aware. Uh, I only just met him. I don't understand why he would tell you that stuff."

"One more thing: I *have* been fully briefed. We've only just met a few hours ago, but this is what I know: after four years at UCLA, you graduated with first class honours, three years of distinguished records in law school, dropped out to travel with Miss Stockard across the country by train to New Orleans, then by boat to St. Martin, returned to learn your mother had passed on, you started contract work a year later doing insurance investigations. You manage to take enough cases to pay the bills, the bulk of your expenses split about equally between your mortgage and your vodka. Satisfied?"

"That's him! That's our Sauce," quipped Hammi. "Not much more to tell, is there Sauce? Except maybe that you are usually unkempt and smell of booze. Not today, though. Nice suit. Amazing how having a girlfriend like Dara Stockard can make a new man out of you!"

"She told you that? That she's my girlfriend?"

"You have to admit you were due for a makeover. She may have a wacko mother, but the girl seems to be entirely sensible when it comes to you."

Sauce looked at BT. "You see what I am up against. Expert con artists and manipulators."

"I hope you aren't including the governor in that grouping."

"No, of course not. I'm talking about Gladys and that man impersonating Gladys. And Dara. She even has Hammi bamboozled. Why do you think she turned up at his place this morning? To cast her spell on him, that's why."

"You are too suspicious, Sauce. She's not at all like her mother. Well, not too much like her. She came by to offer me and my family front row tickets to the Amber Ellis Show next Tuesday. Gladys will be appearing. Miss Stockard, er, Dara, says that it will be one of the biggest television shows of the year, maybe ever, and she wanted me, as your friend, and my whole family to attend. She said it was your idea."

"Don't go!" shouted Sauce, checking his volume to not alarm the waitress again. "Especially not with your family. I don't know why she invited you, but I don't like it. Listen to me, Hammi. People have already died. You can't risk it."

"You're nuts. With all those cameras and a huge audience, nothing's going to happen on the show. Besides, there's no way I would be able to keep my family away. They are already out shopping for clothes to wear." Hammi looked at BT and asked, "What's your take? You seem to have a good read on people. Are Dara and her mother dangerous?"

"Don't know much about Dara; she seems clean and the governor doesn't have a problem with her. I've known about Gladys for some time, though. Harmless, as far as her sheet goes. A few years ago, when I was still in the Secret Service …"

"You are Secret Service?" interrupted Hammi, with hero worship intensity.

"Uh, retired," answered BT, ignoring the affectation. "I was assigned to a detail of politicians who were planning to attend one of her performances in D.C. Background checks on her and the main theatre staff. Usual preliminary stuff. I also had to attend the event, monitor the entrance to the private box. Nothing unusual about the whole thing, of course. Gladys had an unimpressive past, save for a few minor offenses in her youth, shoplifting as a teen in Canada, crossed illegally into the USA twice while still a minor. Standard indications of a rough upbringing. Nothing suggested she was dangerous, though."

Sauce was intrigued with BT's research. "She claims to have helped with legal investigations on more than one occasion."

"Yeah, she has been an informer. But I wasn't satisfied that the information she provided actually led officials in a new direction. The reports suggested she, more or less, corroborated details that were already known. It's possible the officers who wrote those reports obscured details to make themselves appear more efficient. It's hard to trust these things, you know; people are people."

"You see Sauce? Nothing to worry about!"

"I didn't say that," countered BT. "She obviously wants you and your family in the audience, and I can think of only one reason for that."

"Really?" said Sauce. "You're a better man than me if you can guess Dara's intentions. Each time I think I have her number, she pulls another trick from her sleeve. That's why I don't think Hammi should let his family anywhere near Gladys."

"Oh, shut up, Sauce. Every man who's ever been in love is in the dark about how he got there."

"I am not in love!" shouted Sauce.

"You're living with her!" replied Hammi, smiling.

"She moved in while I was … well, indisposed."

"Be that as it may, I want to know what BT thinks is Dara's reason for inviting me to her mom's show."

Sauce gave up trying to dissuade his friend and let BT speak. "Dara seems to know you very well, don't you think?" he asked Sauce.

"She seems to think so. Well, I guess to be perfectly honest, she knows me well enough to get me investigating her mother's manager's murder, despite my resistance."

"Precisely. She has a pretty good read on you, and knows how to get you to do as she wants. Is that fair?"

"It's consistent with what my life has been like these past few days, yeah," answered Sauce.

"Then she probably knows how you feel about her showing up at your friend's house this morning, dazzling his family and giving them an invitation that they wouldn't in a hundred years pass on."

"You're right," said Sauce, nodding his agreement and understanding of the logic in BT's reasoning. "She knows I can't let Hammi and his family attend without being there myself to ensure their safety. The only flaw in your reasoning is that she hasn't even asked me to attend."

"Now she doesn't have to," chimed in Hammi.

"No, she doesn't," confirmed Sauce, sullenly. The men remained quiet for a while as the food was served and eaten. As Sauce was finishing his meal, he pondered on his predicament, his thoughts mostly on Dara and her ability to manipulate him. He retraced his steps of the previous day. Awakening with awful dreams and a terrible hangover. It seemed like weeks ago since he last had a drink, and he suppressed the craving that suddenly invaded his senses.

Hammi pointed to Sauce's shaking hands. "Dara said you'd be a little irritable for awhile."

Sauce followed his gaze to his hand and defensively commented, "Never mind that; it's nothing." He immediately changed the subject, "I suppose you were too caught up in Dara's spell to remember to make a call to Sacramento like I asked."

"On the contrary, Dara told us she hoped I would be able to help you during your recovery, from uh, your illness."

"Illness, shit!"

"Yeah, well, anyway, as soon as Dara left, my wife was on my case. She told me to get to work, take the whole day, and don't come home until I had solved the whole thing for you. She used to hate when I had to work on my day off. Not today. She couldn't wait to get me on my way. She said she was so proud of me. She even told Dara before she left that I am one of the city's finest officers, with lots of friends in the department who would be eager to help."

"Okay, I get it," said Sauce, shaking his head. He saw through the corner of his eye that BT was finding the whole mess amusing and quickly pushed his friend back on topic. "So, what did you find out about the waitress?"

"First of all, I learned her dad used to work for the government. He was a gardener when she was young. Got sick, some bacterial thing, and couldn't work. The family was in a bad state for many years. Her mother left, got remarried at some point. Seems like a motive to me, dad lost his government job, family falls into debt paying medical bills, and the girl blames the governor for the whole thing."

"It's pretty thin," offered BT. Sauce agreed.

"Not unprecedented, though," continued Hammi. "It seems she managed to get a job with a catering outfit and eventually she was serving drinks at government parties, like at the governor's house yesterday. Spends her money on classes at a community college. That's about it."

"Not quite," said BT. "I was provided with a few more details. He pulled out his cell phone, brought up an email attachment, and began to read, "Katherine Bellows; nineteen years old; recent transactions on her credit card place her near the San Francisco University every Tuesday and

Thursday for the past three weeks. Each day there is a purchase at the United Cafe, exactly seven dollars and eighty-six cents."

"Interesting pattern," commented Sauce.

"We'll have to check the surveillance tapes of street cameras in the area. Hammi, could you do that? She may have been meeting someone?"

"Yeah, I'll get on that right away. Don't want to let my wife down, now, do I?" he stated happily, standing.

"Wait a sec," hastened Sauce. "There's one other small thing we need. BT and I found a list of names that we need looked into." BT pulled the photocopied pages from his pocket and handed them to Hammi.

Hammi flipped through the pages. "A small thing? There are a lot of names here. Where'd you get this?"

"They belonged to Beckley," said BT, "Gladys's dead manager. We need to know if anyone on the list may have had enough of a beef to kill him. We are pretty sure they are all local. Beyond that, we don't know anything about them. So whatever you can uncover about each person's occupation or criminal past might be useful."

"This will take a while. My wife will be *so* happy when I tell her that I have to work through the night," said Hammi, sheepishly. He left without offering to pay his portion of the bill.

BT ordered another coffee. "We need to be very careful with our enquiries around the university. Ms. Bellows had associates there, and I am certain one or more of them were involved in planning yesterday's poisoning. She was a pawn, obviously, and probably wasn't told very much."

"Do you think she was set up by Jett?" asked Sauce.

"More likely, someone closely associated with him. Though a young, pretty girl may on rare occasions fall for an old blind man, more often it's a handsome, charismatic, and wealthy gentleman closer to her own age. I think the most curious part is that she was obviously paying for the drinks when they met. She paid each time."

"Perhaps he wanted to give an impression of poverty," offered Sauce. "Some girls can't resist a hard luck story."

"Especially if that story resembled her own past," agreed BT. "Clearly we need more information. The governor is arranging meetings with each of the senators who has already suffered a loss due to the blackmail for tomorrow. Also I really want to meet your *girlfriend*." BT said the last word with such flowery intonation that Sauce couldn't help but cringe.

"What about the guy impersonating Gladys?"

"I would love to, but we can't," said BT. "The governor's instruction, I'm afraid. He's certain we won't learn anything useful from him, or her, or whatever. So Onofrio asked that I leave *Gladys* alone. He said to direct any questions for Gladys to him, and he would get the answers for me. I know, it's not how I like to conduct an investigation, but, as I said, he really believes in Gladys. Besides, we have a lot of other suspects, especially now that we have Beckley's ledger."

"And then there's Jett."

"Yeah. Touchy situation, that one. If he is our man, we don't want to say anything to him to force his hand against those kids. How did you leave it with him the last time you two spoke?"

"That was in my bathroom, yesterday morning," said Sauce. BT raise his eyebrows. "Dara was in the house and I didn't want her to know I was calling him. Anyway, he didn't care if Dara knew. In fact, Jett told me not to hide the call from her, but to make her believe that I didn't trust him, you know, so Dara wouldn't be guarded around me, I guess."

"And you obliged, of course."

"I told her, yeah of course," said Sauce. "Oh yeah, he also said for me not to call him. He said when he needed to talk, he would get in touch with me."

"That's interesting. The man is suspicious, isn't he?"

"Yeah, probably because I told him Gladys tried to hire me to follow him. I also told him Gladys said he had threatened Dara. He denied it, of course."

"Well, if he killed Beckley, then he also threatened to kill Dara. That much is clear from the letter."

"Which letter?" asked Sauce.

"I told you I was sent a copy of each of the blackmail letters. The letter addressed to Gladys was included in the folder. You know, I think the best thing for us to do for the rest of the afternoon is to review all the materials so we are both equally knowledgeable about the case. Then tomorrow we'll be able to make informed inquiries as we begin our interviews with the witnesses."

"That's a plan," agreed Sauce.

CHAPTER 19

BT dropped Sauce off in front of his house at six that evening with a promise to return at eight the next morning. Following BT's suggestion, Sauce immediately reached into his pocket for his old cell phone and reinserted the battery. It was the easiest way for Jett to contact him. Sauce waited at the roadside as the car pulled away. His stomach began to feel odd, and his hands trembled. He sighed and thought, "This used to be when I would pour myself a couple of drinks to help me relax." He fretted that the likelihood of being able to maintain his usual routine was extremely low. He considered walking to the nearest pub or catching a cab to a liquor store on the premise of finally retrieving his car from the restaurant. Curiosity, however, got the best of him as he just had to find out what Dara had done to his home while he was away all day.

He entered the front door, which was unlocked, and stared in disbelief. The dingy beige walls of his living room were painted a brilliant, lime green. His comfortable and inexpensive Swedish sofa and armchair were gone. As were the stained, laminate tables. Sauce admitted to himself, that he loved the new furniture, especially the semi-circular, black leather, overstuffed sectional with a matching reclining chair. The room was centered by a striking, low table, the top a darkly stained one-piece section of a tree trunk that added an ambiance to the room that Sauce hadn't realized was possible. The walls were also adorned with an assortment of prints and oil paintings in a style Sauce found novel, yet inoffensive. The only item of his original furnishings that remained was his mother's hanging lamp, which did not fit in with the new decor, though Sauce was pleased to see it in its familiar location, in the far corner.

"Is that you, honey?" came a sing-song voice from the kitchen.

"Oh, God!" mumbled Sauce at the term of endearment. Loudly, he called to Dara, "Hardwood floors! How the hell did you manage to replace the laminate tile and do all this in one day?"

"Come in here!" she answered excitedly. "You'll love the kitchen."

Sauce approached the kitchen, his nostrils dancing from the aromas of sugar and spice, meats and vegetables grilling, and a hint of freshly baked bread. He entered the kitchen, eyes wide, mouth open.

"You are just in time to taste the gravy. I rarely get a chance to cook anymore, so please tell me if the seasoning is right."

He stared at Dara, standing in bright red high heels. His eyes began at her feet and slowly ascended, taking in the beauty of domestic bliss between paced and punctuated saccades. Her red and white dress, with a tease of crinoline dangling beneath the skirt around her knees, spoke of a fifties ideal that he had seen in movies. Her dirty blonde locks were tussled in a neat bun atop her head. Her makeup was un-Dara like: tasteful, and refined.

"What is all this going to cost me?" was the first thing he said, dazzled by the shiny, stainless steel surfaces of the new appliances, and the brilliant black of the graphite counter tops. "Lace?" he mouthed noticing that the dust-covered, never-once-cleaned window blinds had been replaced with pale, floral curtains, trimmed in pearly-white lace.

"Don't be silly," she laughed gaily. "Come. Have a taste." She dangled a spoon in the air, like Eve with the proverbial apple.

He obliged, placing his mouth over the spoon. Her expression was one of hope and anticipation. "It's good," he answered, wiping a stray, crimson droplet from his bottom lip. "Hot!"

"Thank you," kidded Dara, placing the spoon on the counter and running both hands down the sides of her skirt. Then she grasped both of his hands, raised them, and twirled around, ending with a gentle kiss on his cheek.

"Now our house is a home!"

"Right," said Sauce, coolly. "Remind me. What's my name?"

"Oh, hush," chided Dara, playfully. "Everything is almost ready. You sit right there." She motioned to the seat at the head of the new oak table with decorative walnut inlays, "I'll bring you a drink."

"Now you're talking. I could sure use one," stated Sauce, eagerly following her directions.

She placed a filled, frosted, martini glass at the top of his place setting. Sauce drank the contents in one gulp and asked for another.

"You like it. I'm glad. It's the latest out of Poland. I had a devil of a time finding it on such short notice. It really does taste like real vodka, doesn't it?"

"Real vodka? What the hell is it?"

"It doesn't really have an English name yet. I'm sure it will once the marketing people get their act together. I guess you could call it, un-vodka." She refilled his glass, and Sauce immediately pushed it a few inches away.

Ignored his reaction, she served two plates of sliced, rare steak, roasted red peppers, baked potatoes, and freshly baked, light brown topped buns. She placed a small bowl next to each plate, filled with a lightly dressed tomato and cucumber salad.

Sauce looked at the meal and thought it was unlike any he had ever had in his home. He looked in the direction of the appliance he most used, but saw that his trusty microwave oven had been removed. He felt a tinge of loss, yet had to admit the change was welcome. He immediately started to load his fork with a piece of steak.

"Wait," snapped Dara, seated in the chair right next to Sauce. "Wouldn't you like to say grace, or thanks, for our good fortune? There are so many people who have less than we do."

"Christ, you're kidding right?" Sauce looked at her smiling face and couldn't detect any sarcasm. He put his fork down and pondered what he could say to end this awkward moment so he could eat without feeling guilty. "How about this: today was a good day, better than many I have had, and I guess there are probably some people on this planet who wish they could be in my shoes."

"Okay for a beginner, I guess," joked Dara. She took a sip of her drink and waited patiently for Sauce to take a bite and offer a comment, which he did with a nod, half-smile and a grunt. She then started to eat, seemingly elated.

After a few quiet minutes, she put her fork down and asked, "So how was your first day on the trail with Mr. Torres?"

"I'm eating," mumbled Sauce.

"Multitask," she said in an irresistibly lilting voice.

"All right," he began grudgingly. "Let's start with Hammi. I like him. Please tell his family to stay home next Tuesday. I'll go. You don't need to use them as a lure."

"You're afraid for them. How cute?"

"You win, Dara. I give up. You can take over my home, take away my booze, transform me into whatever kind of man you want. Just keep them out of it. That's the only thing I ask."

"I'm not trying to transform you. I'm just helping you to return to the man you were … before. And on the other point, Tuesday's show is just part one. I'll let you in on the surprise. Everyone in attendance will be asked to return for a

Wednesday evening special where Gladys will announce the name of the real murderer of her manager."

"She will?" said Sauce. "I assume the name she has in mind is Dr. Jett." Dara nodded, politely keeping silent with a mouthful of food. "Have the show's producers never heard of the legal term, libel? They will be sued into bankruptcy."

"The producers don't know, of course. They wouldn't have approved a live, primetime television special of the Amber Ellis Show if Gladys told them about that." Dara rose from the table to get a serving tray, from which she scooped a serving of meat and vegetables and placed this on Sauce's already empty plate. "I'm so glad you have an appetite."

"Thank you, but don't change the subject." Sauce intended to sound sharp and authoritative, but gratitude for the excellent meal softened his delivery. "Why two shows?"

"I'll answer your question, but first let's finish eating. Besides, you haven't even told me about your day. Dinner conversation should be about our day, don't you think? You can see what I've been up to. Beside that short trip to your friend's home, I have been here all day."

Sauce sighed and thought, "She refuses to relinquish control." Despite wanting to convince

Dara to uninvite Hammi's family from Gladys's shows, he decided to remain civil and continue with the discussion under Dara's direction. "How many people did it take to pull off this renovation so quickly?"

"A few. Marcel took care of all the big design decisions. He knew my tastes from the reno I had him complete on Mummy's house years ago. I sent some cell phone photos of the main rooms two nights ago, while you were asleep. He showed up this morning with his crew and viola. Like magic."

"And what about my things? My microwave?"

"These are your things now," answered Dara. "Out with the past, you know. It all had to go. Except for your mom's lamp, of course. Despite what we think of them sometimes, you and I wouldn't be where we are today without our mothers."

Sauce finished the last forkful of food, took a sip of his drink, wincing at the thought of it being non-alcoholic, then pushed his chair away from the table. "I suppose there's dessert?"

"Never serve a meal without dessert, Mummy always used to say."

Sauce detected a hint of melancholy in Dara's voice. "Was that the kind of advice she'd give you over the phone from somewhere on the other side of the planet while strangers raised her young daughter in San Jose."

"You make it sound beastly. It wasn't like that at all," she explained as she cleared the dishes. "Before dessert, let's clean up these dishes. Wash or dry?"

"I thought the new dishwasher you just had installed did both."

"And I thought it would be more cozy if we did it the old-fashioned way, together."

"Whatever you want. I usually just leave them until I run out of clean dishes. It saves time to do them all at once."

"Nonsense. You wash, that way my hands won't get all wrinkly like an old maids."

"Sure," he said, moving to the sink and preparing a soapy bath. "Dinner's over, so how about you answer that question."

"Not so fast! You still haven't told me about your progress today."

"Fair enough." He washed a plate and handed it to Dara to dry. "BT and I searched Beckley's office. It's bugged, by the way, or perhaps you already knew that."

"No, that must be Jett. Why search his office? Certainly you knew the police had already removed his files and notes."

"They didn't remove everything. I came across a ledger of names and numbers. Do you know anything about that?"

"Mummy does! Beckley told her that his professional contacts were locked in his brain. Mummy knew he wasn't that clever and assumed he wrote them down somewhere. Where is it? Mummy really needs those contacts."

"BT kept it. He's going to run some of those names through some legal databases, CIA and Interpol most likely, before we meet tomorrow."

"Well that's a big waste of time. Mummy will know what to do with that list." She reached for the next plate. "What else did you learn?"

"BT showed me those letters."

"And what did you think?"

"Whoever sent them is a crackpot; that's my first impression. The blackmail attempt is futile, totally futile. I mean, expecting senior members of government to take a pay cut is ridiculous."

"And yet?"

"Yeah," he continued, "and yet there is a method to the madness. For example, letters were sent to all voting members of the legislature, yet only six, including the governor, were directly threatened. They were all sent on the same day, too. Except the letter sent to Gladys; that was put in the mail on the day Beckley was killed. BT thinks this fact is proof of Gladys's innocence. While I don't think it exonerates Gladys, I have to admit that a more likely scenario is that someone else killed Beckley to obtain information. And since Gladys was his only client I think the killer found out that Gladys was trying to subvert his blackmail efforts."

"Brilliant."

"Not really. I am still very confused about the endgame here. I can't for the life of me believe the governor even considered giving in to the demands of those letters. He can't. Whoever wrote those letters must know that he can't overhaul the government. I mean he wants to cut all public servant wages to match minimum wage, tell elected officials to abandon their perks and benefits and pay for their own health care. It's insane. I suppose he had to follow through with killing the dogs. But the kids, why threaten to escalate without any hope of obtaining those ludicrous demands?"

Dara placed her hands on Sauce's shoulders and started to rub gently. "Onofrio said that most of the people who received the letters are filled with terror. The police are on alert, but what can they do without any evidence. So far they are sitting on the fence about Jett's involvement. There isn't much they can do, is there? That's why Mummy has decided to force the situation. With the failed attempt on Onofrio's daughter, Jett has to escalate his attack."

"What if Gladys has it all wrong, though? If Jett isn't involved, her plans may aggravate the real killer. It wouldn't be the first time that a false accusation provoked a madman seeking recognition and fame."

"I don't think fame is the objective, though."

"No, I don't either. The letters stipulated 'no publicity.' Oddly, they didn't warn against telling the police. Now that I think of it, I have to wonder why this hasn't reached the press. You'd think someone would have said something. Even in the newspaper article about last night's incident at the governor's house, no mention was made about the letters and their threats. All the blame was placed on the unfortunate waitress."

"The politicians are a pretty tight group," suggested Dara. "Regardless of their party status, they are equal when it comes to threats against their income and lifestyle." She paused for a moment to apply extra pressure on his right shoulder, rubbing hard with both hands. "You are so tense. Leave the rest of the dishes. Let's move to the living room and I'll help you relax."

They only got halfway toward the sofa when Sauce's old cell phone rang. "So *now* it's working," remarked Dara.

Sauce cast a wry smile in her direction as he raised the phone to his ear. Dara reached over and hit the speaker phone button.

"H-Hello."

"Sauce, it's me. I'm still at the station …"

"You're on speaker, Hammi. Dara's here."

"Oh, hi Ms. Stockard. Perhaps I should call back tomorrow."

"Nonsense," said Dara "Sauce and I don't have secrets."

"It's fine, Hammi. What do you need?" asked Sauce.

"That partner of yours, BT, works quickly. He stopped in at the station a few minutes ago. Seems he did some of the legwork for me … went to that coffee shop where the waitress made those transactions. He talked the manager into handing over the digital files for the past few weeks. I quickly looked over the disk, found the time for one of the transactions, and it turns out she *was* meeting someone. Here I'll send over a photo cut from the video. Call back if you recognize her. Oh, also, I'm about a third of the way through that list of names. A cornucopia of trade workers, lawyers, doctors and criminals … well thieves actually, some very high end operators, others with just petty offenses, scam artists, pickpockets, that sort of thing. I don't see anyone who would want Beckley dead."

Dara was about to say something but Sauce help us a hand, stopping her, and quickly replied, "Thanks Hammi. Look forward to hearing what else you discover. We'll talk soon." He disconnected the call.

"You see? He's a good man. He's working hard to help, yet you insist on getting his family involved."

His phone buzzed, signaling an incoming message which Sauce opened. The image sent from Hammi came up on the screen, and Sauce's face revealed instant recognition.

"You know her!" exclaimed Dara.

"Yeah, I do," answered Sauce slowly, not sure how to tell Dara without sounding like an idiot. He prepared himself for gloating and the obvious 'I told you so.' "It's the secretary of the Organic Chemistry department at the university. Jett said he hired her himself."

"You have to tell Hammi. And BT. The police have to pick her up. We finally have a concrete connection to Jett."

"Hammi knows his job. I'll send him a text with the name." Sauce typed into his phone and hit send. He then dialed BT's number. There was no answer, so Sauce left a detailed voicemail. "She seemed clueless when I met her," Sauce mumbled, unable to hide the overwhelming self-deprecation he was feeling.

"You're just a trusting soul, that's all. You see good in everyone."

"That's just it. I think my instincts were just so off. The only one I would have suspected when I visited the university was his arrogant grad student, Mackie. Of course, as the son of a wealthy London banker, what would he care about rich politicians in this country."

He plopped down on the sofa, exhausted. He immediately started to relax in the plush cushions and enveloping aroma of new leather. Dara sat next to him and pulled his head down onto her lap. "You look tired. Relax and close your eyes. While you rest, I'll tell you all about the shows coming up next week."

"Finally," replied Sauce softly. He turned over onto his side and propped his feet over the arm of the sofa as Dara began gently making circles around his temples with her fingers.

CHAPTER 20

"Bacon!" Sauce awoke with this one word echoing in his brain. He was brought back to consciousness by the familiar welcome odour tickling his nostrils and activating his salivary glands. He sat up in bed and looked around. He recognized the overall shape of the room, the proximity of the entrance to the bathroom, the sliding closet doors. Beyond that, however, he was in unfamiliar territory. "Apparently Dara waved her magic wand in this room, too," he thought. He felt like a stranger, a hungry stranger.

"Dara!" he shouted.

He waited a few seconds before repeating his loud call. Dara walked in, smiling and holding a slice of bacon within a set of tongs. She slowly and seductively climbed next to Sauce, on her knees. His eyes were drawn to her low cut blouse and the shape of her hips approaching him on the bed. She extended her hand and presented her offering to him.

"You were so out of it last night, naughty boy. No energy for anything. And I was *so* ready for anything," she whispered this last line then leaned toward him and kissed him passionately.

Sauce pushed her back a little and took the offering. "How'd I get here?" he asked between bites.

"I was talking away, rubbing your head. I saw you were asleep and helped you to bed. That was it. You just checked out for the night. Hurry and get dressed. BT should be here in about half an hour." She gave him another quick kiss on his lips then added, "And I have breakfast ready."

She bounced off the bed and out of the room. Fifteen minutes later, Sauce was dressed and seated in the kitchen sipping coffee while Dara finished his eggs.

"I haven't slept like that in years." He regretted missing his opportunity to learn Gladys's plans. He didn't remember anything Dara said about the upcoming shows. "I'll just have to ask her again when I get home this evening," he thought. He admitted to himself that his certainty about Dara being in his home when he returned after a day's work felt pleasant.

"You needed it." Dara set a plate in front of him. "Eat. I suspect you are probably kicking yourself for drifting off before I could tell you about Mummy's plans. No worries. Here's the abridged version, before you run."

Sauce was about to speak but Dara pushed a forkful of hashed potatoes into his mouth. "First, it was the network's idea to do the two shows on consecutive days, not Mummy's. When she first asked Amber Ellis to do a daytime show, then a primetime special next Wednesday night—you know they've been friends for many years—well Amber can't just make decisions like that without consulting her producers. They recognized how hot the show would be with Mummy as the guest, so they approached the network for more money."

Noticing the time, Sauce ignored decorum and interrupted with his mouth still full of food, "Get to the part that requires Hammi's family to be in the audience."

"I am, just keep eating. Mummy insisted that the primetime special had to be on the Wednesday night. The network came back with a provisional approval. They insisted on scheduling the first show on the day before the evening show, and that posed some logistical issues for Mummy. Mummy had to figure out how to structure the two shows for maximum interest from the audience and maximum safety for herself. She decided that during the first show, she would discuss everything that happened at the séance. That would be the teaser. She'll end the show by telling the audience to tune in on Wednesday night when she will reveal exactly what happened while she was in jail and correct a grave injustice she committed.

"The audience will assume she intends to confess to Beckley's murder. Instead she's going to reveal that Jett is the murderer."

"He won't be pleased."

"Mummy expects that he'll do something to disrupt the show. That's why Hammi will be there. And he'll be motivated to act. He won't let Jett interrupt Mummy in front of his family. Don't you get it? He's Mummy's secret weapon."

"That's manipulation!"

"That's show business. Someone is always manipulated in reality television. Anyway, you will be there as well to make sure nothing goes wrong."

"Give me a break." Sauce was silenced by the sound of the doorbell. Dara pointed at his food, silently telling him to keep eating while she answered the door.

Sauce heard BT's voice say, "Hello Miss Stockard. I'm Beto Torres."

"Sure you are. Please call me Dara. Sauce is almost ready." Moments later, BT and Dara were standing over Sauce who was hurriedly trying to finish the last bite of egg yolk-covered toast.

"Have a seat. Can I get you some coffee?" Dara asked BT.

"We have to go," blurted Sauce.

"We have time," said BT pleasantly. "I'd love a cup, especially if you will stay and join us."

Sauce was surprised at BT's demeanor. He was smiling and flirting like a schoolboy. He finished the food in his mouth, took a swig of coffee, and wiped his mouth on a napkin, all the while watching BT stare at Dara.

"Your home is very nice, Sauce," offered BT, not taking his eyes off Dara. "Really tasteful. It's obvious a woman had a hand in the design choices." He saw Dara point to the small porcelain pitcher of cream on the counter and stammered, "Uh, oh, no. Just black is fine."

"Thank you," said Dara in reply to his compliment on the decor, smiling brightly as she handed a cup of coffee to BT.

BT took a sip. "Excellent. Just what I needed." Dara sat next to BT, who edged his seat slightly closer to hers. "I spoke with Onofrio last night. He reminded me that Jett may try to mitigate the damage caused by his failed attempt to poison his daughter. I agree with him: Jett may shift his attack to the most recent source of his pain. If it wasn't for you two, Jett would have succeeded the other day."

"Mummy deserves the credit," countered Dara.

"Yeah, sure," said Sauce dismissively. In response to BT he asked, "Isn't that partly why the governor asked you to join me during the day?"

"I may be able to ward off an attack on you, but Onofrio is worried about, Miss—uh, Dara." He looked at her and smiled. "Perhaps you would be safer if you accompanied us."

Sauce was shocked at the suggestion. He thought to himself, "I only agreed to spending my days with you because I would be free from Dara."

"No, I have errands to run," Dara said. "I'll be busy all day, around lots of people. I'll be perfectly safe."

"Very well," answered BT. "Just to be extra safe, though, I don't think you should stay here by yourself. Not even for a few minutes. I checked around the neighbourhood when I arrived this morning. The house doesn't seem to be under surveillance, but you can never be one hundred percent certain. I suggest we all leave at the same time, and Sauce can call you right before heading home, so you two can arrive together."

"That sounds prudent," replied Dara.

BT placed his hand gently on Dara's forearm. "Also, I would like to do a quick inspection of your car before we leave." Sauce recoiled at the intimacy in his voice and behaviour.

"I would be very grateful," answered Dara, putting a hand over his.

"What the hell was all that?" snapped Sauce once the two men were finally on their way in BT's rental car. "I would have been right out; you didn't have to come into the house."

"Actually, I did," replied BT calmly. "Onofrio's wife told the governor that she believes Dara is in love with you. I wanted to see you two together to determine if the feeling was mutual. So I flirted a little. Your immediately jealous reaction answered my question."

"I'm not jealous. I was surprised at you; that's all! You were acting like everyone does around Gladys and Dara: gushing, hanging on her every word."

"Come on, Sauce. You're smitten. Anyone could see that. You may compromise our investigation if you aren't clear on your own feelings toward the girl."

"Our investigation will be fine. Just drop it. Where are we headed first?"

BT chuckled softly, then abruptly switched his focus to the morning's business. "Senator Braush is in Washington, but his wife is home and expecting us this morning at their apartment on the hill near the Coit Tower. We'll speak with her then head out of the city to Sausalito. We're scheduled to have lunch with Senator Prouit and his wife at their estate."

Sauce sat silently, still brooding, though trying to shift his thoughts away from Dara and back onto the investigation. Despite these efforts, his thoughts kept drifting back to the morning, waking up refreshed, being well fed, not having a hang-over. "She's been in my life for less than a week, and look at me," he thought.

"What's that?" asked BT.

Realizing that his old habit of thinking aloud had betrayed him again, Sauce quickly shifted the conversation. "I was wondering if you learned anything new about the waitress. Did you get my message about Edith, the receptionist at the university?"

"Oh yes. It took a while last night to find out about her. Not what you'd expect, I'll tell you. I checked her employment records at the university. None of it added up so I ran a facial recognition search on the photo Hammi clipped from the video. Turns out this little girl has quite a rap sheet. The university registrar has her listed as Edith Wharton. Her real name is EB. Yeah, that's right, just the two letters, both capitalized, no punctuation. EB, last name, West. Most of the West family lives around

Baker, California, near the Nevada border. She's been in and out of juvenile hall since the age of seven. Her whole family is messed up. Her father was murdered in a bar fight when she was really young. He had just finished serving seven years for manslaughter.

"I wouldn't be surprised if Beckley was killed by one of the Wests. Many of them, especially her bothers and cousins have a long history of violence and intimidation, often in the course of extortion and drug related activities. I passed the info on to Hammi. He's checking to see if any of them have been reported in the area."

"Isn't he going to pick her up for questioning?" asked Sauce.

"They tried last night. No luck. The address the university had for her was vacant. Seems she cleared out quickly, left most of her things, even clothes and television. Presumably the failed attempt by the waitress sparked her desertion. I called the organic chemistry office this morning and was told she did not show up for work yesterday or today. I can think of one person who probably knows where she is."

"Jett," mumbled Sauce.

"No point in wondering. Chances are Jett has already taken care of her—most likely paid for her to leave the country. I'm sure he wouldn't risk the wrath of her family by hurting her."

"So we may get another chance with her yet," said Sauce.

The car turned just before Telegraph Hill Boulevard, then onto a side street to connect to Kearny, where BT backed up tightly to the curb and turned off the engine.

"Second house on the left," said BT as the two men crossed the street. "She has a security guard outside her front door; he's been informed to let us in."

"Paranoid?" asked Sauce.

"Terrified, I'm told."

Sauce and BT found the guard and were shown in to a bright sitting room with large bay windows revealing a spectacular view of the tower. "Things are looking up," joked Sauce.

"Are they?" answered a raspy, deep female voice from the adjacent hall. She entered the sitting room, quickly shuffled across the room and sat in a corner, out of window view.

"Mrs. Braush, thank you for agreeing to meet with us today," greeted BT.

"It's true, then," she answered, arms crossed and leaning forward. "You got the man who killed my pookie!" She breathed noisily as she spoke, as if she was perpetually gasping for air.

"No ma'am. We have only begun our investigations."

"Oh dear, oh dear, oh dear," she lamented, shaking her head slowly from side to side. "Renata said you would put an end to this sordid affair."

Sauce looked at BT, shrugged his shoulders, and decided to attempt a question. "We'd like some background; would you mind answering a few questions?"

"No, I don't mind. I figured that was why you came. Just don't ask me about that satanic séance!" Mrs. Braush moaned loudly.

"Well, uh, how long ago did you get your dog?" asked Sauce, sitting down on the sofa next to her.

"Fifteen glorious years," she answered. "She was more than a dog, you understand. Ursa was a part of me. We were inseparable. She knew what I was thinking at every moment of the day or night."

"I see," continued Sauce. "I take it, then, you were usually the one who fed Ursa, food, water, snacks."

"She would turn her nose up if anyone else was in the room while she was eating. She was a very proper, private person."

"How then, do you suppose, was the killer able to administer the poison?" interjected BT. "I checked the toxicity report. It was definitely the same unidentified solution that was in little Annabelle's drink."

Mrs. Braush looked at BT. "Are you the young man who's attached to Gladys's daughter?"

BT smiled at the thought of being called a 'young man' while Sauce answered, "No. I guess you might say that's me. I'm Mr. Aase. He's Mr. Torres, a, um, friend of the governor. He's helping with the investigation."

The old lady shifted in her seat to put a little more distance between Sauce and herself. "Oh," she said softly. She clasped her trembling hands and put them in front of her mouth.

"I'm sorry," said Sauce. "We don't mean to upset you. If you could just tell us a little about the day leading up to your dog's untimely passing."

"Has she mentioned me?" she asked softly, looking at Sauce through a sideways glance.

"Uh, has who mentioned you?" asked Sauce, casting a confused look at BT.

"The girl," she answered.

Still unsure, Sauce took a few seconds to review the conversation so far, so he could ascertain an appropriate response. BT attempted to re-ask his question, "Ma'am, we were wondering …"

"Don't interrupt, young man," she snapped, getting increasingly agitated. She looked sternly at Sauce. "I asked you a question. Has Gladys's daughter mentioned me? Or are you sworn to secrecy?"

"No, Mrs. Braush," answered Sauce, perplexed yet intent on trying to instill calm in the old lady. "Do you know her?"

"Ahhhh!" she cried out. She rocked back and forth with her hands pulling her hair on both sides of her head. "I knew it. She told you all about it. She knows! She must know! Gladys told her."

Sauce stood up, frightened that the woman might be senile. He walked over to BT, unsure if they should leave as the woman continued to rock and mumble to herself incoherently.

BT spoke in a soft voice, "Ma'am, honestly, we do not know what has you so troubled. But if there is something you would like to get off your chest, if there's something you know pertaining to this case, you might feel better, and we may be able to help you, if you just tell us. Mr. Aase and I were not told of any relationship between you and Gladys except that which involved the séance in her home."

"It's all going to come out now, isn't it? The gates of Hell have been opened. No one can escape their demons." She stopped rocking and sat silently for a few minutes, tears pouring from her eyes. BT left the room, then returned with a glass of water, handing it Mrs. Braush.

"It's all my fault." She clasped both hands tightly around the glass. "I didn't even want to go to her house. Renata told me I had to go. She said it would bring me closure and may help her little girl. I was so afraid."

"What made you so afraid? Was it Gladys's psychic abilities?"

"Psychic abilities." She scoffed and took a sip of water. "I don't believe in any of that nonsense. I hated her. I brought the hate, the devil, into that house. I knew it at the time, yet there I was bringing the devil in there to meet my poor Ursa."

"You hated Gladys? Why?" asked BT. Sauce, however, thought this was the sanest thing the woman had said to them.

"So your girl didn't tell you about me? About what I did to her years ago? About the threats?"

"No, ma'am," answered Sauce. "Ms. Stockard has not. Perhaps you should start at the beginning."

She took a deep wheezing breath and proceeded to explain. "It's bound to come out now. My husband was shopping for a suit. It was many years ago. We were told by some of his political friends about a tailor in San Jose. He was supposed to be an up-and-comer, you know. Ursa was just a baby. We were in his store and my husband was getting measured, when these three rug-rats—barefooted, screaming, little girls—came in, running around, chasing each other. I pulled on Ursa's lead; she was getting all worked up. This one little girl came around the corner, not looking where she was going and stepped on my baby's foot. What was Ursa to do but defend herself? She gave that little cretin a good chomp on her calf. The little girl screamed and that stupid tailor came running. He looked at the little girl and cried out. You'd have thought Ursa had bitten *him*. He was in such a state, wrapping a brand new wool suit jacket around her leg, screaming at me—*me*!—to get out. My husband pulled on my arm to leave. Oh, the dear man, if only I had listened to him. I was upset, though. My Ursa was shaking. I told the tailor I was going to get the best lawyer in the state and sue his you-know-what off. I used some language that I shouldn't have."

Sauce and BT listened silently. Sauce wondered if this was going to be a typical shaggy dog story with little substance at the end. She continued, "I calmed down after we left his shop and forgot the whole thing by the time we got to our home; we were living in Fresno then. The next day who do you think turned up at my door? Gladys! It turns out that little brat who upset my dog was her daughter. Yeah, that's right! She screamed at me as soon as I opened the door. That just made me angry all over again. She asked me if I had any idea who she was. Of course I knew her. My friends went to her shows religiously. Every time she was in town they'd try to get me to go with them. But not me! I didn't believe in that mumbo-jumbo. I was such a fool.

"I told her I was going to launch the biggest lawsuit the country had ever seen, or something like that. That was when she became really calm. I admit I haven't had a day without fear since that moment. When she looked at me, calm and intense, I knew I was messing with powers beyond this world. She told me I was not going to tell anyone about her daughter. Instead, she told me, I was going to see death: see it every day for the rest of my life. She said that my future had violence, pain and loss. Nothing but pain and loss. Then she left. I was shaking."

"Did you sue her?"

She looked at BT with squinting eyes. "Did you hear a word of what I just said? Other people talk about 'Good Gladys the loving, caring Gladys.' I saw her for what she really is. A conduit for the devil. I felt death and knew she was going to send it to my home. No! I stayed away from her and didn't tell another soul about it. But she still got her revenge."

"Gladys did not kill Ursa," said BT calmly.

"Perhaps not directly, but she invited evil to my home. I don't know how. I just know that it was because of Gladys that Ursa was chosen, then poisoned."

"Then why did you go to her house for the séance?" asked Sauce. "You could have said no."

"I had to be there. Call it greed, or whatever. Renata said that I might get to speak with Ursa one last time. I couldn't pass on the possibility, the slim chance that Ursa might reach out to me. I wanted one more moment with my baby. I didn't know how these things work. I had no idea then how powerful hate is."

"I'm lost. What did you do at her house?" asked Sauce.

"Not just me, you stupid man. Me and Ursa. I sat at the table, holding hands, concentrating on my hate. I asked Ursa to come and get her revenge: take away that little girl's mother, just as she took my Ursa from me. No sooner had I completed my prayer than the lights went out and bam! She was gone, and that hideous creature was there in her place."

"He says he is Gladys," said BT, entirely unaffected by the old lady's hysterics.

"That's exactly what the devil would say, isn't it?" retorted Mrs. Braush. "Gladys created the door to the underworld, I invited the devil in, then Ursa pushed the devil through. You see it now, don't you?" She squeezed her eyes tightly closed and extended her arms, as if she was expecting to be put in handcuffs.

"I think we are done, for now," said Sauce to BT. "Mrs. Braush, thank you for your time. I don't think we will need to bother you again."

She opened her eyes and stared at the two men as they walked out of the room.

CHAPTER 21

In the car on their way to Sausalito, Sauce voiced a comment he was dying to say ever since Mrs. Braush's last statement: "She thinks her dog went to Hell."

"She would know, wouldn't she?" chuckled BT. "Not the most reliable witness."

"Funny. I used to think Gladys mainly appealed to crackpots like her. Yet she hates Gladys. And the governor, an otherwise reasonable, logical man, he … well, he doesn't."

"One thing I've learned over forty plus years in law enforcement is that people are weird."

Sauce looked at BT and laughed. "That's it, huh? People are weird. I didn't realize I was riding with a philosopher."

BT looked slightly miffed about the sarcasm. "All right I may have learned a few other things. She was seriously disturbed. I just don't have the energy to offer a more detailed critique of her or people like her. I was up most of the night scanning the pages of that ledger."

"You scanned the whole thing?"

"Yeah … had to if we were going to keep a copy of it in our possession. Onofrio told me to courier it to him immediately. Besides, I have a friend at Interpol who agreed to check out as many names as he had time for on their database. I emailed the scanned pages to him. Who knows? We may get lucky."

BT accelerated past a few cars and pulled abruptly into the right hand lane as they approached the end of the Golden Gate Bridge. "We'd better hurry or we'll be late for our next appointment. Onofrio emphasized that this is our last opportunity to meet with the senator and his wife before they leave the country for a month."

"Opportunity," mused Sauce.

"What's that?"

"I was just thinking about those letters. The demands don't make any sense."

"No. I was saying the same thing to Onofrio this morning," agreed BT. "Even if this Jett character is just trying to instill terror, there must be hundreds of ways to do that. Why this particular method? For that matter, why single out these six politicians? Onofrio's men have spent weeks crosschecking their past meetings and histories and couldn't find a policy or platform link, or anything connecting them specifically to Jett. Did you know Jett was involved in a congressional task force on research spending? It was only for a year, though, before the funding for the task force was cancelled. As far as we can tell, there wasn't any hard feelings afterward to provoke this kind of action. Also none of the target politicians were involved, so it's really a dead end."

Sauce sat up excitedly. "Maybe that's not the point. We know he had someone on the inside at the governor's home, the waitress. That gave him the opportunity. Perhaps that is the common link. Jett may have six of these insiders, each with access to a politician's family. These six targets may have been selected simply because Jett had the opportunity to strike them at close range. I'll call Hammi right away and suggest he run new background checks on the people closest to the other five politicians."

"Excellent thinking, Sauce! Miss West may have met with some of them as well. He should also check her apartment and credit records. We need to learn of her movements in the past few weeks to see if she met with other potential accomplices. I'll call the governor and let him in on your theory."

Sauce and BT spent the remainder of the drive on their cell phones. Sauce ended his call to Hammi and waited for BT to hang up. "Bad news. The District Attorney told him they did not have enough on EB West for a search warrant."

"Typical, isn't it?" commented BT. "It's always some shithead attorney or judge putting handcuffs on the cops instead of on the criminals."

"He said they were still able to bring her in for questioning. Unfortunately, they can't find her. He also said he found some interesting leads in those pages of Beckley's ledger. He wants to meet with us tonight but isn't sure what time he'll be free—his captain has assigned him to a prisoner transfer detail. One of the risks of hanging around the office on your day off, he says."

"Just his luck." BT sat silent for a minute, then suggested, "As I see it we have two avenues to pursue. One is Ms. West's apartment, of course. We can't let a bloody search warrant stop us from gathering evidence that could potentially save lives."

"I'm in!" confirmed Sauce. "We could swing by her place after lunch and have a look around."

"A look around, yes, exactly. That's all we'll be doing, just having a look around. We also need your girlfriend to employ her ample resources to track down EB's cell phone location."

"I get it," snapped Sauce, casting a knowing smile at BT. "If she can track my phone, then she may be able to do the same for EB's. Good thinking. I'll give her a call and ask."

They pulled into the long driveway of a palatial estate located on the outskirts of Sausalito. Sauce inserted the battery into his old phone and was about to dial Dara's number. He hung up, however, before it was answered; as they approached the house the first thing that caught Sauce's eye was Dara's yellow Porsche parked near the entrance. "I guess I'll ask her in person, instead," he stated gruffly.

As their car slowed to a stop behind the Porsche, they saw Dara standing on the veranda waiting to greet them. "Just in time," she announced quietly as the two men ascended the entrance stairs. "Keep your voices down as you go in. Mummy is in a trance."

"Gladys is here?" said BT, sounding enthused to finally meet her.

"She was asked to attend our luncheon by Senator Enid," Dara responded. "He's here too with his wife. They sent their daughter Valerie to Europe with the other children mentioned in Jett's letters, to keep her safe. After the attempt on Annabelle, none of them want to take a chance on Jett changing his timeline and attempting to poison the kids earlier than he initially threatened."

"Prudent," commented BT.

"Follow me through the house to the backyard."

"One second," said Sauce, pulling Dara to the side of the porch. He ignored her request for quiet and asked, "How are we supposed to conduct an interview with so many people here? And you promised to leave me alone during the day! Shouldn't you be at my house building a new wing or something?"

"Harsh," scowled BT, showing discontent with the acidity of Sauce's attack.

"It's all right," said Dara to BT. "He just needs some time to get used to the changes I made to our home."

"Our home," said Sauce softly, throwing up his hands looking at BT, who was chuckling.

"Don't worry about that," whispered Dara. "Besides, I was here first so technically you're following me this time." She giggled softly and marched into the house. BT shrugged, looked at Sauce, and motioned for them to follow Dara.

They passed quickly through the house, exiting through double glass doors off the dining room, onto a faux marble patio, centered by a teardrop-shaped pool. Seated around an oval glass-topped table were the hosts and guests of the luncheon. Gladys was seated, eyes closed, head tilted backward, wearing white slacks and a crisp, open collar sky-blue shirt. Senator Prouit and his wife, Millie, were seated to Gladys's left. Millie was wearing no fewer than forty pieces of the cheap costume jewelry she had been selling through home parties for more than twenty years, amassing a fortune in the process. Senator Enid, tanned like a baseball glove, and his pale Norwegian blonde wife, Innes—at least thirty years younger than her grey-haired husband—sat on the other side. Sauce and BT respected the silence at the table, took seats at the side farthest from Gladys and waited.

Sauce was annoyed at the scene around the table. No one had even acknowledged his arrival; they just stared at Gladys in anticipation. Sauce scanned the surrounding grounds of the backyard noting the plethora of security cameras mounted high on poles around the periphery and the half dozen burly guards, stone-faced with their arms at their sides seemingly prepared to draw their side-arms at any moment. The people were silent, though a pounding noise echoed across the yard, skipping over the surface of the pool like a smooth stone, emanating from a small cottage on the far side of the estate.

Dara, having taken the seat next to Sauce, saw him looking in the direction of the cottage. She leaned close to Sauce's ear and whispered, "Guest house".

Sauce nodded his understanding, turned to her, and mouthed the word, "Who?"

Dara shrugged and mouthed back, "You'll see," just as the silence around the table was shattered by the ringing of Sauce's cell phone. Gladys's eyes popped open, and everyone turned toward Sauce, glaring their disapproval.

"Uh, sorry," apologized Sauce, while hurriedly reaching into his pocket for the phone. He had neglected to remove the battery after seeing Dara's car. He looked at the call display and saw Jett's name.

"I have to take this," he said, showing the display to BT, then rising from the table. He walked a few feet away and answered, "Dr. Jett?" He sensed that many eyes were watching him, yet tried to ignore them and act nonchalant.

"You are a difficult man to get in touch with," began Jett. "I've been trying to call you all day."

"Why?"

"Are you alone?"

"No."

"Ditch whoever you're with. We need to meet. I am being falsely accused. You have to help me." Sauce perceived impatience in Jett's voice.

"Sure, uh, where? At your office?"

"That would be best. How soon can you get here?"

"Not for a couple of hours. I'll call when I'm near." Sauce heard the phone click as Jett ended the call without responding.

Sauce turned around, looked at the staring faces, and calmly commented, "Jett wants to meet with me."

Gladys spoke up first. "If he offers you a drink, refuse it!"

"Or anything to eat," blurted Dara.

"Don't shake hands with him, either," suggested Senator Prouit.

"Probably not a good idea to touch anything in his office," added BT.

Sauce noticed that not one of them had posited that he should not meet with Jett. "Really? You think if Jett wanted to kill me he wouldn't find a way? Once I'm near him he could simply stab me with a needle if he wanted to."

"Don't be absurd," said Dara. "He's the one who's blind, not you. You could easily keep him at a distance."

"Not if he has an accomplice. His research assistant could sneak up behind me …"

"Unlikely," interjected Gladys, with a smile. "You needn't worry about that. His parents will vouch for him, I'm sure. They should be here any moment."

"Here? The banker?" inquired Sauce, looking behind him.

"Sure," answered Millie Prouit. "My, but we've forgotten our manners. Welcome to our home, Mr. Aase, Mr. Torres. You must have heard the ruckus that boy of theirs has been making in the guest house. His parents asked us to take care of him while he studied in the city, so we let him use the guesthouse. Now, well, given the circumstances, he has been put under house arrest, you could say."

Dara approached Sauce and put an arm around his waist. "Come have a seat and we'll explain." Sauce stared at the little cottage as he took his seat. He felt confused—he hated that feeling. "Why am I always in the dark with these people?" he thought to himself. He shifted his gaze to Gladys, who was staring back at him with a blank expression. He cast a glance at BT, who raised his eyebrows and shrugged his shoulders. "At least I'm not the only one with questions this time," he thought.

"Why the séance in the middle of the afternoon?" BT asked.

"Séance?" queried Dara. "You mean Mummy's trance? That's not a séance. She was simply reaching beyond for assurance on the safety of the little girls."

"I asked her to, uh, well you don't believe, do you?" began Ms. Prouit. "No, I can tell neither of you believe. But the governor assured us that non-believers make the best investigators, so I'll forgive you. Gladys, I'm so sorry you were interrupted." She cast a menacingly hateful glance at Sauce. She then turned back to Gladys and in a warm apologetic tone asked, "Do you need to begin again?"

Gladys took a sip from her water glass, then wiped her mouth. "Don't blame him. That call to Mr. Aase was extremely important and meant to happen while we were all present. I wasn't able to learn anything about the girls. I suspect the incessant noise from that rebellious young man may be blocking my reception."

"Excuse me for interrupting," said BT. He glanced around at the unfamiliar faces. "I'm Torres, assisting Mr. Aase with investigations."

"Yes, we know," said Senator Enid. "The governor told us about your involvement. We appreciate your help in putting an end to our distress."

"If I may make a suggestion," continued BT. "Why don't you just call your children? Or better yet, keep them near you so you can see for yourself?"

Gladys smiled at BT and put up a hand to prevent others from answering. "Our friend makes an excellent point. Why didn't we think of that?" Gladys looked around the table with a quizzical expression, hands outstretched, palms raised, then burst into laughter. "I'm sorry. This is no time to joke but I couldn't resist a brief reprieve. You are serious, of course, Mr. Torres. Believe me, the girls are better off this way. They are en route to Europe as we speak. Their parents will join them in a couple of days. Unavailable during the flight of course. Hence the request for me to seek information on their progress from other-worldly sources."

"I see," commented BT. "All four, together with their chaperones and bodyguards?"

"No," answered Ms. Prouit. "We thought they would be safer on two separate flights."

"Separate flights? That's not the usual protocol. I've overseen numerous protection details, and we have always found a single group of assets was easier to protect than multiple groups. Who recommended this particular agenda?"

"I assure you we acted in the children's best interests," harped Senator Prouit, obviously angry at BT's insinuation.

Ms. Prouit added, "Gladys herself recommended this arrangement and I wholeheartedly agreed with her suggestion. After all, two targets are harder for a criminal to follow, don't you agree?"

Sauce could tell that BT did not agree and was noticeably agitated at the lack of professional standards that had been employed in the transport of the children. He was about to offer his own opinion when he saw the banker and his wife enter the backyard, escorted by two guards.

"Mr. and Mrs. Mackie!" yelled Ms. Prouit, causing everyone to shift their attention to the new arrivals.

Sauce joined the others by standing. He pondered on the foolishness of the situation: wealthy foreign parents arriving to claim their son from captivity in a politicians backyard guest cottage. He was intrigued to learn how these parents would handle such a situation, and how their son's wardens would react in turn. He did not have to wait long to find out.

"Bring me my son!" shouted Mrs. Mackie. Sauce was startled, partly by the venomous verbal tone, though mostly by the depth of the vocal pitch.

"She's a baritone, if not a bass," thought Sauce. He was startled by the contrast: Deirdre Mackie was a waif in every way, except her voice. She was no more than five feet tall, thin everywhere except her bosom, which appeared surgically altered to project unnaturally at least six inches beyond her fragile frame. Her wispy platinum hair formed tight ringlets around her scalp. These physical features, combined with her pale pink, form-fitting dress, suggested that a high whiney sound would escape in hushed, airy syllables. Instead, her frosted pink lips parted to unleash thunder.

Sauce wasn't the only one taken aback. BT was noticeably stifling a laugh. Dara, too, was looking at their hosts with an expression of muffled titillation.

"We're old friends," hastened Senator Prouit. "There's no need for a confrontation."

"I'll give you much more than a confrontation," boomed Mrs. Mackie. She gave her husband a slight nudge.

He walked two steps closer, raised his chin, and in a commanding tone, said, "My son? Now!"

Sauce was impressed with his brevity. He also saw that both Mackies were staring at the senator. They avoided making eye contact with Gladys. "Fear?" he pondered. He would have preferred to monitor the drama while comfortably seated, perhaps enjoying a cocktail. He mused, "Can't sit while everyone else remains standing, and Dara wouldn't allow me to enjoy a drink anyhow."

He shifted his weight uncomfortably onto one leg and watched as Derek Mackie was silently led by one of the security guards from the cottage to his parents.

"Shut your mouth and listen!" shouted Mr. Mackie as the boy approached. Derek reached his parents and accepted his instructions like an obedient son, a public persona perfected over the years.

"Derek, listen to your father and do exactly as he says," insisted his mother as she extended a hand to fuss with the boy's hair, pushing his bangs away from his eyes.

"Son," began Mr. Mackie, "I want you to make it clear to these people that you had nothing to do with the unfortunate events leading to the passing of their dog. Tell them that your involvement with university faculty is confined to matters involving your studies and research. As well, thank the senator for his previous hospitality. We have arranged a suite in town for the remainder of your studies. Be quick about it, and we'll be done here."

"You can't tell him what to say! Are you not interested in the truth?" interrupted Sauce.

"Who the hell are you?" shouted Mrs. Mackie.

"Mr. Aase is an investigator on the case," explained Ms. Prouit. Then turning to Sauce she added, "We are not in the habit of insulting our friends, Mr. Aase."

"Insulting? Mr. Mackie tells Derek how to answer our questions and I'm the one who's insulting?"

"Yes, quite," commented Senator Prouit. "If Mr. Mackie says he is innocent, well, then, there we are."

Sauce looked at BT for support but received only a blank stare in return. BT made a subtle downward movement of one hand, signaling for Sauce to accept defeat, for now. Sauce realized that BT had a lot more experience around politicians than he had and probably recognized that arguing facts was futile with people whose world was governed more by perception than reality.

"Investigator, eh?" answered Mrs. Mackie, looking up and down at Sauce. "Have we taken this to the next level? I thought we were still on civil terms. Should I have brought council?"

"We are civil," answered Ms. Prouit. "It was the governor. He insisted that we allow Mr. Aase and his colleague Mr. Torres here today to learn the circumstances of Kiefer's passing … because of the attempt on his daughter. You understand. These men are not here about Derek. They're here because of the recent escalation in the threat … as is Senator

Enid and his wife. Their daughter was also threatened, you know."

"Right," replied Mr. Mackie. "Derek, do as I told you and we'll be off."

Derek turned to the senator and began, his voice embellished with sarcasm and self-righteousness. "Thank you for the *hospitality* over the past year. I hope your troubles come to an end soon."

"Do you? Do you really?" asked Gladys, softly.

Derek's smirk was immediately replaced by a confused frown. He turned to his parents, hoping they would answer, but they were dumb with fear. He looked back at Gladys and mumbled an affirmative answer.

Gladys walked around the table toward Derek, who retreated close to his parents. Gladys stopped within inches of Derek, looked straight into his eyes, and remained motionless for a few seconds before speaking.

"You want our troubles to come to an end. When our troubles end, yours will as well."

Mrs. Mackie's deep voice trembled as she said, "Derek's troubles. No! You don't mean … is he in danger?"

Gladys looked briefly at Mrs. Mackie, then turned back to stare into Derek's eyes. "There is a dark shadow over his soul. That is clear. As soon as you entered my presence I was approached by no fewer than a dozen spirits, trying to tell me something. Their voices are muddled, but they seem to be trying to get a message to you."

Derek, with a nervous giggle, pleaded with his parents, "Come on. We don't believe any of this crap. Don't we have to go? We can go now."

Mr. Mackie quickly chided him. "Quiet lad! This is serious. Gladys, what does this mean? Is our son's life in jeopardy?"

Gladys tried to take Derek's hand, but he instantly withdrew.

"Derek! Don't be a fool," shouted his mother. "Do as she says!"

"But Mom, he's just a con-artist," pleaded Derek.

"Shut it!" shouted Mr. Mackie. "All that education and you think you know everything. Do as Gladys says, or so help me I'll cut you off, disown you!"

Derek grudgingly offered his hand to Gladys.

CHAPTER 22

Gladys lifted Derek's hands up to shoulder height, staring into his eyes. Everyone remained silent. Some due to fear. Others, Sauce and BT in particular, remained silent out of curiosity, eager to see Gladys in action. They knew Gladys was adept at manipulation, and this situation certainly called for the use of that skill.

"Ah yes, yes, I hear you," said Gladys, still staring at Derek, though obviously speaking to someone else. Gladys continued, "Sedge, Sedgwick. Oh, I see … your son."

Mrs. Mackie let out a gasp and clung to her husband's arm in fear. Mr. Mackie began to cry and wrapped his arms around his wife.

"Yes, of course, we are grateful," said Gladys after a few minutes of silence. "I hope so, too."

Gladys released Derek's hands and looked at his parents, frowning and shaking her head. Gladys then turned, walked around the table and sat down.

Gladys stared at the Mackies coldly, silently. Everyone waited in suspense.

"What is it?" snapped Ms. Prouit, unable to contain herself any longer. "What did you learn?"

Gladys looked at Ms. Prouit then back to the Mackies. "More than I could have imagined."

Mrs. Mackie stammered, "Y-you have to understand. We were desperate."

"It was all my fault," added Mr. Mackie, putting his hands on his son's shoulders. "Derek didn't mean any harm. We should have known you would find out. Is it revenge? Is that what he came to tell you? He has to know that we are truly, truly sorry. He does know, doesn't he?"

"He is not vengeful," answered Gladys. "He did have a warning for Derek. And I will tell you. First, you must share your secret. Sit down and tells us about Sedgwick. Then I will let you know what he told me."

"Mom, Dad, this is silly," pleaded Derek. Turning to Gladys, he leaned on the table and pounded his fist in frustration. "I don't know what you think you know about Sedgwick, but it doesn't matter. He's dead, gone, nothing! And we're all better for it."

"And what about Lisle?" asked Gladys, unemotionally. "I guess if she doesn't matter then we really can drop it."

"Wh-what about Lisle?" asked Derek.

"You first," Gladys answered.

Derek paused and looked back at his parents for support. He took a deep breath then looked around the table. "We didn't do anything wrong. Sedgwick was a letch, a blackmailer. He contacted me at Cambridge, when I was in first year. Said he was my real father, and he would keep quiet about the circumstances of my birth but wanted to be part of my life. I told him he was bonkers and that I would 'ave him up on charges. That was all that happened. I never heard about him again until an investigator came calling a few weeks later saying Sedgwick was dead and that my name came up during the investigation. I told him what had happened and that was it. So you see, there is nothing really to tell."

"Nothing?" interjected Sauce. He could see from the expressions on the faces of Mr. and Mrs. Mackie that they knew more about Mr. Sedgwick than had already been disclosed.

"Son," began Mr. Mackie softly, "there is more to the story. We couldn't allow your life to be derailed by mistakes we made. Sedgwick contacted me after you dismissed his inquiry. He seemed sincere enough. He told me he only recently learned that he was the father of the child we adopted, you—that is. Nevertheless, I tried to buy him off, as we had done with your natural mother, a sex trade veteran, numerous times over the years. I told him to leave you alone and offered a few thousand pounds. I didn't realize he was so unstable. It seems he was profoundly affected by the insinuation, and committed suicide. He left a lengthy note of explanation. My friends on the force kept it all quiet. But there it is, our dark secret."

"I'm the son of a whore?" cursed Derek at his parents.

"No, you're our son!" answered Mrs. Mackie. "We wanted a child, and I … I just couldn't do it. The weight gain, the labour, all that comes with it … well, it wasn't for me. But a friend told me about this young woman who had given birth—a horrible excuse for a human being, she was. Well, as you see, things worked out for the best. We rescued you from that life. We gave you life. Don't you see?"

Derek stared at his parents for a few moments. As if remembering why they had been forced to disclose this family history, he spun around and glared at Gladys. "Happy? You got your damn confession. Now tell me about Lisle."

"Who's Lisle?" asked Sauce.

Gladys looked at Sauce. "Lisle Garrety, Derek's girl in London."

"They don't care," Derek said. "Just tell me why you brought up her name. What are you up to? And don't give me any of that crap about Sedgwick speaking from the grave."

His mother gasped and shook her husband's arm. Mr. Mackie snapped at Derek, "Be civil! You don't have to believe in Good Gladys, but you can at least show some decency. Your mother and I know she is totally selfless."

"She?" interrupted Derek. "This is a man!"

"There's still time to save her." Gladys's tone was confident and unperturbed. Her statement had the desired effect, bringing silence to the estate. Silence and anticipation.

Gladys smiled broadly. "Are you sure Sedgwick and I didn't have a conversation? Are you absolutely confident he didn't tell me about your secret rendezvous … planned for the end of the week … here in San Francisco?"

"Derek you have a *girlfriend*?" beamed his mother, revealing years of suspicions about his orientation. Mr. and Mrs. Mackie looked profoundly relieved by Gladys's revelation.

"She's just a colleague from years back," answered Derek. His reddening cheeks betrayed a deeper relationship. "She has research that I need; that's all."

"So you don't care what's going to happen to her on Friday?" asked Gladys.

"If you lay a hand on her so help me …" Derek raised a fist.

"Calm down, lover boy," said BT taking a step toward Derek. He looked at Gladys and demanded, "If you know about a crime that is going to be committed against this young man's friend then you must tell us."

Gladys smiled broadly, sat back in her chair and did not reply. Nearly a full minute passed before Derek shouted, "All right! What do you want?"

"I want you to come here and kneel down in front of me," answered Gladys.

"Really?" Derek looked at the others. His father nodded in agreement with Gladys. His mother made a shooing motion with her hands. He started shuffling his feet, moving slowly toward Gladys.

He knelt at the side of Gladys's chair, his face bright red. Gladys gently placed both hands under his and guided Derek's hands so they were held at the level of his eyes. She then tilted her head back and moaned softly.

Sauce looked at BT and chuckled softly seeing him roll his eyes at Gladys's performance.

Gladys quickly tilted her head forward, stood up from the chair with her eyes open wide, staring sternly at Derek. She still held his hands at the same height, but her back was arched slightly forward, so Derek had to bend back in order to maintain eye contact.

"Lisle will die this Friday," Gladys began. "You have angered the spirits. They will not tell me anything except that she will die."

Sweat began to bead on Derek's brow. A large drop traveled to his nose and hung there, for all to see. He tried to pull free but Gladys would not release his hands.

"The itch must be driving him nuts," thought Sauce.

Tears welled in Derek's eyes. "Is there nothing I can do?"

"Perhaps," whispered Gladys, "if you were to do a selfless act. There are dark forces acting on the people here, and the spirits tell me that you are hiding crucial information from them."

Sauce followed Derek's eyes to his parents. "They look gripped in terror at what he might confess." He wondered if Derek would adhere to his father's words from earlier telling him to admit nothing.

"Jett! I know, it's Jett, isn't it?" Derek gazed at Gladys. "You want to know what he is up to."

"We know what he is up to," countered Gladys. "You can't tell us anything we don't already know about him."

"Did you know his career is sunk? Bongo, caput. Did you know that?" He looked around at the glazed expressions on everyone's faces. "I heard rumours while completing my Master's degree. I happened to attend a talk that Jett gave at UCL. I sat near the back and a couple of doctoral students were chatting about Jett's failed publication attempts and rejected funding applications. I saw the opportunity. In academia, if you can't publish, you can't get grant money and your lab quickly becomes someone else's. My grades sucked, but I figured I could get into the PHD program here simply by waving my family's wallet in Jett's face. And I was right."

Sauce asked, "So, you bought your way into his lab?"

"Bribed. I didn't actually buy anything. He's a washout. A bitter, disgruntled has-been. He hates everyone. There was no way I was going to give him a red cent. I made promises; that's for sure. When he gave me the grand tour, before I joined, he bragged about the new equipment he was going to purchase when his most recent NIH grant was approved. Mass spec, blah, blah. I mentioned that my dad would cover those costs so he could allocate his funds in more productive ways. I could see on his face that I had him. Besides, no other students would apply to work with him. Word was out. Unofficially of course, but rumours spread, you know.

"Since coming here he keeps hinting about the cost of this or that. His grant was rejected, no surprise. He went into a rage when he got that letter. Screamed about how he did his time on some stupid government committee and deserved the money. He often talks about government waste robbing his lab of what it's due. He hates politicians." Derek paused and looking at Gladys he added, "Well, almost as much as he hates you."

"Me?" asked Gladys. "What could I possibly have done to him?"

"I don't know. The day after he accompanied me to one of your shows he started nattering on about you. He said something about you meddling in things that were none of your business. Called you a thief, pickpocket … didn't say why he hated you, though."

Gladys started to shake, released Derek's hands, tipped her head back, then collapsed into the chair. After a few moments, she relaxed and took a deep breath. "That was sufficient. The spirits have softened their position and have given me detailed instructions that Lisle must follow precisely to survive."

"I'll do whatever you say," answered Derek.

"Tell Lisle that a Black Cab, car forty-one, will be outside her residence at precisely six-thirty on Friday morning. It won't wait for her so she must be ready when it arrives. It will take her to Gatwick; that's right, not Heathrow. She must go to the Air Canada terminal. A ticket for Toronto will be there in her name. In Toronto she will transfer to United and fly to LAX. Pick her up at one o'clock on Saturday morning and she will be out of danger."

Derek listened intently, then answered softly as he rose to his feet, "Thank you."

"Go," commanded Gladys looking at the Mackies and waving dismissively. "And Derek, one last thing: do not go back to the lab for a week. In fact, do not have any contact with Dr. Jett until Lisle is gone."

"Okay," answered Derek. He walked to his parents and received a strong hug from his mother, who mouthed, "Bless you" to Gladys. They turned and left without saying another word.

CHAPTER 23

"That was a bust," commented Sauce as he and BT proceeded to drive away from the estate.

"As far as learning anything directly from the senator or his wife, certainly," answered BT. "We learned more than I expected, though, thanks to Gladys. What a display?"

"Didn't quite get a confession from that little shit."

"The kid was never going to admit to killing the dog. Mackie senior saw to that. Gladys didn't waste any time on trying to force the issue, did she? She's obviously been around people like that too long to expect too much." BT chuckled. "I've worked most of my career around wealthy people like them. They're like kids: you can't predict what they'll say next. Despite my experience, there's no way I could have managed that situation better than Gladys did."

"That's Gladys's gift, isn't it?" snarled Sauce. "And Dara's, for the most part."

"What did she say to you that made you so sour?"

"Oh, you mean just before we left the estate?" began Sauce. "Am I sour? Well, maybe I am. But you'd be too. She handed me these." Sauce pulled an envelope from the inner pocket of his blazer. "She said, in that saccharine tone that I hate, for me to give them to Hammi: the passes for Gladys's television appearance."

"You going to give them to Hammi?"

"I might've, before, but she couldn't leave it at that. This time she has gone too far." Sauce was sitting erect, tense, and red-faced as he recalled his conversation with Dara.

"Come on, what'd she say?" asked BT with a broad smile on his face.

"She told me not to be too late coming home. She said we were going to have a relaxing night, soaking in the Jacuzzi being installed in our bedroom. A Jacuzzi! And she called it *our* bedroom!"

"And earlier she said, 'our house'," commented BT, playfully.

"Precisely! She's taking over my life."

"The women we love do that."

"Don't start," cautioned Sauce, suddenly aware of the absence of empathy coming from BT. "You can't possibly believe I am enjoying having her in my life. She is just like Gladys."

"Not all bad from what I saw this afternoon," offered BT. "Derek told us much more than he wanted to. I was most impressed by the amount of forethought and planning that went into the ruse: researching the girlfriend, then arranging the flight itinerary. Derek's info gives us clear motive for Jett's actions—certainly worth the price of a couple of airline tickets."

"You mean you don't believe the spirits interceded?" asked Sauce sarcastically.

BT laughed softly. "Are you going to burn the tickets and hand her the ashes later in the Jacuzzi?"

"I *should* do something like that." Sauce put the envelope back in his pocket. "We'll see."

"Do you think you're ready to speak with Jett?"

"Not yet. I don't want to spook him, riding up with you in the car. It's about time I get my car back from the restaurant where I left it before you became my personal chauffeur."

"I'm no one's chauffeur," kidded BT. "But you're probably right about the car. In fact, I have some things in my hotel room we should retrieve on the way. If I put a GPS tracker and mini-microphone in your car, I can follow from a safe undetectable distance. That should decrease the likelihood of Jett becoming suspicious and making you his next victim."

Sauce smiled. "Yeah, I was hoping to avoid that."

"Besides, Dara would kill me if you gave me the slip and arrived home in a drunken stupor."

"Right. Nice to know you have faith in me."

Sauce insisted that BT drop him off two blocks away from the restaurant where his car was parked. The idea of becoming Jett's next victim haunted him while he sat in the car waiting for BT to retrieve his electronic surveillance gear from his hotel room. When BT returned to the car, Sauce insisted on a crash course on how to install the items so BT would not be seen by anyone who may be watching for Sauce to retrieve the car. BT agreed, showed him how to mount the electronics, and helped fasten a shoulder harness on Sauce. Sauce was grateful to be wearing a concealed handgun, considering the circumstances.

Except for a folded pink piece of paper resting under a wiper blade, his TR7 seemed to be the same as when he left it: top secure, windows intact. He pulled off the note, unlocked the driver's door and sank into the seat. He turned the key and the engine resisted a little then roared, coughing black smoke and idling a little too quickly. "Oh shut up," yelled Sauce. "I've only been gone a few days. There's no need for the theatrics." He slammed the door shut, revved the engine a couple of times, then sat back, and read the note. He sighed and reached under the dash to attach the tiny magnetic GPS unit and microphone, ensuring both were turned on.

"Looks like you are ready for a little drive up to the university," he whispered, continuing the ruse of talking to his car. "What do you say? Ready to finally leave this restaurant?"

His phone vibrated once, then stopped: the signal they had prearranged that meant BT was able to hear him.

Sauce squealed his tires as he hit the accelerator. He didn't waste any time, driving as quickly as he could safely manage, hoping that if he was being followed by anyone, BT would notice and alert him. His heart was beating faster than normal for most of the trip but started to race uncontrollably as he pulled into a parking stall near the chemistry building.

"No campus security today," he mused as he turned off the ignition. "Deep breaths".

He walked through the main doors, past the office, which was empty as he expected and proceeded to the outer door of Jett's office. He listened at the door and was sure he could hear two male voices. They seemed to be arguing, though Sauce couldn't make out the words. Recognizing one of the voices as Jett's, he knocked hard against the door.

A few seconds passed then the bolt clicked and Jett poked his head through. "No need to pound the door down; I'm blind, not deaf."

"I didn't realize, sorry. I was just trying to get your attention since you seemed to be having quite a heated discussion in there."

"Well, come in," said Jett, seemingly annoyed. "We're not going to discuss this in the hallway, are we?"

Sauce was more apprehensive than before, given the cold reception. He told himself to stay strong and as he entered the office, he asked, "Would you prefer I leave. It *was* you who requested this meeting."

Sauce noticed immediately the hulk of a man seated in Jett's office chair. Even seated, Sauce could tell he was tall, at least six and half feet tall. His pectoral muscles protruded from his barrel-shaped chest like balloons. The sleeves of his black leather jacket appeared to have been ripped off exposing muscular arms covered in a spider-web design of tattoos that extended from his shoulders to the tips of his fingers. He had a thick mustache and at least two-days growth of beard over a jutting square jaw. His hair was long and greasy, tied back into a braided ponytail.

He sneered at Sauce. "This is the guy?"

"Ah, yes," said Jett. "Mr. Byrne Aase, this is my attorney, Mr. Vincent."

Sauce wasn't sure how to answer, so he nodded toward the imposing figure. He had never met anyone who looked more un-lawyer like than Mr. Vincent.

Jett continued, "Mr. Vincent, Byrne almost completed his legal studies some years ago. So you, uh, kind of have something in common, I suppose." He fidgeted with a pile of papers on his desk. "I, uh, asked Mr. Vincent to sit in on our discussion. You know, just in case we require a formal legal opinion on how to proceed."

"That's right," Mr. Vincent stated. "He asked me here. So let's get on with it."

Jett said nothing. He just stared at Sauce with a look of anticipation. Sauce looked back and forth at the two gentlemen and said the only thing that came to mind, "Did you try to kill the governor's daughter?" He regretted the question as soon as it left his mouth.

Mr. Vincent chuckled menacingly and slowly turned his gaze onto Jett. "Well?" he asked, folding his hands in front of him.

Sauce noticed the plain gold band on his left hand, and, instantly, memories brought him back to days when he would meet a girlfriend's parents and see the look on their hopeful faces that said, "My daughter is dating a lawyer!" He remembered thinking that they were already planning the wedding. "I imagine his poor wife's parents had a similar expectation when their daughter told them she was bringing a lawyer home for dinner. What I wouldn't give to have seen their faces when *he* walked in the door."

"Byrne, you know I didn't," pleaded Jett. "You sound like one of those infernal policemen. They barged in here asking the same thing. Of course they have nothing connecting me."

"If they have nothing on you, why did they come directly to you after the crime?" asked Sauce.

"You know precisely why." He turned to Mr. Vincent. "Long before the incident at the governor's house, Byrne came to warn me that I was being set up. I thought it was absurd at the time. Why would anyone try to set me up for a crime? I mind my own business. I spend all my time on my research. Frankly, I thought Mr. Aase might have been playing some silly joke on me. Well, that's what I thought until the police came accusing me of orchestrating a murder."

"So you came here before the hit on the governor's daughter?" asked Mr. Vincent. "Where were you when the failed hit took place?"

Sauce felt his knees weaken. The word "hit" echoed in his head. "I, uh, I was with the governor. At his house, that is." He immediately felt guilty. Quickly, he added, "I stopped it, in a way. I kind of, um, inadvertently knocked over the tray carrying the poison meant for the girl. It was the waitress; she was the one who brought the poison."

"Did she confess?" snapped Mr. Vincent.

Sauce shook his head. "No. She pinned it on, uh, someone else."

"Me? She told the police it was me?" asked Jett. Sauce looked down and said nothing.

Mr. Vincent stood up and slammed his knuckles down on the desk. "Answer him! Who did she say was responsible?"

"Gladys," mumbled Sauce.

"Aha!" yelled Jett. "I knew it. That bitch is out to get me. She's the one who put the police after me." Turning to Mr. Vincent, he added, "Byrne told me she was trying to pin her manager's murder on me, too. She probably told some lie about me having an affair with that waitress so she'd do my dirty work."

Sauce looked at Jett, the frumpy old man that he was, and thought what a ridiculous couple he and the pretty waitress would have made. "Actually, it was the evidence that led the police to you. They found footage of the waitress meeting your office secretary in a cafe. Her name isn't Edith, by the way. It's EB West."

"Really? Of course that's her name. I knew about her past, and her family's run-ins with the law. She told me all about it. But she said she was straight. That just shows how trusting I am. I believed her; still do in fact. She must be innocent. I bet the waitress was telling the truth and it was all Gladys. Actually, I bet the governor and Gladys are in this together. What better way to gain the sympathy of the voters before an election than to contrive a conspiracy against yourself?"

"You think the governor tried to kill his own daughter?" asked Sauce.

"It wouldn't surprise me. Those politicians are more evil than any convicted murderer in prison. And Gladys! I heard she is good friends with the governor. She's a clever one. I bet the whole thing was her idea, right down to pinning this on an innocent girl like EB. Has she told the police her side of the story yet?"

"No, she's missing. Ran off, they think. But we'll find her. And soon, I'm sure."

"You sound like you're in deep with the cops," said a scowling Mr. Vincent.

"And with Gladys," commented Jett. "Are you still living with her daughter?" At this, Mr. Vincent started walking around the desk toward Sauce.

Jett continued, "I could blow the lid off the whole scam she's been running these days. All that bullshit about being turned into a man. I know Gladys is hiding out somewhere. And I know who that man really is."

"Why don't you tell the papers?" asked Sauce. "I'm sure they would love a juicy story like that."

"I would if I thought they'd actually print it. She has them under her thumb. There's no way the public would ever hear what I have to say."

Sauce reached into his blazer pocket and pulled out the envelope. "Perhaps there is a way. I have passes to the live television show Gladys will be doing in a couple of days. You can have them, stand up while the cameras are running, and get the story out to millions of people before they'd have a chance to stop you." Sauce handed the envelope to Jett.

"I like this idea," commented Jett. "Perhaps I was wrong about you. This could really solve my problems."

Sauce thought he had best retreat quickly while he had the opportunity. "I don't think you have anything to worry about." He slowly started walking backward towards the door. "Like you said, you're innocent. The police will find EB and conclude that she was just acting on her own. After all, the Wests are all a bunch of brainless criminals, right? When the police find her, they'll realize it was all her, and you'll be free and clear."

"Are you leaving?" asked Mr. Vincent.

"Yeah." Sauce turned the door handle. "I think I should get back before Gladys's daughter gets worried and sends the cops out to find me. She knew I was meeting with you."

"I'll walk you to your car," insisted Mr. Vincent, pushing Sauce through the door. They walked silently at a brisk pace into the parking lot toward Sauce's TR7. Sauce noticed a large, black SUV was parked next to him and feared the worst.

"Can I borrow your phone?" asked Mr. Vincent when they reached the rear of the TR7.

"My phone?" Sauce reached into his pocket, removed his old phone and surrendered it. He grabbed his keys and took a few quick steps toward the driver's side door. He unlocked it and pulled it open. Suddenly he felt a hand on his shoulder pulling his upper body up and back. In one motion, Mr. Vincent ripped Sauce's blazer off his shoulders and snapped his gun harness.

"Nice piece," he mused, holding the gun high in the air. "Let's leave that in the car with your phone." He threw Sauce's gun and cell phone onto the driver's seat, then patted the rest of Sauce's pockets to find the phone BT had given to him.

"A second phone! You won't need that either where you're going," said Mr. Vincent, tossing it into the car as well.

"Are you taking me in your black Escalade?" said Sauce loudly, hoping BT was still listening to the microphone stashed in the car.

Mr. Vincent slammed the door of Sauce's car closed. "We're not taking *your* piece of shit; that's for sure."

He forcefully grabbed Sauce's arm and slammed him against the side of the SUV. The doors of the truck opened and two large men stepped out. They pushed Sauce into the backseat, with one man sitting on each side of Sauce.

Mr. Vincent took the driver's seat and casually drove them away from the university. For the first ten minutes, no one said a word as they cruised through the streets of San Francisco. Mr. Vincent's cell phone broke the silence. He mumbled a few words to the person on the other end of the call, then hung up with a slight chuckle. Mr. Vincent pointed to the rearview mirror. "It looks like we picked up a tail."

Sauce turned and saw BT was following a few cars back, trying to appear inconspicuous. Briefly he felt a surge of hope. Then he saw a huge dump truck pull up beside BT's car and abruptly cut to the right. BT's car propelled right through the glass window of a flower shop.

"Guess I was wrong," snapped Mr. Vincent, and all three men laughed.

The remainder of the ride was uneventful and silent. Sauce watched the roads, carefully noting where they turned so he could find his way home if he managed to escape. He was a little perplexed when the car entered an ordinary, middle-class residential neighbourhood and pulled into the driveway of a split-level family home.

"Is it too much to ask why you abducted me?" asked Sauce as he stepped out of the SUV.

"Yes. It is too much to ask," answered Mr. Vincent. He pointed toward the house as the other two gentlemen got into the front seat and proceeded to back out of the driveway. Mr. Vincent gave a friendly wave to his accomplices, then pushed Sauce toward the front door.

The two men entered the house to shouts of "Daddy!"

Sauce did not expect this. Two boys, Sauce estimated them to be about seven and ten, ran across the living room and jumped into Mr. Vincent's outstretched arms. He gave them each a kiss on the lips,and a tight squeeze.

"Oh, I missed you guys," he said warmly. "I hope you're being good for your mom."

"We are," answered the older one, "not!" The boys laughed and each grabbed one of their father's hands.

"Come and see what we built," the younger one said.

"In a minute," said Mr. Vincent. "First I want to introduce you to our guest. This is Mr. Aase. Say hi."

"Hi Mr. Aase," said the boys in unison.

"Byrne, these are my greatest treasures. The little guy is Gus, and this rascal is Vinnie Junior." His older son squirmed as Mr. Vincent ruffled his hair.

Sauce didn't want to alarm the boys so he merely said "Hi, boys."

"Mr. Aase and I have some talking to do, so you guys go play. Where's you mother?"

"She had to go out," answered Vinnie Jr. "Auntie called and told Mommy to go to the store. She said she'd be right back."

"Well then, if she's coming right back we'll just sit right here and wait for her."

Mr. Vincent pointed to the sofa. The two men sat down and watched the boys play with a large Lego collection on the carpet in the center of the living room. Sauce could see an assortment of family photos on the walls and many, many toys scattered all around the room. The room connected to the kitchen and a hallway. "Domestic bliss in a house ruled by a kidnapper," thought Sauce.

At the sound of a vehicle pulling into the drive Mr. Vincent pulled the sheer drapery open a little and exclaimed, "Yay! Mommy's home."

He stood and motioned for Sauce to do the same. The door swung open, and in walked an average looking, casually dressed, slim—though not in an attractive way—brunette, carrying two large paper grocery bags.

"Oh hun, do you mind? These are heavy."

Mr. Vincent jumped into action, taking both bags from her hands and planting a kiss on her cheek. "No problem. What'd you buy me?"

"It's not for you. Your cousin called and suggested I get these for our guest. When your brother told her you were bringing home a prize, she called me and suggested that I pick up something to soften him up before she gets here." She looked at Sauce. "I didn't know what you like so I bought rum, whiskey and vodka. Is that all right, Mr.?"

"Byrne. His name is Byrne Aase."

"I don't drink," said Sauce, unconvincingly.

"You do today," answered the brunette. "Oh, you *sure* do."

Mr. Vincent walked into the kitchen with the bags. His wife approached Sauce with an outstretched hand. "I'm Gabe, Vin's wife."

Sauce took her hand and attempted to reason with her. "Look, I don't know what you've been told but I need to get home." He was still being cautious of his language with the children in the room.

"Hell no!" Gabe yelled. "We are going to have a party!" Sauce felt chills run down his spine, partly from her tone, but mostly from the giggles of the children who were looking at their mom with anticipation.

Vin returned with a couple of glasses and three bottles. "Have a seat Byrne, and we'll get started." Sauce sat down on the sofa as Vin placed the bottles and glasses on the coffee table. "Well, go ahead. Pick your poison."

Sauce looked at the vodka longingly and felt sweat bead on his forehead. His hands began to tingle and twitch.

"Honey look at him," giggled Gabe. "I know that look. Damn sure do. He's on the wagon. Ah, honey, how long's it been?" she asked tenderly, brushing the hair from Sauce's forehead.

"I really can't … I mean, thanks, but I don't want anything right now," said Sauce. "Maybe later."

Vin chuckled and turned to the children. "Hey kids, come here." The two children dutifully ran to their father's side. Vin gave them a warm embrace and asked in a soft parental tone, "Do you remember when Mr. Nadir came over."

Vinnie Jr. smiled and answered, "Yeah. He was fun."

"Do you remember those funny gurgle, gurgle sounds he made?" asked Gus. The kids and their parents laughed at the shared recollection. Vinnie Jr. and Gus kept emulating the gurgle sounds they had heard.

Vin continued, "That was pretty funny, wasn't it? But remember before that. He was screaming and crying. That was funny too."

"Yeah," said a smiling Vinnie Jr. "But he told you, didn't he? He didn't want to, but after you whacked on his fingers with the hammer, he didn't want to keep secrets anymore."

Gabe pointed a chastising finger at Sauce and sternly said, "I told him it's wrong to keep secrets, didn't I?"

"Yes, Mommy," Vinnie Jr. answered. "But Mommy, why didn't he just tell you his secret? I don't understand why he wouldn't tell you."

"Oh, baby," answered his mother, "not everyone is smart like you. And also some people didn't have parents who love them like you do, and who teach them what's right. Now listen to your father. He has something very important to tell you."

"That's right; I do. You'll never guess why Mr. Aase came to visit us," said Vin playfully. "Mr. Aase has a secret."

Both kids started bouncing and yelling, "Yay!"

Gabe giggled, then made an effort to settle down the kids. "Come on guys. Your dad hasn't told you the best part yet. Go ahead Vin. Tell them."

"No, you should. It was your idea."

"What Mom? What?" the kids pestered.

"Okay! Well, remember, I'll have to ask your Aunt EB first. But we think you're both old enough, so if she says it's okay, we're going to let each of you do one of Mr. Aase's hands."

Sauce felt sick watching the children bounce up and down, screaming with glee.

"Should I go get my hammer now?" asked Gus.

"What did your mom just tell you?" chided Vin. "We have to check with Aunt EB first. Besides, you know we don't do that stuff in here. It would mess up your mom's carpet. But I'll tell you what. You two can go set up the garage before your auntie arrives."

"Okay Daddy," said a beaming Vinnie Jr., wrapping his arms around his dad's neck.

Sauce watched as the two kids walked out of the room with the older child saying, "I'll lay down the plastic and you can get the hammers ready."

Gabe looked at Sauce. "Now, which bottle would you like opened first?"

Sauce pointed to the vodka and thought, "There's no way I'm going to stay sober today."

CHAPTER 24

Vin filled a glass with vodka and slid it across the table. Sauce lifted the glass and downed the entire contents in one gulp.

"See now," said Gabe in a sweet motherly tone, "you were thirsty after all." She refilled his glass. "Drink up, honey." She pushed the glass to his lips and Sauce consumed the entire contents a second time. Then she refilled his glass again.

"It's clear that you are new to this, so just tell us what Gladys is up to. We know she has a big play on the go. This charade with a man pretending to be her seems really clever. Somehow she's even got the governor in her back pocket too. Normally, we don't mess with other people's cons, but she shouldn't have tried to set up EB as her patsy. She knows we take care of our own. First we'll hit her where she is weakest." Gabe pointed a finger at Sauce. "Then we'll keep on hitting. Is it possible that she has forgotten how we deal with traitors?

"She's one of us, after all. Oh, you didn't know that, did you? Well, she is. She may have figured out how to milk those fat cats and finagle her way into the jet set life, but she's playing the same game my family has played since before she was born. It's the same game no matter if you are in with the politicos and financiers or just doing ordinary smash and grab."

"Look, I don't know what you're talking about," stated Sauce.

Gabe interrupted him by pushing another glass of vodka toward his mouth. "Oh, honey, it doesn't matter either way to us. You saw how excited the kids are. If you don't tell us now, they just might have their fun after all. The last time we had a guest like you over, they were only allowed to watch. But Vin and I have raised some really intelligent boys. I'm pretty sure they will be able to get you talking. They looked really excited to give it a try. Don't you think?" She and Vin shared a huge laugh. Then Gabe refilled Sauce's glass.

Sauce felt really ill. His mind flashed back to the beginning of all this mess, Dara's visit, with the lawyer depositions and the invitation to the court room. "If only I had held firm to my convictions," he thought. He looked at the vodka glass and suddenly he heaved and spewed vodka and stomach acids all over Gabe and her nice carpet.

"Oh shit, Vin! Do something!" screamed Gabe, wiping some of the splashed effluent from her blouse. Vin ran to the kitchen to grab towels. Sauce continued to retch and spew until he passed out.

He awoke in a daze, face down in the living room, looking at an assortment of feet around him. Sauce remained motionless, listening to the arguing voices above him.

"Fuck you, Vin! No one gets wrecked like that after a couple of glasses. Did you stick that infernal fireplace poker down his throat? I know that's your signature thing. I told you no rough stuff until I got here."

"Don't go accusing Vin," snapped Gabe's voice. "Listen, EB. We told you what happened. He must have been sick before he arrived. That's the only explanation."

Sauce felt his stomach churning, and despite trying to remain calm, he resumed vomiting, shooting out juices over the tan, suede high-heeled shoes in front of him.

"God damn it!" screamed EB, delivering several swift pointed toe kicks to the side of Sauce's head. "I just bought these. Couldn't you have at least dragged him into a bedroom until he settled down?

We're not going to get anything out of him when he's like this."

"Yeah, sure," said Vin. "Marv, give me a hand."

Sauce was exhausted and offered no resistance as two men grabbed his legs and dragged his body backwards across the carpet, then onto a linoleum hallway floor and finally into a bathroom. They lifted him in the air, then dropped him into the bathtub, banging his head hard against the porcelain, knocking him out.

Sauce felt a cold wet cloth pass across his face, then a soft tapping on his cheeks.

"Come on buddy. I need you to wake up." Sauce recognized BT's voice and opened his eyes.

"Keep quiet. I snuck in through the backdoor. Took down one guy, but I need to know how many others stand in our way out of here."

Sauce whispered, "I think two men, two women, plus two kids."

"Well, let's hope that's all. I watched as the husband and wife drove away, so that leaves one woman. Let's get you out of that tub. Carefully now, your head has a nasty gash, but you'll live."

BT pulled Sauce to his feet and wrapped one arm around Sauce's back to support him. They walked to the bathroom door and BT peeked around the corner. "Can you manage on your own? I may need both hands."

"Yeah, I can," answered Sauce, bracing himself against the wall for support and breathing heavily.

"Sit tight. I'm gonna see if I can find the other one."

Sauce closed his eyes as BT walked down the hall, checking the other rooms. Sauce heard a short scuffle. Then BT returned. "Let's get out of here."

BT had EB in a half-nelson with one hand and a gun pointed to her head with his other hand. "Say anything or try to fight and I won't hesitate, bitch. Let's go!"

They cautiously proceeded toward the living room which was now empty. They crossed halfway to the main door when they heard a shuffling coming from the kitchen. They turned in the direction of the noise just as two screaming boys started running toward them. Obviously hoping to rescue their aunt, the boys headed straight for BT, yelling loudly, each holding a carving knife up high, ready to strike.

BT spun around just as the boys reached him and both knives plunged deep into EB's chest. BT threw EB onto the boys, and screamed, "You want her? You got her!" He grabbed Sauce's arm, and they ran out of the house and into a panel van. Dara was at the wheel and she didn't hesitate to hit the accelerator as soon as they were in the vehicle. Sauce rested his head on the floor of the van and passed out again.

CHAPTER 25

Sauce could hear someone walking around in the adjacent room and considered whether or not he should get out of bed. He had slept for two days, occasionally waking to drink some soup or water provided by his caring nurse, Dara. He reached back and felt the bandage at the base of his skull. That area still throbbed when he thought about it. He lifted one edge, stuck a finger under it, and felt along the length of the gash. Bumps and sharp edges. He didn't remember getting stitched or even anyone else visiting his room except Dara.

Sauce smiled weakly, pulling his hand down quickly as she entered the room carrying a tea tray. "Don't scratch it!" Dara scolded. "You'll pull out the stitches. It was hard enough to get a doctor to make a house-call once."

"Not for you it wasn't," quipped Sauce, tilting his head and raising his eyebrows.

"Okay. You're right. It wasn't that hard. I could probably have a dozen in your room within a half hour if I wanted. But that was hardly the point." She placed the tray down on the bedside table next to Sauce and began pouring tea. "You look much better," she offered.

"Still feel like I was hit by a truck. Man, I don't think I have ever been that sick in my life. My insides still feel raw."

Dara handed him his cup and in an exaggeratedly nagging tone said, "It serves you right for drinking alcohol after all I did to sober you up. You should be ashamed of yourself."

Sauce took a sip of his tea. "Thanks." He recognized the debt he owed to Dara. "I don't think it was alcohol. They must have laced the bottle with something else."

"No, I'm positive it was just booze."

Sauce noticed the edges of her mouth curl slightly and knew she was keeping something from him; he could tell she was inwardly trying to hold back laughing. "What? What are you not telling me?"

"Okay, but remember, you were in pretty sad shape only a week ago, and now look at you." Sauce considered his condition, lying on the bed, head in a bandage, internal organs ravaged, weak and sore all over. "Some improvement," he joked.

"You know what I mean. Getting off the bottle was the best thing for you."

"And you take credit for that."

"I guess I should also take the blame. Now don't get mad." Dara sat on the edge of the bed and put one hand on Sauce's outstretched leg. "You needed to sober up. You agree with me, don't you?" She paused as Sauce waited blank-faced and impatient. "You know those drinks I've been preparing for you: the faux martinis, the coffee, even the lemony-water you drank during our dinner with the governor. I've been, um, well kind of spiking them with disulfiram."

"Disulfiram?"

"Yeah, you know, Antabuse. It makes your body allergic to alcohol. You were supposed to get sick, well a little sick, if you sneaked a drink. I was worried when you didn't get sick after stealing my glass of wine at the governor's that the dose was too weak. I upped the dose, slightly, after that. I suppose I might have been giving you too much. Or your body may simply have had an unusually strong reaction to the drug. Now that I think of it, you have been a little too sleepy lately. Either way, there you have it."

Sauce started to chuckle, then laugh, but the pain in his sides turned his laughter into winces. "Ow, ow."

"Oh, I'm sorry," said Dara with genuine remorse in her voice.

"No, no. It's not you. Laughing really hurts." He took another sip of his tea. "I was about to be turned into mince meat. If I had not become so sick before EB arrived, they would probably have allowed their two little brats to pound the shit out of my hands. Did you see that note in my jacket pocket?"

"Oh, yeah. It's over here." She walked across the room to retrieve the pink slip of paper.

"It was sitting under my windshield wiper when I retrieved the car at the restaurant. I didn't understand it at the time. But Vin and his wife made the meaning abundantly clear to me."

Dara opened the note and read aloud, "Get out of the game or that finger you're pointing at me will get stepped on."

"Your elixir may have saved my life." Sauce chuckled at the irony.

Dara smiled sympathetically, then smirked. "Well, of course. That's why I gave it to you, silly!"

"So what came of EB and her murderous clan?"

"Oh, they are in the wind. Except for EB. Her body was discovered by the police. BT gave Hammi the *anonymous* tip about the house. Those poor kids. Their lives are going to be so messed up after killing their aunt."

"Messed up? They just passed their entrance exam for the family business. I'm sure the Wests will find a use for those sadistic cretins."

Sauce lifted himself onto his elbows. "I'm feeling much better today. I appreciate how you've been taking care of me, but I think I should probably have a shower and get dressed. Isn't Gladys's first show today?"

"Tonight; the network thought an evening show would be better for ratings. I'll have to be leaving soon. But not you. I already gave you a sponge bath while you slept this morning. Just the fact that you slept right through it—and believe me I was very attentive to certain parts of your body—" she winked and gave a devilish smile, "should tell you that you still have some healing to do before you get out of bed. BT will be here soon. He'll be staying with you tonight to keep you company. He said he'll set the TV on the dresser so you don't miss the show."

Sauce handed his teacup to Dara and lay back. "I suppose you're right. How is BT? And Hammi? Oh, that reminds me. I guess I have a confession to make, though I'm sure you already know. I didn't give the passes to Hammi."

"I didn't know. He didn't say anything, though I suppose he might've thought it rude to remind me about my offer. Does that mean the Wests have them?"

"Ah, no. I gave them to Jett." Sauce waited a few seconds, expecting to have to explain. He shrieked from the pain as Dara pounced on him, giving him a tight squeeze and a flood of kisses on his face. "You are amazing!"

"I don't understand," he confessed, pushing Dara off him.

"Mummy wanted Jett to attend. In fact, Jett's attendance is an integral part of tomorrow night's show." Sauce still looked confused. "Oh, don't worry, you'll find out why tomorrow. She has a number of schemes in the works to ensure he attends. But nothing is guaranteed, of course. One of them involved me pressuring you to rebel against me. The redecorating, taking over your home, the Jacuzzi, and of course, inviting Hammi to the show against your wishes. Mummy hoped you would use your relationship with Jett against me, and you did."

"It wasn't really like that, but I suppose you may be partially right. So you had no intention of moving in with me?"

Dara grabbed Sauce's hand and pressed it up against her heart. "I guess a confession is in order. Especially now, before BT arrives. I'm afraid he's a lot smarter than Mummy hoped he would be. He figured out everything about Mummy, Beckley, even the trial and Mummy's disappearance. Mummy should have told the governor to pick someone else to guard you, but that's water under the bridge, isn't it?"

"You mentioned a confession."

"Yeah, I did. You're sweet, really sweet. And I have a special place in my heart for you. But I can't stay with you. We're from two very different worlds. I've enjoyed our time together. Just like when we went to St. Martin. I enjoyed spending time with you then. It's just that if I stayed around you, I'd eat you alive. You are too good a person, and I'm too good at what I do." Sauce frowned at the implication of being stupid. "Don't get sour. I love you. I really do, in a way. Well, more than I have loved any other man. So that's something isn't it?"

"Yeah, it's something," said Sauce.

"It is. It really is. And you have to remember that when you and BT talk. Please, don't hold it all against me. I'm sure you had some fun over the past few days playing house."

Sauce looked down at his broken body and joked, "Some fun!"

Dara giggled. "I meant before that, silly. Oh, dear, I never ever wanted you to get hurt. I thought that with BT near you you'd be safe through all of this. And you are now. Safe, in your own bed, in your own home."

"With no stupid Jacuzzi in my bedroom," said Sauce with a smile.

"That's right. With no stupid Jacuzzi in your bedroom." She laughed softly. "Listen I have to finish getting ready to go to the studio. Mummy needs me there. But BT has a key and will be here soon." She leaned over and kissed him softly. "You might want to have a nap so you are able to stay awake for the show tonight. "I'll come around to tuck you in later. Okay?" Dara rose to leave.

"I am feeling a little groggy. Did you put something in my tea?" asked Sauce with mock concern.

"Sauce, I'm insulted. What kind of girl do you think I am?" She turned and stamped her feet loudly as she left the bedroom. Sauce couldn't help but laugh, despite the pain.

CHAPTER 26

The muffled sounds of voices and music playing began to invade his dreams, until he finally opened his eyes to see the TV screen on the dresser. He scanned the room and saw no one else was there. He assumed BT was nearby, as Dara had promised.

Sauce sat up. "BT are you here?"

The toilet in the ensuite flushed. BT poked his head through the open door. "Hey man. You're awake just in time. I'll be right there; just let me wash up."

BT came in holding a towel, wiping his hands. "Hungry?"

"Not really? You been here long?"

"Couple of hours, maybe. The show will be starting in a little bit. I'm going to grab a beer. Do you want anything?"

"A glass of water, I guess. Maybe some toast."

"Good, you're starting to get your appetite back. No problem. Be right back."

Sauce closed his eyes and remained half awake until BT returned. BT placed Sauce's plate and glass on the bedside table, then sat down on an easy chair he had previously moved from the living room. He took a long sip of his beer then asked, "Do you feel like talking, or would you prefer peace and quiet?"

Sauce thought about his conversation with Dara and decided he had been in the dark long enough. "Tell me about Dara and Gladys."

BT leaned in. "You know, I haven't told anyone yet. Except Dara. I had to get her reaction. And I also knew how you felt about her. I had to see if it was all a ploy, or if she had any feelings for you at all. So before I go any further, you should know that her feelings for you are genuine. She may not love you in the way you'd like, but she loves you in her own way."

"Wow. I must have come across as a total idiot to you and Dara to deserve all this coddling. I'm a big boy, Daddy," he said with childish scorn. "Fuck the preamble and get on with it."

"Yeah, you're right." He took a long swig of his beer. "After getting smashed off the road, I called Hammi for some assistance in finding you. I've met thousands of cops over the years, and he's as good as the best I've seen. He had persisted on checking names from Beckley's ledger and found some intriguing connections. He followed up on a few of those leads, asking questions, cashing in favours, and making some key assumptions. He was still perplexed about most of it when I met with him. I don't mean to brag, but my years of protecting presidents provided me with a way of looking at these things from multiple angles at once. The pieces just seemed to fall into place, and I could see the whole, contorted, messed up picture. I confronted Dara with my interpretation of the facts. It was obvious from her expression that I was, at least partially, on the mark. I could tell she was conflicted. She wanted to preserve the mystery of Good Gladys. She realized, however, that the only way we were going to be able to save you was if she cooperated with me, which required her to divulge some of her secrets. There was no way we would have rescued you so quickly if she hadn't."

"Because she cares about me?" said Sauce, rolling his eyes.

"As I said, I think she does. She is complicated; I'll give you that. Anyway, before she would help, she insisted I promise one thing: not to tell anyone else about her, or Gladys. She promised she would tell you herself, and do so right after tomorrow night's show. I am confident that Dara will keep her word, so please don't ask me about things that I cannot divulge."

"Fair enough," answered Sauce. "What about Hammi's research, can you tell me about that? Maybe I'll put the pieces together like you did."

BT chuckled. "Yeah, I guess you might. Hammi didn't. I called him after we got you out of that house and filled him in on the Wests, so he may have figured out the rest by now. Don't get any ideas. Hammi said Dara called him this afternoon and asked him to promise to keep his findings to himself. Dara also told him that after tomorrow night's show, he and I can tell you everything if we want."

"How did Dara know where I was being held?" asked Sauce.

"That I *can* tell you. First let me explain what I did after the damn dump truck smashed into me. I was pissed, not hurt, fortunately, but determined to get even, and get you back, of course." He smiled and took another sip of beer. "Oh look, the Amber Ellis Show is about to begin. They always start by posting the phone numbers: one for positive votes, the other for negative votes."

"So you're an expert on this show, are you?"

"This show has been on for years. Many of the brainiac politicians I was assigned to protect spent hours watching daytime TV. There was this one guy who had the number for a negative vote programmed into his phone and he would just hit redial, over and over. It didn't seem to affect the show, though. Most voters tend to follow the crowd. Gladys might have something to worry about if the show allowed voting to play out naturally. If the tide was allowed to turn against her, this could be a bloodbath."

"Hyperbole aside, I don't imagine Gladys left much to chance," suggested Sauce.

"You're right. She thinks things through. That's one of the things that sets her apart from the other criminals in this game."

"Game?" asked Sauce. "The Wests called their racket a game, too."

"Con game," said BT. "That's what all of these psychics or mediums are doing. I could never understand why the law hasn't cracked down on them. Anyone who takes money claiming to talk to the dead has committed fraud. By not prosecuting each and every person who makes that claim, the Justice Department is basically stating they believe talking to the dead is possible."

"So you agree with me that Gladys is a thief?"

"Oh, she's much more than that. She was probably just a small time crook before she found Ned West. Yeah, that's right. She used to hang out with the West family. Married into it, in fact. If you ask me, she sought them out. Like I said, she is thorough. Ned provided financial backing for her to start the Good Gladys routine. He's long dead, though. Right after Dara's birth."

"Dara told you all this?" asked Sauce.

"No, Hammi did. He found some of the Wests in Beckley's ledger. Gladys employs many of them whenever she performs in the area. Hammi found a lot of curious connections in the ledger. He crosschecked some of the more interesting names with Beckley's bank records and uncovered some sizable payments. For example, there were forensic experts, judges, and police officers in almost every city receiving money from Gladys. In addition there were employees at search engines, telephone, and cell companies listed in the ledger. The psychic game went big time when the internet came into existence and information became a commodity. You wouldn't believe the extent of her network of paid contractors."

"Why would they work for her?" asked Sauce.

"Face it, buddy. Rich people can buy almost anything because there are so many people who want more than they already have. Greed feeds the beast, and the beast is Good Gladys." BT laughed at this new axiom he just created.

"Gladys is the beast?" asked Sauce with a shrug.

"Not Gladys the person. I'm talking about Good Gladys the global enterprise, because that's what it is. Good Gladys is shows, marketing, news stories, and books. It was her books that first propelled Gladys into the jet-setting spotlight. Her first book, Good Gladys Embraces the Dead, is in its eighteenth printing. The enterprise employs hundreds of people and takes in millions each year."

"So this show isn't going to make a dent in that," commented Sauce. "What if someone presented irrefutable evidence that Gladys is a fraud, right there on live television?"

"History shows it wouldn't make a bit of a difference. Houdini, one of the most famous men alive years ago, wrote a book detailing how each of the top mediums of his day were frauds. The book was a best seller. Ironically, those same mediums did better because of the exposure Houdini gave them."

Sauce started to laugh, then noticing BT's confused expression explained, "I was just talking about that book the other day when I met the governor."

"It's one of a kind."

"Can you turn up the volume?" asked Sauce. "Amber's introducing Gladys. I have to hear this."

BT pressed the button on the remote. "This show is merely a set-up for tomorrow. Dara said the trick will be to convince the audience at home that the man on stage really is Gladys."

"That may be challenging for the many viewers who aren't familiar with Gladys but not for the legion of Good Gladys believers," said Sauce. "Even the governor had no problem believing in the transformation." They both kept silent for a few minutes to hear the once beautiful, though now noticeably middle-aged Amber Ellis on the TV.

"For the past month, we have been getting in touch with people from all over the world who knew Gladys and could swear to her identity. Many of those people are here, in the audience tonight."

"Oh look, people are already texting in their votes," commented Sauce. "I didn't realize the Fan Response Meter was used on the host as well as the guests."

"It's used throughout the show." BT pointed at the changing numbers on the screen. "See that; it's suspiciously instantaneous, so the votes apply to whatever is on the screen at the time."

"Amber is getting close to ninety percent positive votes," commented Sauce. "She must be happy about that."

"Don't believe everything you see," suggested BT. "Remember, this is television. Everything is about shaping the audience. Talk show producers are masters at controlling the crowd."

"Is nothing sacred in this world anymore?" asked Sauce.

"Not that, anyway. Hammi told me the meter was introduced during Gladys's very first appearance on this show. I wouldn't be surprised if it was her idea."

Sauce turned his focus back on Amber, who was saying, "After the commercial I will introduce some of these audience members so they can tell their amazing stories of how Gladys changed their lives forever."

"And emptied their bank accounts in the process," said Sauce.

"She only did that early in her career," said BT. "You don't need to be so cynical. After her first appearance on this show, her book sales took off, and her performances moved from individual's homes to football stadiums. She didn't need to liquidate any one person's assets. Though there was plenty of that at the beginning of her career."

"Were the Wests part of the enterprise, too, back then?" asked Sauce.

"Actually, the Wests never left Gladys, in a way," answered BT. "They had a more integral role early on. But as she became a global enterprise, she needed to broaden her list of criminal contacts. That was when Beckley came into the picture. He had a knack for finding the right people."

"And the ledger kept track of those contacts."

"He didn't trust computers. Too old school, kind of like me, I guess," said BT with a smile. "Gladys needed pickpockets, magicians, computer hackers, and numerous other lowlifes to produce the desired effect during each performance. She also needed sympathetic and greedy law enforcement officials at various levels to guarantee that no one in her entourage would be risking prosecution. Good Gladys became a very coordinated machine that rarely made mistakes."

"There were mistakes though, right? There always are," said Sauce with a knowing smirk.

"I think you may have had a eureka moment."

"Tell me if I'm wrong, but on the night Jett was in attendance, there was a mistake wasn't there?"

"A monumental, rookie mistake," answered BT. "That was one of the things that threw me off. An old colleague once told me that blind people are always safe from pickpockets. The criminal needs his mark to be able to see the distraction, to focus on something other than the location of their wallet. Blind people are less distractible and more sensitive to touch. They are higher risk than most people. Gladys knows this. Yet something must have happened to Jett during the show he attended, for him to set his sights on Gladys."

"So what went wrong?" asked Sauce.

"Beckley often hired over twenty people to manage the preshow show. That's the part of the show from the moment people start to line up, until they are seated in the theatre. The preshow involves a highly coordinated process of distracting, lifting a wallet, and passing it to someone who searches through to find pertinent information, like identification, and personal details. The wallet is returned to the lifter and reinserted in the exact pocket or purse where it originated. It should all happen very quickly, to minimize the risk and maximize the number of marks that Gladys will have in the audience to work her magic on.

"At the show attended by Jett, the crew was two men short due to a bad winter flu that was going around. They brought in some inexperienced talent to fill the void. Gladys wasn't told until after the damage was done. Jett's wallet had been taken. Inside was a slip of paper with all of his computer passwords. I know most security experts say it's the best thing to do to keep track of passwords, but I always thought that writing down passwords was foolish. Before Gladys had even taken the stage, her hacker network had scoured his home and office computers, found the letters to the politicians, and passed the information to Gladys."

"And Jett knew his wallet had been compromised," said Sauce.

"He must have figured it out partway through the show. Dara said his eyes were throwing darts at Gladys throughout the second half."

"Listen to these stupid testimonials. Are all of these people plants?" Sauce pointed at the television.

"Some of them are. Gladys probably has this down to a science, knowing the precise golden ratio of legit believers to paid confederates that produces the maximum overall effect. Gladys should be out right after the next commercial. Dara said Gladys will only be on for about fifteen minutes tonight."

"You're kidding? People are tuning in to see Gladys and that's all they get?"

"Don't worry. The viewers will get enough of Gladys to peek their interest so they won't be able to resist tuning in tomorrow night. Tonight's show is cleverly designed so people will discuss it at work and on social media, helping to maximize the size of the audience for the big show tomorrow night."

"One thing I don't get," began Sauce. "If Gladys is a West, why didn't they just ask Gladys to leave EB alone instead of abducting me?"

"In their eyes, Gladys went rogue. She's not a blood relation, after all. And Gladys hasn't had direct contact with them for a long time. They certainly didn't believe that the man calling himself Gladys was the real thing. Dara said that Gladys never allowed her to meet the Wests. As you noticed, the Wests can become violent on occasion. Gladys wanted Dara to have a straight life. She certainly had enough money to ensure that Dara didn't need to learn the trade, like she did growing up. The Wests only ever communicated with Gladys or Beckley. When Beckley wouldn't tell them where Gladys was hiding, he was killed.

"When I told Dara that her mother's family had you, she called Gladys. It only took a few minutes for Gladys to find the address where you were being kept."

"You mean she called the real Gladys?" Sauce sat up at this development.

"Don't get all excited. I wasn't on the line. All I know is that she said Mummy a lot into the phone, and of course, the address Dara was given was the right one."

"Oh shit, we're like a couple of old ladies," snapped Sauce. "Gladys is talking and we're going on and on and not paying attention to the television."

CHAPTER 27

Sauce leaned forward and pointed at Glady. "Who in their right mind would believe that is a woman?" Gladys was sitting cross-legged on the sofa in the center of the stage. The soft blue lighting bounced off her hair creating a halo-like effect. Her suit was black and tight. Even her open collar dress shirt was too tight and pulled on the buttons creating small gaps through which a few hairs on her chest could be seen when she turned to the side. Enormous view screens above the stage allowed the audience to see everything shown to viewers at home.

"The same people who believe Gladys can talk to dead people, I imagine," answered BT.

Amber was also seated on the sofa, one hand holding a photograph, the other stretched out toward Gladys across the back of the couch. She was relaxed, wrapped in a loose fitting lavender dress that hid most of her middle-aged lumpy body. Her voice was authoritative without sounding bitchy.

Amber learned toward Gladys. "You've been a man for a few weeks now. Tell me; what is the biggest difference between living as a woman and living as a man?"

Gladys chuckled playfully. "Invisibility." The audience responded with subtle laughter. Gladys winked at the camera.

"How so?" asked Amber.

"Show the picture again," suggested Gladys. The camera zoomed in on the photo in Amber's hands of Gladys in a gorgeous ball gown. "That was me, before. Look at that cleavage!" The audience applauded louder than before. The fan meter, which had been teetering around a thirty percent positive rating, jumped up to sixty percent. "Now look at me. For the first time in a long time, I can shop at Safeway without getting asked to connect with a dead aunt or parent for someone. Don't get me wrong; I love to help people. Lately, though, I've learned the value of having a little time to myself."

The fan meter dropped below fifty percent briefly before Amber said, "That takes us to the question on everyone's mind. How did it happen? I am sure we would all love to know!" She raised her arms enthusiastically. The camera panned around the audience, pausing on people who were typing on their phones, registering their votes. The fan meter jumped up to ninety-eight percent approval.

"Look at those numbers," commented BT.

"Gladys wouldn't even tell the governor this part," said Sauce. "Timing is everything in her business. Now she has millions of gullible minds to infect with her vision of reality."

The camera zoomed in on Amber. "Remember everyone, keep voting, and stay on this channel. We have to take a short commercial break. When we return, Gladys will tell her incredible story of how God took her away from this world, then sent her back to us as a man!"

"I need another beer," grunted BT.

"Yeah me too," said Sauce. BT smiled sheepishly, obviously unsure if Sauce was kidding or not. Sauce lifted the empty plate from the side table. "Another toast, I mean. And a cup of tea if you don't mind."

"Oh, yeah. Sure."

A few minutes later, BT returned with his beer. "The kettle's on. What do you think of the show, so far?"

"I think there are too many commercials. And no substance, really. Gladys hasn't said anything yet.

It's like a long, drawn out introduction for an infomercial."

BT laughed softly. "I bet the network is happy, though. Amber and Gladys look like a happy married couple up there. It's all kind of surreal."

"And probably exactly what their audience loves. Not that I'm an expert."

"You're probably right, though," added BT, leaving the room to silence the whistling kettle.

"Better hurry," yelled Sauce. "It's starting up again. You can get my tea during the next commercial break."

BT quickly returned. "Holy shit, I just looked at my watch. There are less than twenty minutes left in the show."

"Gladys had better hurry or she'll miss her opportunity to tell the biggest lie of her life on national television," joked Sauce.

The show resumed with the camera in tight on Amber Ellis's face. "I am here with Good Gladys, once a beautiful woman adored all over the world for her ability to speak with the dead, and now the tragic victim of a heavenly test, trapped in a man's body. During a private séance in her own home, she was whisked away from our Earthly plane, into … well, I don't know. Gladys, do you even know where you were taken?"

The television screen showed a wide shot of the stage. Gladys rose from her seat and approached the edge of the stage to tell her story. As she moved forward the camera gradually zoomed in on her. "I am Gladys. I have to correct Amber, though. I am not a woman trapped in this body. I am a man, with the same feelings, desires, and thoughts of a man. I can't explain how it happened. I can only tell you what I experienced and hope you believe."

"And fork over your money to buy my books and tickets to my shows," commented Sauce.

The fan meter showed a perfect split in the votes. "I was in a relaxed state, conducting a séance for a few prominent government officials. I must respect the anonymity of my clients, you understand, though I think a couple of them are ready to share their stories, and I'll leave that up to them. As I said, I was beginning to relax and seek a connection with the other side. I kept repeating the name of the loved one I had been asked to contact, when another name came into my head … my own. It repeated over and over, echoing in my mind's ear.

"Suddenly I felt warmth on my arms, like sunlight on a summer's day. I opened my eyes, and I wasn't in my house anymore. I was … the best way to describe it is like the backyard of an old ranch house, with overgrown thistle bushes on one side and a large plum tree in the middle. There was some fallen fruit on the ground, bruised and rotten, sending a pungent aroma into the air."

"Don't you love the detail?" asked BT, chuckling.

Gladys continued. "An old man was sitting in a white wood-slat deck chair and he called to me, 'Hey, you! Gladys! Run in the house and get Eve, would you?' I quickly ran to the house and poked my head inside. It seemed to be an ordinary farm kitchen, complete with a metal basin on the table that was being used to prepare freshly picked green beans. I called but got no response, so I walked farther into the house. Then something weird happened."

Sauce and BT looked at each other and laughed. "*Then* something weird happened?" Sauce repeated.

"I heard a disgusting grunting sound coming from behind a door." Gladys's face grimaced. "It lasted a few minutes, and then a toilet flushed. I just stood there like an idiot. When the door opened, I must have been red as a beet, because the grey-haired old woman hastened into the kitchen repeating 'Oh dear me, dear me' over and over."

The television briefly showed the fan meter, which hovered around sixty percent approval, then the image returned to Gladys. "Don't forget to vote people," mocked Sauce.

Gladys walked across the front of the stage. "I quickly apologized for intruding, and she waved her hand and said, 'Young lady, we are the ones intruding. I hate coming here. Every time He sends us to meet one of you, my IBS goes haywire and I spend most of our visit in the bathroom.' At the time I didn't know what to say, but looking back I can't help but laugh. I mean Adam lounging in a deck chair while Eve struggles with irritable bowel syndrome? It just seems so fantastic. Yet there I was."

"My God, yet another psychic with an Adam and Eve encounter," said Sauce.

"She kind of has to stick with the script," commented BT. "It's familiar, so people believe it. Besides, she has added a new spin to it this time."

"Eve ushered me outside and took a seat next to Adam," continued Gladys. "I asked them if I was dead. Adam said very clearly these exact words, 'Good Gladys is part of the world now and forever.' I had no idea what he meant. Eve must have sensed my confusion because she explained why I was there. She told me I had abused my gift. She said I was being punished for taking without giving. I tried to explain myself, tell her that I thought I had been a generous person. Adam got angry and said, 'Do you think Eve and I enjoy getting sent here to talk to you? If He says you are selfish, then you are.' I couldn't very well argue with that. So I asked them if there was a way for me to correct the situation. The image of James Stewart from the movie *It's a Wonderful Life* popped into my head. Adam snapped again saying, 'This is real life, not a movie. You were given one of the greatest gifts, the knowledge of death. You should have used it to save life. People could have changed their diet, their lifestyle. You would know if their lives had been extended.' I suddenly realized how foolish I had been. Adam was right. I was selfish."

The audience gasped loudly and scattered boos could be heard from a few members of the audience. The fan meter dropped to its lowest point that night, close to ten percent.

"Yes it's true," yelled Gladys, silencing the crowd. "In my defense, I explained to Adam that most people did not want me to tell them the day they were going to die. I even discussed that in my book, Good Gladys Embraces the Dead. I asked them how could I help people when most didn't even believe in me. Adam said I should have tried harder. We talked on and on for hours. They pointed out specific situations where I could have made a difference, and honestly I cried so much my eyes were burning.

"Eventually, they said it was time for me to return. They told me there were two things I had to do before my powers would be restored to me. First, I had to prove my sincerity by correcting a major injustice in the world. And secondly I needed to help reduce the fear people have of dying. Adam suggested that I make public the date of my own death. I promised I was a changed person. In my enthusiasm, I told them I would be able to help a lot more people if they sent me back with irrefutable evidence of this heavenly encounter. That was probably the stupidest request I have ever made of anyone. Suddenly, I was back in my house. It was immediately apparent that, despite the hours I felt had passed, no time at all had elapsed here on Earth. My guests were stunned. I looked at my hands, my body, then saw my reflection in the wall mirror and knew that this was how God had answered my plea."

Gladys looked over at Amber, signaling it was time for her to intervene. Amber looked into the camera. "We'll be right back to take a few questions from the audience and have a quick look at what you can expect from tomorrow's show."

"My God!" shouted Sauce to BT, who was already halfway to the kitchen to fetch the tea. "Do you think anyone believed that load of crap?"

BT shouted back, "Oh, only about ninety-five percent of the viewers." Sauce laughed, realizing BT was probably right.

BT returned a few minutes later with buttered toast and a cup of tea for Sauce. "You look much better. You should watch this show more often."

Sauce spilled a little tea on his blanket. "Don't hand me a hot drink then make me laugh. I actually think her spiel was kind of inspired. I've never actually seen Gladys on stage, but you look at the faces of people in the audience while she's talking and they are totally mesmerized, like zombies."

"Did you see the fan meter when she finished her story?" Not waiting for an answer BT continued, "It was at twenty-seven percent. The camera work was really clever. It showed the meter then people in the audience with looks of awe and admiration."

"That's what I mean. Gladys's speech combined with the meter and audience reactions are kind of dissonant. It's basic psychology. Just liking or disliking doesn't really amount to anything. People need to feel dissonance, feel like something is just a little off, to be motivated to do something. How can any of them reconcile her statement that her *powers* were revoked, with the news reports of her time in prison saying she used her powers on an inmate and a guard?"

"They'll be motivated to come back tomorrow night; that's for sure," added BT.

"We're back," stated Amber, "and Morise has our roaming mike in the audience to get a few questions for Gladys."

The camera panned around the audience showing many excited hands raised and waving in the air. It zoomed in on a tall black man holding the microphone. He pointed to a tall, pretty, young woman. "Amber this is Marcy Denton from Fresno."

"Hi, Marcy," said Gladys, who was back on the sofa next to Amber.

"Hi Gladys. Hi Amber. I just wanted to know, well, um, I know the court let you go, but still, did you kill your manager?"

"Oh, I'm sorry Gladys," began Amber. "We don't screen these questions, as you know. You don't have to answer that …"

"No, it's all right," interjected Gladys. "Marcy, you're very brave to ask that question. I expect it's a question everyone has been thinking about all night long." The fan meter rose to seventy-five percent. "The answer is no. I loved Beckley like an uncle. He protected me and helped build my career right from the start. In fact, I can say with one hundred percent certainty I would not be where I am today had it not been for him. I just wish to God he had not made me promise years ago to never tell him when he was going to die. As the day approached, I tried to warn him subtly, so as not to break my promise, but he would not listen."

"Thanks, Marcy," interrupted Amber, obviously intent on getting more questions answered before their time was up. The camera stayed on Marcy as she looked for a place to set down the microphone. "That's okay, honey," said Amber. "Morise will take the microphone."

Morise moved down a few rows and stated, "Amber, this is Blair Simco from San Diego." There was a smattering of applause at the mention of the city. The camera briefly showed Amber and Gladys giggling, then returned to Blair.

"Hi, Blair. Do you have a question for Gladys?"

"Hi, Gladys. I don't know if you can answer this but here goes. If God thought you had wasted your gift, why did he let you return? Couldn't he have just given the gift to someone else?"

"Like you, you mean," joked Amber. Blair laughed and nodded, and the audience clapped. The fan meter rose again to eighty-two percent.

"Thanks for the question, Blair," said Gladys, smiling broadly. "I suppose that despite my history, God just isn't finished with me yet. As I said before, he did take my gift away, for now. I hope to fix that tomorrow night, by explaining where I've been for the past several weeks and how I have been helping the police prevent a major disaster. You must have heard about the attempted poisoning of the governor's daughter. I helped prevent her death, and have been working with the governor to keep his daughter, and the other children who were threatened, safe. By tomorrow night's show, I should be able to reveal the perpetrator of that crime. I will also fulfill the second part of my punishment. I will tell you when I am going to die. I have known all my life when that will be, and by tomorrow, everyone will. I don't know if my gift will be restored, but I know I will be well on my way to becoming a better person."

"It looks like our viewers agree with you there," commented Amber as the fan meter rose to ninety percent. The audience also voiced their approval with loud applause.

"Thank you, everyone," said Amber. She started to stand, then sat back down, appearing to have been shown a message from the producer off camera. "Oh, it seems we have time for one quick question. Morise, can you find someone with a short question?"

"I sure can, Amber," answered Morise. "This is Michael Jenson, from Eureka."

Sauce adjusted his position on the bed, inadvertently sending his toast plate onto the floor. "Damn!"

"Just leave it," commented BT. "With only a couple minutes left, I am sure this is the most important part of the show."

The gentleman holding the microphone was dressed in an Armani three-piece suit and well groomed, looking like a thirty-year old male model. He stood tall, but said nothing.

"Do you have a question for Gladys?" asked Amber after a few seconds of silence.

"You don't remember me, do you? I knew you were a fraud. I thought to myself, there is no way the Gladys I knew would have pissed off God. She was a good person. I owe my life to her, so don't tell me you are Gladys after having been punished by God." Morise tried to take the microphone away from him but the man held on to it firmly. "I'm sure you researched all the stories about Gladys so you could fool everyone, but my story wasn't in the news. The only people there were me, Gladys and God."

"Your name isn't Michael," snapped Gladys standing up and approaching the man to get a better look. "My goodness, my goodness. Thomas, is that you?"

The camera briefly zoomed in on the man's face. He looked stunned.

Gladys walked down from the stage, then up the stairs into the audience until she was right next to Thomas. "Amber, this man's name isn't Michael, or at least that's not the name he gave me, oh, what was it now? About ten, twelve years ago? He told me he was Thomas."

"Yes ma'am, you're right. I am Thomas. It was twelve years ago." The camera zoomed in really close to show the tears falling from his eyes.

"Thomas, of course I remember you. It was right after a show I did in Boston. I decided to walk to my hotel and you approached me for money. I touched your hand and immediately knew you were going to die that very night. I felt so sad. You walked away, but I followed from a distance. I watched as you entered an alley. You were about to insert a needle."

"You stopped me!" he shouted. "You told me who you were and about your gift. You said I was supposed to live for many more years. You told me God had a special place for me when I die and I was going to earn that place by helping others."

"Yes, that's right. I lied to you. My gift told me you would die that night, but I couldn't tell you that."

"You gave me hope." He dropped to his knees, wrapped his arms around Gladys's legs and started crying. "Because of you that night, I turned my life around. I went back to school, earned good grades, and was accepted into medical school. I am now a doctor, helping others. Everything you said came true."

The audience was on their feet crying and cheering, and the fan meter was at one hundred percent approval.

"Thomas, do you remember? You gave me something. A photograph of your mother. You said she had passed on. You wanted me to tell her that you felt sorry you were never able to make her proud." Gladys reached into her pocket and pulled out a wallet. "I still have it right here."

Gladys handed the photograph to the man. He kissed it gently and said quietly, but loud enough for the microphone to project it over the airwaves, "Thank you Mom for sending Good Gladys to me when I needed her." He stood up and gave Gladys a long hug.

The camera focused on Amber. "What an amazing night! Our time is up, but you don't want to miss tomorrow's show, with Good Gladys."

"Like you said," commented Sauce as soon as BT turned off the television, "her audience will definitely be back tomorrow night."

CHAPTER 28

"Do you hate me?" asked Dara, lying close to Sauce in his bed. She was dressed, on top of the covers; he was still in the pajamas he had been wearing during BT's visit the night before, under the covers.

"I was having the strangest dream," said a groggy Sauce, having just been awakened by Dara.

"You're back in the real world now." Dara giggled.

"I thought you said you were going to come over after the show."

"Technically this morning is after the show," she kidded. "I came in here last night, but you were sleeping. So I just curled next to you and here we are."

"After last night's show, I question whether I am in the real world or not. That performance was … let's just say, out of this world."

"You liked it?" she sang merrily. "I hoped you would. Mummy is amazing in front of a live audience, isn't she?"

"Once you see it you can't un-see it."

Dara gave Sauce a hurtful, pouting stare. "I'm not being critical. I mean, I have a better understand now why Gladys has become so famous. The experience of watching Gladys is very real. When Thomas broke down crying, even I began to get a little misty-eyed. And I knew it was all fake!"

"Oh, you silly cynic," chided Dara, giving Sauce a little punch on his arm. "It's not fake if everyone believes it!"

"Not everyone." Sauce rubbed his arm. "BT didn't believe it. Neither did I. And I bet there are a whole bunch of angry Wests, your kin, who didn't believe it either."

"So BT did talk to you last night." Dara sat up with a serious expression on her face. "I'll have to thank him for holding to his promise."

"How do you know he didn't tell me all about you and Gladys?"

"You didn't throw me out of the bed as soon as I woke you, for one thing. Also, you would have wanted to discuss that instead of the show."

"Sounds like I am in for an earful after the show tonight, then. Is Gladys going to tell everyone that one of your family killed Beckley?"

"No, she wouldn't betray her family," said Dara indignantly. "Besides, Mummy tried to contact the Wests yesterday to clear up the whole thing and smooth things over. Mummy is confident that eventually she'll be able to convince the family that Jett was behind everything."

"After they tried to kill me?" snapped Sauce.

"Well, they have their faults."

"And what about Jett? I gave him Hammi's passes for the show, yet he didn't show up."

"He couldn't. Mummy arranged a plumbing problem in his home. He was probably drying out his carpets all night. Mummy didn't want him to disrupt the show. Tonight, however, I'm sure he'll be there."

Dara stood up and grabbed one of Sauce's hands. "Get up. We have one last day to continue pretending that we are madly in love with each other."

Sauce reluctantly climbed out of bed. "We were never madly in love with each other. Why would we start pretending now?"

"Oh, go have a shower. I was just being silly. Let's go out for breakfast, okay? Do you feel well enough?"

"Yeah, I feel great," answered Sauce, exaggerating. "What about you? Are you feeling okay?"

"Me? I'm fantastic." Dara twirled on one foot. "I feel like a little girl. Let me have that for a little while longer, all right?"

Not quite sure what she meant, he nevertheless agreed, and walked to the bathroom to get ready.

Coming out of the shower fifteen minutes later, he could hear a heated argument. He put his ear to the bathroom door to hear Dara and BT shouting. Sauce hurriedly dried himself, put on pants and a shirt, and ran into the kitchen.

"Oh shit!" he screamed, quickly hopping on one foot to a chair. "Why is there glass all over the floor?" He lifted his left foot to examine the source of the pool of blood collecting on the kitchen tiles.

"Sorry, that was me," said Dara. "I was just about to clean it up, but BT barged in and distracted me."

"So really it's my fault? You're insane!" BT was incensed. He threw Sauce a towel. "Wrap this around your foot!"

"Thanks," said Sauce unsure how to respond to the lack of compassion shown, given the amount of blood he had spilled. "What was all the shouting about?"

"Nothing," answered Dara, pouring water on a dish cloth, preparing to clean the floor.

"Nothing?" snapped BT loudly. Dara glared at him, causing him to pause. Reducing his volume he continued, "The governor is furious at Gladys."

"Oh, he'll understand," said Dara dismissively.

"He doesn't *understand*," retorted BT. "Gladys won't even take his calls to explain. She should have given him a warning before announcing to the world that he was working with *Good Gladys*." His voice cracked each time he said Gladys's name.

"I'm sure Mummy has her reasons for not preparing the governor. He's still coming tonight isn't he?" Dara didn't wait for an answer. "Tell the governor to come to Mummy's dressing room just before the show and she'll explain everything."

"Or perhaps," he cast a quick glance at Sauce, "you could insist that Gladys call him right now."

Dara smiled devilishly and changed the subject. "Sauce and I are going for breakfast right now, aren't we?"

Sauce pulled a large piece of glass from his foot and wiped the wound with a cloth. "I think I had better get this checked by a doctor. It looks like it needs a few stitches."

BT suddenly acted sympathetically, bending down to look. "Oh my. That *is* a bad gash. Come on, buddy. I'll take you to the hospital. I'm sure

Dara should be helping her mummy prepare for tonight's show anyway." He looked at Dara and added, "I *promise* to have him at the studio on time for Gladys's big finale." He put an arm under Sauce's and helped him to avoid the rest of the broken glass on their way to the living room to retrieve Sauce's shoes.

Dara pleaded with them to stay, but BT kept moving Sauce toward the door. Just before they left, BT looked at Dara very seriously and calmly stated, "Make sure Gladys calls the governor, or he may not even show up tonight. She wouldn't like that, would she?"

On the way to the hospital, Sauce sensed that BT was calming down. He fidgeted with his sore foot, and maintained the silence, waiting for BT to start the conversation.

BT still hadn't spoken when they pulled into the parking lot of a medical clinic.

"Don't you think I'd be better off at a hospital?" asked Sauce.

"It's just a scratch, you big baby," scoffed BT, obviously still quite upset. "This guy will be able to put in a stitch or two. Trust me, you'll live."

"Man, you are in a mood today," asserted Sauce.

BT put an arm under Sauce's and guided him into the clinic without saying anything. Sitting in the waiting room, he finally offered an explanation. "Listen, Sauce. I like you. You're a decent guy, with a good heart. I'm sorry for going on and on. You know, I wish I hadn't made that damn promise to Dara. But it is what it is. I can't change the past. But you have to believe me that you do not need to be spending any more time around Dara than is absolutely necessary."

"What's this have to do with Dara?"

"I don't think I am compromising my principles in saying that come tomorrow, Dara will probably be out of your life forever. She'll have moved on, and you need to start thinking about your life and your career."

"She still has a closet full of clothes at my house," countered Sauce. "She's not going to just disappear."

"Forget it. Let's talk about your career. I've been thinking. We have worked pretty well together for the past week or so. We make a good team. You know, I was getting kind of bored with retirement. Would you consider a partnership? We could split the work fifty-fifty. You have the knowledge of the area and the law, and I have the investigative skills and experience."

"Experience in auto-insurance?" quipped Sauce.

"I was thinking that we might expand your range of services a little."

"Something doesn't quite add up," said Sauce suspiciously. "You're hiding something."

BT smiled. "You're right, but this goes no further. Agreed?"

Sauce considered the ramifications briefly, then shook hands with BT.

"Here are the real reasons why I was so angry with Dara. The governor's mad because he's afraid of losing votes if Gladys's plans go south. Me, I've always been a law man. So it burns me that Gladys won't give up the guy in her family who killed Beckley. She worked with Beckley for years, yet she has no intention of seeing that he gets justice. That's the kind of thing that really gets me hot."

"Yeah, I can see that. But those Wests will get their comeuppance. They keep getting put in jail for one thing or another anyway, so eventually the guy who did Beckley will do time."

"You don't get it. I need to be the one to put him away. I took this job, expecting to complete it. Unfinished business just doesn't sit well with me."

"So that's why you want to partner up. You figure we will eventually get a case involving the Wests and you'll be able to settle the score."

BT laughed softly. "That's part of it. There's one other thing as well. You know the ledger, the copies I scanned into my computer, sent to my friend at Interpol?" Sauce nodded. "They're all gone. Every shred of the ledger has vanished. Even Hammi's copies at his precinct, gone."

"When did that happen?"

"I noticed it when I got home last night. I wanted to look up those people in the audience at last night's show … see if their names were in the ledger. The notes and names were gone from my computer, even gone from my sent mail folder. So I called my buddy back east, and he claims they were all erased from his computer as well."

"Sounds very coordinated and thorough."

"Almost perfect, wouldn't you say?" added BT. "And it all starts here. A global underground crime network, with its roots attached firmly to Good Gladys. You and I already have a head start at chipping away at the infrastructure. I say we team up and keep digging."

"Who will hire us? My contracts were only with insurance companies, and they were never enough for one person to live off, and certainly not two."

"We'll get work; don't worry about that. Once word gets out that you lived with Good Gladys's daughter, we'll get lots of work."

"I'm not sure I like that kind of exposure."

"Think about it. I'll be around for a few more days. We'll discuss it again before I leave."

"I might be more amenable if you take me out for something to eat once we finish here," suggested Sauce. "I missed breakfast thanks to you."

CHAPTER 29

"I'm just going to close my eyes for a few minutes while you finish helping Gladys get ready," said Sauce, leaning back on the sofa in the studio's green room.

"All right, honey," said Dara, quickly running out to work on last minute preparations.

Sauce's mind shifted from one thought to another as he tried to compartmentalize facts and reinterpret his emotions. He was also exhausted from his first day outdoors since the kidnapping. He realized he needed a nap or he might not be able to remain conscious for Gladys's show.

"There you are!" rang a familiar voice. "He opened his eyes and thought, "Damn!" but enthusiastically said, "Hammi!" instead.

"Great to see you up and about," said Hammi.

"Thanks in no small part to you, so I've been told." Sauce got up to give his friend a hug.

"Ah-ahchoo!" shouted Hammi.

"Bless you." Sauce stopped before reaching his friend.

"Oh, keep your distance." Hammi pulled a tissue from his pants pocket and wiped his nose. "Oh, man I hate my job."

"Really? I thought you loved being a cop."

"Okay, I do most of the time. The last two days, however, I've been assigned to supervise rookies, on the graveyard shift, walking the beat near the docks. Do you have any idea how foggy and damp it gets in the morning near the water? Then I get home and my wife wants me to spend quality time with her—help fold the laundry, go shopping. Don't mind me, I'm getting rundown, that's all."

Sauce smiled at the image of domesticity painted by Hammi. "Better you than me," he thought to himself.

Hammi continued. "She just wants to reconnect. It all started when Miss Stockard visited the house. My wife sees me in a whole new light, I guess. Man, was she angry, though, when I told her she wasn't coming tonight."

"I'm surprised you came," commented Sauce. "You should have stayed home to rest and recover."

"Believe it or not, I'm on the job. Gladys specifically requested that I was part of the extra security assigned to this thing. The governor's here."

"Oh, he did come?"

"You knew he was planning on it? I didn't find out until this afternoon when the captain told my wife to wake me early enough so I could get here by five. I've been walking around this place since then, making sure everything's secure."

"I feel safer already," joked Sauce.

Hammi moved a few steps closer to Sauce and whispered, "I'm not sure that *I* do. Dr. Jett is in the audience." Hammi paused for a few seconds, reading Sauce's face. "Why am I the last to learn these things?"

BT burst into the room and shut the door behind him. "Hammi, you will want to alert some of the other officers to be extra vigilant tonight. I was just coming down one of the access corridors and I could have sworn I saw one of the Wests. I swear the guy looked just like the one I watched leave with a woman, right before I found you in their bathtub."

Sauce sat heavily on the sofa. "Vincent! Round two, I suppose."

"No way," said Hammi. "Not on my watch. If the Wests try anything, we'll be ready. Don't worry."

"And I'll be right beside you most of the night as well," said BT.

"Most of the night?" queried Sauce.

"Yeah. Dara told me you and I could watch from the wings, except for a small part of the show when I would be needed on stage. She said Gladys is planning a little game, and I would be needed as an expert witness to make sure no one cheats."

"You're going to go onstage?" asked Sauce.

"She said the cameras won't even be running. It will be during a commercial; that's all."

"Check your watches, guys," said Hammi, playfully. "Ten minutes and counting. I'd better get in position. I should be able to see both of you. I'm supposed to stand right next to the lower stage camera, near the governor."

"Aren't you special?" mocked Sauce. "Just don't get too mesmerized by Gladys or she may have you clucking like a chicken."

Hammi chuckled. "Now that wouldn't be very professional." He sneezed one more time as he left the room.

"Let's find out where they want us to stand," suggested BT.

Gladys and Amber were already on stage when Sauce and BT arrieved on the right wing. They watched for a few minutes as microphone levels were tested and spike marks were adjusted according to Gladys's specifications. To Sauce it looked like Gladys was in charge. That was until he and BT discovered they were standing on the wrong side of the stage. The stage manager, whose demeanor suggested he considered himself to be the boss, told them to stand on the left wing.

Sauce peeked out at the audience and could only see the people in the first couple of rows: the rest of the studio was too dark for him to make out any faces. The governor was in plain sight in the center of the second row surrounded on all sides by linebacker-sized men in black suits. Hammi was also visible, standing next to the camera closest to Gladys on the right side of the stage.

Suddenly a two-second, loud blast of music shattered the proceedings. Sauce noticed Hammi and the governor's security detail reach for their guns. He looked at BT and asked, "Did you just reach for your gun, too." BT didn't answer. "Tension is high tonight," whispered Sauce.

The audience was restless after the outburst. A few screamed from shock, many laughed, and many more talked loudly, abandoning their serene patience of a few moments earlier. "This house is ready to explode," thought Sauce.

The stage lights dimmed and brightened, then dimmed again, and the stage manager came out to the front of the stage to address the audience. "Ladies and gentlemen!" he bellowed, with his hands motioning for the crowd to settle and listen.

"Welcome to the second primetime episode of the Amber Ellis Show." He paused, allowing the audience to applaud for a few seconds. "I am Serge Marchant, stage manager. The show will begin in a few moments. I would like to remind you of some rules before the show begins. We will be filming throughout the show, using the cameras you see around the studio. At various times, some of these cameras will be directed at you, our audience. Please be aware of this so as to avoid any embarrassing gestures reaching our viewers at home. Yes, ma'am," he pretends to address a question from a pretty girl in the front row, "that includes picking your nose." The audience dutifully laughs. "I can tell we have a great crowd tonight. Please be aware of our audience prompter located above the stage. When it says silence!" he shouted the word into his microphone so that it echoed loudly through the room. "Yes, very good, that means we need everyone to be absolutely quiet. When it says applause?" He raised his hands unnecessarily as the audience immediately reacted with boisterous cheers and clapping. "Brilliant! Should we try that again?" He paused for a second, then answered, "No. I can tell you are ready for the show. Please wait for your cue. When Amber makes her entrance, please stand and give her love. Thank you." He exited the stage to a smattering of cheers.

"Here we go," said BT as the house lights brightened. He slapped Sauce on the back. "You sure you're up to this?"

Sauce ignored the question and commented on the behavior of the audience, now clearly in view. "They're already texting in votes, before there is anything to vote on! I bet viewers at home are, too." He looked at BT. "How the hell can psychologists hope to understand people when they keep doing crazy things like voting on something that hasn't even happened yet?"

BT laughed a little and pointed to Amber and Gladys on the stage. "I don't think they give a damn about psychologists. They know how to control people and have no need to learn why their methods work."

"Oh, there's Dara," said Sauce pointing to the opposite wing. He cringed at her makeup, which was caked thick, bright, and gaudy. He realized that this was her usual style, but since moving into his home, she had scaled back and become more conservative. She walked up to Gladys and whispered something in her ear. Gladys smiled broadly. Dara started to walk offstage when Gladys grabbed her arm and pulled her back to say something. Dara nodded her agreement.

Gladys stood and walked to the edge of the stage, dragging a resisting Dara beside her. She said something, but the microphones were not live. She then got a signal to proceed and spoke in an exaggeratedly deep voice. "My friends. Before the show begins I wanted to introduce you to my daughter, Dara. This is her first time in front of an audience so please give her a warm reception."

Dara pretended to be shy. She gave a quick curtsy, then fled back into the left wing. Sauce caught her eye. She smiled at him, raised her hands, and mouthed the words, "Que sera, sera."

The show's theme music began. Make-up girls and technicians quickly fled the stage, and cameras steadied on Amber.

Sauce scanned the seats and located Jett, sitting near the exit on the edge of one of the uppermost rows. He also noticed Vincent West, standing at the exit closest to Jett, and suddenly felt weak-kneed and nauseous. He leaned on BT for support and whispered this news in his ear.

BT pulled on Sauce's arm and the two of them walked to the hallway offstage. "You look pale," said BT as soon as they were on their own.

"How'd he get in here?" asked Sauce. "There's going to be trouble."

BT thought for a second then said, "It's too coincidental, don't you think? I'll bet anything I know who invited him."

"Gladys," said Sauce. "It has to be. We'd better get back out there."

"Are you okay?"

"A little weak. I don't want to miss this, though. I have to find out what she is up to."

They walked back to the right wing just as the house lights were dimming to begin the show. Dramatic music echoed throughout the studio, and the audience quietened down. Sauce kept alternating his gaze between the limited direct view of the stage and the view provided by an offstage monitor.

"Welcome to the Amber Ellis Show," she began in a somber, subdued voice. "In my fourteen years of doing this talk show, I have never seen such a response to a guest as we had last night. Over eighty million votes poured in during last night's telecast with Good Gladys, the world famous medium who proved to us that she was indeed transformed by heavenly forces into a man. I am here again for the second night with Gladys. I expect tonight's show will set a new record for votes. When we return after the break, I will turn over the stage to Good Gladys. Be prepared for an hour you will never forget."

"I bet they're charging a fortune for commercial time right now," commented BT.

"What was it you said last night about greed feeding the beast?" asked Sauce with a nervous smile.

They watched as the stage was cleared of chairs, leaving Gladys standing alone, center stage, in her familiar black two-piece suit and white open-collar shirt. The offstage monitor showed a close-up view of her face. She had her eyes closed, obviously preparing to give the performance of a lifetime.

The music rose again, then faded. "Hi, everyone," began Gladys. "Thank you all for joining the Amber Ellis Show tonight. I am Good Gladys. I may not look like Gladys. I may not sound like Gladys. Nevertheless, that is who I am. Last night I explained how I was transformed into the man you see before you. Before sending me back to Earth like this, God demanded that I do two things for him." She paused dramatically. "Tonight, with all of you as my witnesses, I will satisfy God's requests. My wish is that doing so will restore my gift, so I can begin a new chapter in my life giving peace and hope to all of you in body, and, after my passing, in spirit."

Gladys walked along the edge of the stage and continued. "I used to believe that my gift was the ability to talk to people who had passed on from this world. As you know, people call me the woman who embraced the dead. My gift also allowed me to touch someone's hand and know when they would die. I often thought this particular ability was a curse, the flipside to my gift. Some people would avoid getting close to me, for fear that I would touch them. I too feared that aspect of my gift. Now I know different. I know the real gift was the ability to use my unique knowledge to help people change their lives for the better. I should have embraced that ability. Last night we met Thomas, one of the few people I helped using that gift. I knew he was going to die, yet he changed his life and lived. I was wrong to view my gift as a death sentence, instead of a death warning. I was afraid and shouldn't have been.

"In his infinite wisdom, God charged me to convince everyone they should not be afraid. I have known the day of my death all my life, and now you will know it too. The secret I have kept hidden is … this will be the last time you see me. Tonight is in fact, my last in this world. Tonight, I am supposed to die."

Sauce heard the audience react with surprise and confusion. He wished he could see what was showing on the fan meter located above the stage. By the audience's reaction, he imagined it must be either registering a really low approval or a really high approval. "One thing is certain," thought Sauce, "Gladys has the audience's attention."

Suddenly a woman in the audience screamed, "We love you Gladys. You can't die!"

"I am not afraid," answered Gladys, "and you shouldn't be afraid either. Death is just a door to another plane of existence. Yet I am hopeful, that my actions tonight may somehow allow me to live beyond this day. Last night we heard how Thomas was able to change his fate. But even if the event I have anticipated my whole life, my own death on this day, does happen, I will leave this planet knowing I have used the few remaining minutes left to me in the service of justice and love."

Sauce heard scraping noises behind him and looked back; stage hands were moving chairs and equipment toward him. He alerted BT just in time for the two of them to move aside as the props were pushed to occupy their places, in readiness to be moved onstage.

"I can see the stage manager telling me it is time for another commercial break," said Gladys. "I guess even though my time on this planet is limited, we still have to take care of Amber's sponsors. Please return after the commercial break, so you can help me fulfil God's second request."

Sauce edged his way around the back of the stage to the right wing. He reached the other side, noticed Dara wasn't there, then raced out to the hall, looking for her. Dara was in Gladys's dressing room, drinking a bottle of water.

"I wanted to warn you. I saw Vincent West in the audience." He was breathing heavily from running and leaned forward with his hands on his knees.

"Oh, honey," said Dara in motherly tone. "We know. You shouldn't be so worried. You heard Mummy, didn't you? She knows she is going to be killed tonight. It very well may be the Wests who kill her."

"And you aren't going to do anything?" snapped an exasperated Sauce.

"Like what? Have him escorted out? That won't change anything. If we do that then someone else will take Mummy's life. It doesn't matter what we do, Sauce. Don't you see? Mummy has known all her life that tonight it would happen."

"So you aren't going to do anything?"

"Mummy *is* doing something. She is going to catch the person who poisoned that poor waitress and tried to kill those children. That's why she is here. To stop this madman from hurting anyone else."

"But—"

"I can't stay," said Dara opening the door. "The commercials must be over by now. I just came to get a bottle of water. I have to be near Mummy, just in case, so I can say goodbye." She ran out and down the hallway toward the stage.

Sauce walked back to his place next to BT. "I had to warn Dara," he explained in answer to BT's questioning glare.

The show had resumed. Sauce saw two chairs had been moved to the center of the stage. One was occupied by Gladys, the other by the governor. They were in the middle of a conversation.

"You are not very popular with the Amber Ellis audience," joked Gladys. "The fan meter dropped to twenty-five percent approval when I announced your name."

"I'm a politician not a psychic," he quipped in return. "Though sometimes I wish I was both. I know that many voters expect us to be both."

"If you had the gift, governor, how would you use it?"

"That's a good question, Gladys. You know the budget is always a concern. Divine intervention could make things a whole lot easier. On a daily basis, I have to decide to fund one program or another, recognizing that our state has a limited amount of tax dollars each year. Inevitably, there are many important initiatives we just cannot support. That's the beauty of democracy. If voters think I am making mistakes with their money, they can express their dissent in the voting booth. There will always be some people who aren't happy with some of our decisions in government. I'm just glad I don't have to look at Amber's fan meter on a daily basis." He gave a reserved.

Gladys smiled too, then became very serious. "Some voters prefer to voice their dissent in other ways, though. Of course I am speaking about the attempted murder of your daughter."

"If you don't mind, Gladys," began the governor, deepening his voice to sound more authoritative, "that is a personal matter better left to the proper legal authorities."

"Governor, the law is inefficient and slow. By the time an investigation is conducted, someone, perhaps your daughter, will die. Even if the police apprehend a suspect, and the person goes to trial, twelve people, just twelve, may decide to release the perpetrator so they can threaten more lives."

"That system is thc best we can do, Gladys."

"Perhaps it's the best you can do, but let me show you something." Gladys stood up and pointed above the stage. "Look at the fan meter. Right now it says fifty-four percent. Yet if I ask the viewers, would you like me to name the person who tried to poison the governor's daughter … There see that: seventy-five percent. And if I ask our viewers, should I reveal the man who has been blackmailing the government, threatening to kill the children of six top officials if they fail to enact new laws based on his personal agenda, effectively destroying democracy in the process? Well? There, Governor, see the support you have? Ninety-eight percent approval. That is far better than a twelve-person jury. That is millions of people of all races and ages. Tonight we can turn the Amber Ellis Show into the most efficient and representative court of law in the world. What do you say, everyone? Do you want to solve a crime?"

The audience erupted in support of Gladys. The fan meter registered one hundred percent approval.

The governor immediately stood up. "Wait, everyone. This won't do. We can't accuse someone publicly. That would be slander. It's against the law."

Gladys was beaming and waving her arms to keep the audience cheering to drown out the concerns of the governor.

Finally, Gladys motioned for the crowd to calm down. She took the governor's hand and conceded. "Okay, I suppose the governor is right." The audience began screaming "No!" Gladys laughed and again motioned for silence.

"Let me finish," she yelled above the noise. She waited a few seconds. "I just said that he was right. I didn't say I was going to listen to him! But we must be fair, right?" Gladys turned to the governor. "You would prefer if I did not shout the name of the person responsible for this heinous crime, is that correct?"

"If you name him on the air, then you and the Amber Ellis Show will most likely be sued for libel, defamation of character, and a host of other crimes. So yes, I would prefer if you kept the name of the person you suspect to yourself."

"I don't care about getting sued. I'm going to die tonight, anyway." Gladys looked at the audience and smiled. They laughed at her morbid humour. "I do care about my good friend Amber, though. I don't want to leave her with an expensive mess to clean up once I am gone." She looked behind at the fan meter and frowned.

"Look at Gladys's face. The meter must show a lot of disapproval," commented Sauce.

"She better be careful," whispered BT. "A hyped up crowd like this could quickly get ugly."

Gladys looked at the audience. "Oh don't be so hasty. I'm not going to disappoint Amber's audience. I have a solution that will appease your thirst for blood and address the governor's concerns. And I will tell you what it is, right after this short commercial break."

CHAPTER 30

Sauce watched as the governor tried to convince Gladys to reconsider turning the show into criminal theatre. Gladys sat back in her chair as a makeup artist worked on her face. She would say a word or two, then the governor would excitedly continue to explain his position. Sauce couldn't hear a word, but could tell Gladys was not giving in to the governor's demands.

Gladys stood up and beckoned Sauce to approach. He wasn't sure if she wanted both of them, so he pulled BT along, just in case. The four men stood in the center of the stage, nodding and arguing for a few seconds. The stage manager yelled "Ten seconds!" BT escorted the governor back to his seat then ran to the left wing to rejoin Sauce.

"This is nuts. I didn't sign up for this," asserted BT. "The worst part is Onofrio suggested I go along with it to ensure it is done without trickery."

"Are you a registered polygraph expert?" asked Sauce.

"Years ago, I was. But that was on a real one. There are conditions that have to be met, behavioural controls to establish. This thing she has planned isn't real!" shouted BT. He was hushed from various voices behind the curtain.

Gladys stood at the edge of the stage and motioned for the cameraman to zoom in close to her face. On cue, Gladys began talking, as if the viewers returned while she was in the middle of a sentence, "… we have a responsibility to learn the truth. The great poet John Keats wrote, 'Beauty is truth, truth beauty.' Together, we will learn the truth. The truth of who has threatened to kill little girls, who has attempted to control the government." Gladys smiled and added, "Trust me, no one will be falsely accused. No one will be unduly harmed. You trust me, don't you?"

Gladys looked behind at the fan meter and smiled broadly. "I appreciate the vote of confidence." Turning to the right wing, Gladys extended an arm. A beautiful woman in a skin-tight dress approached Gladys, pushing a cart. On the cart sat a glass fishbowl filled with scraps of paper.

Gladys then pointed to the left wing. A group of stagehands pushed past Sauce and BT with six chairs and six large rectangular boxes on wheels. The chairs were aligned at center stage. The boxes were positioned behind each chair, then lifted to reveal flat-screen television displays, each connected to an electric console outfitted with two long coils of wire.

"Can we have the house lights on, please? Ah, thank you." Gladys ran her fingers through the papers in the bowl. "On each slip of paper in this bowl is a number that corresponds to a seat in this theatre. I will draw six numbers. If your number is called, please come to the stage and take one of these six chairs. One of the six people who will be seated in these chairs is our criminal. I won't tell you which one. You will decide by voting."

She looked from side to side smiling devilishly. "You are all nervously hoping I don't call your number, aren't you?" Gladys reached into the bowl and pulled out one number after another, until six were called. Sauce and BT were behaving just like the audience members, scanning from side to side to see who would be joining Gladys on the stage.

The first person to stand was a pear-shaped woman, in her mid-fifties, with blonde, though slightly greying hair. She bounded down the stairs with her arms raised, happily screaming like she was about to be a contestant on the game show The Price is Right. She attempted to jump onto the stage near Gladys

Hammi stopped her at the bottom of the stage.

Gladys called to her, "Please, for the benefit of both of us, do not approach me. Please go straight to one of the empty chairs."

Hammi released the woman, then helped her up the side stairs onto the stage. She chose the chair closest to Gladys. She looked too happy and full of nervous energy to be a murderer.

Sauce watched as one after another descended toward the stage. Then he noticed Jett stand slowly after his seat number was called and look longingly at the exit. Vincent was still standing at the top of the stairs. "Escape is not an option," thought Sauce. Jett pushed his white cane into the stairway and stumbled down onto one knee.

Gladys called out to Vincent. "Young man! Yes, you by the door. Can you please come down and help this gentleman reach the stage?"

Vincent answered, "Oh sure, yeah, no problem." He hopped down the stairs and placed a hand under Jett's arm. Without saying a word, he guided Jett down the stairs and onto one of the chairs on stage.

Sauce watched as Vincent slowly walked back into the audience. He was halfway up the staircase when the theatre darkened and dramatic music filled the room.

"My friends," said Gladys to the three men and three women onstage, "you do not need to be nervous. I don't bite. I won't harass or manipulate you into giving a confession. You won't even have to speak. I don't even want to know your names."

She paced slowly as she spoke. "If I still had my gift, I would attempt to contact the waitress who nearly succeeded in killing the governor's daughter. She could have earned heavenly forgiveness and inner peace by revealing her mentor. I don't have my gift. Instead we must rely on a less elegant, though I am sure, equally effective methodology."

"No gift, she says! If Derek Mackie is watching, he must feel like a complete fool," whispered Sauce to BT.

She waved at BT, signaling for him to approach her. "To assist me, I now ask on stage the investigators who have worked day and night to solve this crime. Please welcome private investigators Beto Torres, a retired Secret Service agent who routinely put his life on the line to protect the President of the United States, and Byrne Aase, considered by many in law enforcement to be San Francisco's Sherlock Holmes." Sauce hesitated for a few seconds, then followed BT onto the stage. The crowd cheered enthusiastically, giving the two men a celebrity's welcome.

They reached the first chair and stopped in response to Gladys holding up her hand. Sauce looked behind at the fan meter and smiled at the eighty-four percent approval that he and BT received.

"These experts," said Gladys, "will secure our six volunteers to the lie detectors located behind each of their chairs. Once all six are properly connected, each person's blood pressure, heart rate, and other indications of honesty will be collated onto a single graph. That graph will be displayed on the screens above their heads. Lying will appear as jumps on the graph. Telling the truth will result in a flat line. It is that simple. Except I will not ask them to answer questions. We already know that all six will deny being the murderer."

Gladys paused, walked up to the edge of the stage, reached into the pocket of her suit jacket and removed a folded set of papers. "I have in my possession, two letters that were written by the murderer. One is a copy of the letters that were mailed to six of California's most esteemed politicians. This letter attempted to blackmail these politicians to pass certain laws and alter the constitution of this great land. I became aware of the existence of these letters during my last performance in Los Angeles some months ago. I immediately offered to help the governor and his colleagues to find this person. No sooner had I become involved in the investigation, though, than I received this letter," she held up the second letter, "in which the murderer threatened me and threatened my daughter."

BT watched Jett, seated in the middle of the six chairs, fidget and look away from the cameras. He whispered into Sauce's ear, "You know him better than me; how long do you figure before Jett speaks out?"

"I thought he would have already. I don't understand what he's waiting for."

"If he's waiting for Gladys to stop talking, then he'll be waiting all night. She never comes up for air." joked BT.

Gladys walked up to the seated volunteers. "This is the first letter." She proceeded to read the letter, quickly and calmly. She then read the second letter, again without emotion. "All we need now is for our expert investigators to connect these individuals to the lie detectors and ask them if they wrote the letters. They don't need to answer; their desire to either tell the truth or lie will appear on the graph. The murderer's natural instinct for self-preservation will reveal him or herself to us. After that it will be up to you. Send in your votes to show that you approve of my methods and agree to help determine which person is our culprit."

"What a load of bullshit!" shouted Jett. He stood and faced Gladys.

The audience immediately reacted with a chorus of boos. Gladys looked up at the fan meter and smiled. "Sir, I don't think an outburst like that is going to earn you any votes. Look," she pointed up, "fifteen percent! They're already against you."

"Perhaps they are against you," he replied. "At least they will be against you when they learn the real truth about Good Gladys. *You* are the criminal! This whole charade is merely your latest attempt to treat the public like fools." He turned to the camera. "Gladys is not even here. This person in front of you isn't Gladys. He is the real criminal. First, he killed Gladys's business manager. Then he and the governor masterminded this clever deception. That's right. The waitress's murder, even these talk show appearances, all concocted out of greed by a sorry excuse of a politician and a fame hungry con artist."

The audience quietened to a low murmur, obviously unsure how to interpret these accusations. Gladys, however, smiled and appeared unperturbed.

"Clearly, this man did not watch last night's show," Gladys joked to the audience, getting a renewed wave of applause and a spike in the fan meter. "I proved that I am Good Gladys."

"You proved nothing," asserted Jett. "Ladies and gentleman, you have to believe me. Last night was a show, a television show. There was no reality involved. The people giving testimonials, including the moving account by the man called Thomas, nice choice of name by the way, *doubting Thomas*, were all shills. They were hired by the show."

Gladys again turned to the audience. "He seems to be quite sure of himself, doesn't he?" Gladys waited for her question to garner a chorus of dissention from her loyal audience then looked at Jett and asked, "If I am not Gladys, then please tell us all, who am I?"

Jett looked at the fan meter. It sat at ninety percent. He looked at the camera and stated, "The studio audience met Gladys's daughter at the beginning of the show. Some of you may have seen her picture in the papers during the trial where this man conned the court into letting him go. Yet before a few weeks ago, no one had even heard of her daughter. Gladys was remarkably keen on keeping her children, yes that's right, *children* out of the public eye. The man standing on this stage, pretending to be Gladys, is one of those children. In fact, his name is Patrick West, Gladys's son."

He looked at the fan meter and frowned that it sat firmly at forty percent. Gladys met his gaze. "Not the response you expected? People know me and trust me. You, on the other hand, are a nobody. Why would they believe you?"

Jett's face was beginning to redden with anger. He shouted, "You fools! Imbeciles! I am a respected professor. A man of science. I am telling you a fact. Don't be so stupid. Look with your eyes at this man. I am telling you he is Gladys's son, Patrick!"

Gladys threw her arms up and cast a look of disgust at the audience. "Well it looks like the only way we will be able to continue with the show is if I come clean. This man is correct about one thing, I do have a son named Patrick. I protected his identity, and his sister's, all their lives. I'm sure you can understand. I chose a life in the public spotlight. They did not, and I wasn't going to force them into the limelight. Dara has grown into a beautiful, independent, confident woman who decided, on her own, to accompany me during these difficult weeks after my transformation into a man. There was no need for Patrick to be exposed, and he wanted to preserve his privacy.

"He is here, though. He has to be. I am supposed to die tonight. He wanted to be near me, so he could say goodbye when the time came."

"You never stop!" Jett pleaded to the camera, "You have to see he is just spinning another tale. We deserve the truth. Vote right now if you want Gladys to bring out her son. Tell Gladys you don't believe her. Demand she produce Patrick!"

Sauce motioned for BT to look at the fan meter which rose to ninety-two percent and whispered, "Gladys is in deep, now. Jett even has the audience on his side."

"I already said," pleaded Gladys, "he does not want to be known publicly. Please respect his privacy. I have already proven I am Gladys, so there is no need for Patrick to come forward."

Jett smiled. He looked at the fan meter, which now showed only seven percent approval at Gladys's refusal to expose her son.

BT nudged Sauce's side and leaned toward his ear. "I don't like how this is going. The crowd is bouncing from approval to disapproval too quickly. This could get ugly."

"It looks like the show's over Gladys," he said smugly. "You're finished. I hope the police in this room arrest you and the governor. I'm sure they'll be able to find ample proof of your guilt, now that I have shown everyone who you really are."

Gladys stood resolute and calm as Jett walked toward the stage stairs. He smirked as he passed

Gladys and stated, "You should never have messed with me."

Just then a young man in the front row stood up and shouted, "I'm Patrick!"

"No!" shouted Gladys. "You don't have to say anything."

"It's okay, Mom. I want to." The young man wiped tears from his eyes and looked into the camera. "You gave me everything I needed in life, yet I selfishly kept quiet, wanting to preserve my anonymity. But I won't let this monster destroy your reputation with his lies. I am Gladys's son and I will provide the police with all the proof they want."

Jett looked at the fan meter which showed that eighty-eight percent of the votes supported the young man. He turned to the audience and yelled, "No! He's not. He's lying. You idiots! You can't possibly believe him."

Gladys mouthed a heartfelt thank you to her son. She looked at Jett and asked, "Are you finished berating my audience? These honest people don't deserve your abuse." She looked into the camera. "How many of you would like this man to return to his chair?" She turned to the audience, enthusiastically raised her arms and asked, "Would you like to see how he fares with the lie detector when I ask if he wrote those two letters?"

The fan meter jumped to one hundred percent approval. Jett glanced at it and screamed, "The letters are fakes, too!" The governor stood to offer a rebuttal. Jett looked at Gladys and corrected himself, "Well at least the letter to you was a fake."

Gladys quickly pounced. "You're right. Audience, he is correct. Only one of the letters was sent by the murderer. In fact, I wrote the second letter." Gladys put her hand on Jett's shoulder and stated loudly, "But only one person knew that besides me: the man who blackmailed the government, attempted to poison a little girl, and killed his accomplice!"

The audience started to shout obscenities and cries of "guilty!" at Jett. He lunged at Gladys and wrapped his hands around her throat, saying, "I'll kill you!"

A single gun shot rang out, sending the audience into a frenzy. Some ducked under their seats, others raced for the exits. The five volunteers onstage, all with splatters of Jett's blood and brains on their clothes, ran for cover offstage.

Sauce and BT ran at Jett and pulled him away from Gladys. Blood was pouring from the side of his head, a large portion of which had been blown away by the blast. He was gasping for air. Sauce looked across the stage and saw Hammi in a crouched position, his gun still extended in Jett's direction. Stage hands ran from the wings in the pandemonium to try to help. BT removed his shirt and applied pressure to Jett's wound in a futile attempt to keep him alive. Jett's head turned to the side and he was dead.

"Everyone!" The stage manager's voice echoed through the studio. "Please stay in your seats and remain calm. The police have the situation under control."

A woman screamed, and all eyes shifted to Gladys. The cameras which had been focused on Jett, turned to the body lying motionless at the edge of the stage. Sauce and Hammi ran to Gladys's side.

Sauce first saw her body. The suit was the same, but the shape was not. The legs of her pants extended well beyond her feet. Her hips were wider, her chest full. He looked at her face. The makeup was amazing, but Sauce wasn't fooled. He gasped softly, "You're Gladys?" In her neck was a syringe, it's plunger fully depressed.

Sauce felt dizziness overcome him, and passed out.

CHAPTER 31

Sauce awoke in his own bedroom. He looked around the room and saw BT sleeping in a chair next to his bed.

"Hey!" he called.

BT opened his eyes, sat up, and smiled. "You gave us a scare. You obviously shouldn't have gone out last night."

"What?" said Sauce. He searched for the right words to say, then shouted, "Gladys! You knew!"

"Let's not get into that just yet. We have an appointment. You should hurry and get dressed. Are you feeling up to it?"

"Not get into it?" Sauce shook his head in disbelief. "But Jett, and the show. It was all a set up. Dara?"

"Not now. Trust me. Just get dressed," repeated BT. "Hammi said to give him a call as soon as you woke up. We're meeting him to discuss what happened. I promised not to say anything until we are all together."

Sauce replayed the events of the previous evening in his head as he quickly showered and dressed. His head still throbbed, but he was determined not to complain. He didn't want to delay connecting with Hammi so he could find out what happened after he fainted.

"I made us sandwiches for the road," said BT as Sauce entered the kitchen.

"Make yourself at home," said Sauce sarcastically.

"Bitter? I suppose I would be too, if I was in your shoes."

"You mean if you had been beaten, dumped in a bathtub, then a few days later stood by as two people were murdered? And Dara, she played me like a violin. How could I have believed she was interested in anything but her mother? I guess some might say she got what she deserved."

"Now who's feeling sorry for himself? I'll bring our breakfast. You get your shoes. We have to be on our way."

"So you're not going to tell me anything? What about all that crap about a partnership? This isn't a good start, is it?"

BT silently opened the door and proceeded to walk outside. Sauce followed, locking the door behind him. "If you're not going to talk, I may as well take my own car. Just tell me where we're going and I'll make my own way."

"Don't be an impatient ass. Get in the car. You have a concussion, you idiot. At least that's what the doctor said last night. You can't drive."

"So I was visited by a doctor last night. That's a start. Don't stop there. What else did I miss?"

"Ha ha," said BT as he dropped into the driver's seat. "Get in!"

The men ate their sandwiches as BT drove through San Francisco, toward the coast. Sauce recognized the path they were taking and assumed he knew their destination. His suspicions were confirmed as they pulled up to the tall, black metal gates in front of Gladys's house.

As they got out of the car, Sauce quipped, "So it takes losing her only daughter for Gladys to finally show her face?"

"Sauce!" came a familiar voice from beyond the open gate.

"Hammi!" answered Sauce. "Are you going to tell me what we are doing here? BT hasn't been especially helpful."

Hammi shrugged his shoulders then pointed to the house. "We're supposed to let ourselves in," he said, ignoring Sauce's question. "She's meeting us in the library."

"Hammi, it's me. We've been friends for, well, a long time. I know you. You can't just keep quiet about last night. You killed someone, for Christ's sake. You have to want to talk about that!"

"I've never killed anyone," replied Hammi. "I drew my gun, but Gladys was in my way. The bullet came from somewhere else. Probably one of the Wests. Half of his head was blown off, Sauce. Ballistics will probably determine that a high-caliber sniper rifle was used. Who fired it? Your guess is as good as mine. We may never find the answer to that one. That's all I'm saying, sorry. The rest of the answers are in there."

Sauce impatiently walked ahead of the other two men, threw the door open and quickly walked past the dead ancestors to the library.

"You!" uttered a surprised Sauce. "Dara, I thought—"

"Wrong!" said Dara with a broad smile. She was seated on one of the leather loveseats with her knees together, back straight, in a dark pinstriped blazer and skirt. Her face was softly adorned and her hair pulled back in a bun.

As BT and Hammi entered, Dara suggested they all have a seat. BT walked up to the globe in the center of the room and ran his hand across the inscription. "I hoped I would get to see this: Kaos's sculpture."

"It is beautiful," commented Dara.

"And huge," added Hammi. "It's something you'd expect in the lobby of a fancy hotel or in a museum."

"It fits here. It's perfect here," said Dara softly.

Looking at Sauce, BT stated, "I don't know if I would have figured it all out if we hadn't come across Kaos. After that insane afternoon in Sausalito with the senators and the Mackies, I started to have suspicions. But later, when I was talking to Hammi, I remembered the globe and it all became crystal clear."

Sauce sat next to Dara. She took his hand and warmly said, "You made it all happen."

"Whoa! I don't even know *what* happened, so you can stop lying already. I certainly didn't want Jett dead."

"Oh, he was as poisonous as the mixture he tried to give to little Annabelle. I am telling the truth. This room is all about truth, like the inscription at the base of the globe."

Sauce looked at the fake books and raised his eyebrows.

Dara noticed his skepticism and added, "Okay, so the room isn't all about truth." She grinned and looked down. "It also isn't the place to mourn the dead. Not someone like him anyway. The past is the past. Let's just leave it at that."

BT looked at the globe and asked, "Isn't this room the perfect place to discuss the past? You promised to tell Sauce everything."

"Everything?" said Dara sternly. "I like Sauce, but not enough to tell him everything."

Sauce was beginning to feel fatigue set in again and wanted to leave. "So I came here for nothing more than to find out you are alive? Obviously the syringe in your neck was merely part of the show. I thought at the very least I could give Gladys a piece of my mind. You and she can just go to hell as far I'm concerned."

Dara sat silent and resolute. She turned away from Sauce.

"You weren't the only one who was played last night," said Hammi. "You passed out just before I became famous." He looked at Dara and pointed a finger. "You had me fooled for a minute. Of course, a minute was all the camera needed. The news channels have been running that clip of me over and over all night. My wife recorded it Sauce, so I'll show you later. There I was kneeling at her side, and I pulled out the syringe. I then checked her carotid pulse and looked up. The camera was zoomed in on my face as I shouted to the world, 'Gladys is Alive'. It wasn't until a few minutes later that I realized it was really you lying there and not your mother."

"Plastic and paint," said Dara. "The hardest part was getting the male Gladys out through the trapdoor and me into position without anyone seeing. I didn't expect you to pull out the syringe, though. When you did, I thought you might have noticed that it was a stage prop. "

"It was a clever circus act," added Hammi. "They whisked you off that stage in seconds. Everything happened so fast." He looked at BT. "And you! So smug and silent. You knew all the time."

"Not all the time," said BT. "My first impression of Miss Stockard came from a photo in the paper of her coming out of the court house during the Beckley murder trial. She looked hideous." He looked at Dara and added, "Sorry. I mean your makeup was extremely overdone. I thought then that you were wearing a mask. When I finally met you, in Sauce's kitchen, I saw your natural face, and thought why would a girl cover up such beauty. I should also mention that I observed your face transform when you looked at Sauce that morning. No girl lights up like that for someone, unless she really cares about him." Dara looked at BT and giggled gently, wiping a tear from her cheek. She looked at Sauce, who was still angry, and her face darkened again.

"At the time, I assumed the mask was part of her lifelong strategy to maintain her privacy. No one knew Dara Stockard before the trial so it seemed reasonable. She wanted to be able to return to her old life once this ordeal was over.

"Then there was the arrangement of the flights for the four little girls. Two separate planes? In my experience that is just wrong. If I'm protecting multiple assets, I want them together where I can easily keep track of them.

"Yet even with that information I didn't put it all together until Hammi filled me in on his research into Beckley's ledger." He patted Hammi on the back and said, "you want to tell Sauce what you told me?"

"Sure. I began kind of half-hazardly, just searching one name at a time in the police database. Of course there were several members of the West family listed. Each name, however, seemed to be a dead end. Lawyers, bankers, even dentists. It seemed like a motley collection of meaningless contacts. There were a lot of names too, so I didn't see the few that should have popped out from the beginning. Judge Wheeler, for instance."

"From Gladys's trial?" asked Sauce, casting a suspicious glance at Dara.

"Yeah. His name in the ledger got me thinking that perhaps I was going about the investigation the wrong way. So I then examined a copy of the trial transcript and the notes from the investigating officers. I found some revealing connections. For instance, the lab tech in charge of the DNA analysis, and the forensics expert in charge of the fingerprints. Both men were in the ledger. I wondered how deep this went. I asked BT to use his connections to get me access to Beckley's banking records—a subpoena could have sent red flags to other co-conspirators. Besides, I didn't know who to trust. BT came through, fortunately, but only for a single bank account, and I'm sure Beckley had many. I did, however, discover large payments made to two SFPD veterans, whose names were also in the ledger. That kind of scared me a little. I told BT and he seemed to immediately bristle with excitement. I thought he was going to kiss me. I am still not clear on everything else, so I'll let BT tell you the rest."

BT looked at Dara and asked, "Do you have anything to add at this point?"

Dara answered, "You're doing so well. Please, go on."

"From the beginning I was sure this whole thing, the transformed Gladys, the trial, all of it, was a massive charade. I was also pretty certain Jett's involvement came about quite accidentally. Sauce, you were the one, actually, who suggested how the two events became entangled with your insight about Jett taking advantage of his opportunities. Good Gladys did the same thing. The transformation took a lot of planning. It wasn't conceived overnight. I figured they had this scheme in the works for months and were waiting for the right moment to begin this phase of her career. When Gladys uncovered the letters on Jett's computer, she and Beckley saw the opportunity and put the wheels in motion."

"Wait a second," interrupted Sauce. "You're saying Jett's blackmail scheme wasn't part of Gladys's plan?"

"Of course not," shouted Dara. "How could you think that I would allow two innocent dogs to get murdered? That happened before we learned of Jett's plans. I never set out to hurt anyone."

"Except for Jett," replied Sauce, self-righteously. "You did have him killed."

"The Wests killed him," answered Dara sharply. "I didn't care if he lived or died, but I knew if they were in the studio, Jett wouldn't be able to hurt me." She paused for a second, adjusted her skirt and with renewed conviction proceeded to explain. "Mummy protected me from them for years. You met the only father I cared about, the tailor Francis: a decent, hardworking man with an ordinary life and ordinary family. That's what Mummy wanted for me, an ordinary life. She didn't even tell me about the Wests until I was sixteen and able to decide for myself if I wanted to know them or not. I chose to keep them at a distance. At the same time, I wanted to spend more time with Mummy. So I started to work with her, and learn the trade from the sidelines, hidden for the most part.

"You saw for yourself how protective the Wests are of family. Jett convinced them you were a threat to EB, my cousin. They wouldn't have even been involved in any of this if it wasn't for Jett trying to stop Mummy from messing with his plans. He approached Beckley first, threatening to tell the world Mummy used pickpockets during her show. Beckley just laughed at him. So he decided to hire an assassin to kill Mummy. The idiot happened to find one of Vincent West's brothers. Vincent was already worried about Gladys, who hadn't returned any of his calls for the past few years, so he told his brother to take the job—you know so Jett didn't hire someone else, and he was going to warn

Mummy, who was still family after all. He also insisted Jett hire his cousin EB to prevent Jett from running without paying once the hit had been carried out. Her real job, of course, was to keep the family informed about Jett's activities.

"Vincent said he went to Beckley's office and demanded to be put in touch with Gladys. Beckley couldn't do that and wouldn't explain why—it would have messed with our plans. Vincent got a little carried away and accidentally stabbed Beckley."

"You don't seem too upset about that," chided Sauce.

"I'm not. Mummy was good at keeping Beckley in order. He knew that one phone call from her to the Wests and he was a dead man. But over the past few years Beckley had been taking advantage of me, skimming more and more off the top. He held all the cards."

"I don't get it," said Sauce. "Why didn't Gladys stop him?"

"She's dead!" blurted BT. "That was what I figured out. All the pieces added up to that conclusion. Why two planes for the kids? Because Dara insisted on it. She's afraid of planes. The kids had to go abroad for their safety, so she figured at least if one plane goes down, some of the kids would survive."

"How did you know?" asked Dara.

"Your trip to St. Martin with Sauce: first by train to the east coast, then by boat. Only people afraid to fly travel by train anymore. The senator said Gladys insisted on the flight itinerary: that had to be you. That was my eureka moment. Gladys is dead; this whole charade was designed to be the grand finale in the Gladys story. Dara emerges and Gladys fades away with a glorious final send-off on live television."

"You've been pretending to be your mother? For how long?" asked Sauce.

"Almost six years," answered Dara. "I hated it at first, but didn't have a choice. We were in Mexico, at Mummy's estate near Playa del Carmen. She had a massive aneurism and died almost immediately. Beckley came down to help with the arrangements, cremation. He said we were broke. It turns out he lied, but I didn't know that at the time. He concocted this scheme for me to portray Mummy. The whole thing just steam-rolled from there. Beckley had all the contacts and controlled everything I did. Finally, three years ago I was becoming so bitter and disillusioned. I needed a break. So I hired one of Mummy's team to pretend to be me, well pretend to be me pretending to be Mummy. That's who you met the first time you came here. I escaped with you. It was the first time I got to be me in years. I fell in love and began to really like myself again too. It was the best time of my life; it really was.

"Beckley found out and tracked me down. He forced me back. Last year, I finally convinced him to let me go. He planned the transformation ruse with Amber Ellis. Her show was falling in the ratings and since she gave Mummy her first big break, it seemed fitting to use the transformation to boost her show back on top. A Good Gladys book is already written about the ordeal and would have been published posthumously, with Beckley getting all the profits. He was going to retire very wealthy."

"And your brother went along with it too?" asked Sauce.

Dara laughed. "I don't have a brother, silly." Then feigning confusion added, "I can't for the life of me fathom how Jett got that ridiculous idea in his head."

BT and Hammi laughed at the joke, but Sauce was still processing all he had just heard. "So there is no Gladys?" said Sauce softly.

"Sure there is," answered BT. "She's right here with us now."

Sauce looked at him askew. "Dara doesn't have to keep up the charade. Beckley's gone."

"That's not quite what I mean. The real Gladys, Dara's mom, is here in this room," said BT. "Remember I said the existence of the globe was an essential fact that helped me piece together the evidence. As things started to fall into place, I asked myself, where is Gladys? Then I thought about the globe, with its hidden compartment inside. An image sprang to mind of Gladys lying in there."

"Just her ashes," explained Dara. "Mummy was very proud of the enterprise she built. She would tell me that Good Gladys is a part of the world and always would be, long after she passed on. So when I returned home, I told Beckley how I wanted to keep her memory and he arranged for Kaos to create this beautiful vessel. You know despite his shortcomings, I think he really cared for Mummy."

Sauce sat quietly for a few minutes. Hammi then broke the tension asking, "So what's going to happen to Dara Stockard now?"

"You mean Gladys, don't you?" answered Dara abruptly.

Sauce looked at her in amazement. "You're not going to continue with this? You are free. You said yourself you wanted to get away from this life."

"That was last year. I was tired of being told what to do by Beckley. But I like being Gladys. I guess I always have. People love me. And I'm really good at it, better than Mummy ever was."

"But it's a lie!" shouted Sauce. "You're better than that."

"People don't see it that way. I give them hope. Even more so now. Good Gladys is the only psychic in the world who has been to the other side and returned. I think I will have more fun as Gladys than I have ever had."

Sauce felt beaten. He realized Dara was not going to change. He also knew he was a better person for having met her. Before he left, he gave her a gentle hug and wished her well. She told him to keep in touch, and he was sure that he wouldn't.

In the car on the way home he and BT kept to themselves. In front of his home, he told BT he would give him a call in a couple of days, after he had some time to think things through. He entered his home and went to the bedroom, longing to sleep. Opening the closet to hang his blazer, he immediately noticed that all of Dara's clothes were gone, removed while he was at Dara's house. He lay down on the bed and drifted off to sleep.

He woke abruptly to the sound of a pounding on his front door. He looked at the time on his phone, which showed that it was six in the morning: he had slept all night. He walked to the front door, and saw BT's face through the peephole.

"It's early," said Sauce upon opening the door.

"Look at you," replied BT. "Did you sleep in your clothes?" He pushed past Sauce, heading straight to the kitchen carrying two cups of coffee, a newspaper under his arm, and a bag of donuts.

Sauce followed. "I thought we agreed to give each other some space."

"We could do that. Or we could get to work. I figure the best thing for you right now is to get back on the horse. So, I brought you coffee, breakfast and a proposition."

"You're not still thinking about teaming up?"

"Hell! As far as the public's concerned, we're already a team. If it's in the papers it must be true." He chuckled, throwing the newspaper down on the table.

On the front page was a picture of Hammi kneeling at Gladys's side with the caption, "'Gladys is alive!' exclaims Office Hammi of the San Francisco Police Department moments after Good Gladys was transformed back into a woman on live television." Below that was a smaller picture of Sauce standing with BT on the stage at the Amber Ellis Show. Sauce started to read the accompanying article.

"You can read that later. Flip to page three." BT turned over the page, pointed at a paragraph in the middle, and read aloud: "Jett may have succeeded if not for the help Gladys received from two of the nation's top private investigators, San Francisco's own Sherlock Holmes, Byrne Aase (called Sauce by his friends) and his assistant, former Secret Service agent, Beto Torres."

Sauce lifted the paper and read the line over again. "It doesn't say I have only handled insurance claims."

"Don't be a cynic," countered BT. "This article is in dozens of papers around the world. We're famous, like it or not. The question is, are you prepared to act? With a start like this, Torres and Sauce may actually be able to make a difference in this world."

"Sure, if only we could convince Gladys to magically fix every case we come across."

BT's face widened into a suspicious grin. Sauce gave him a nudge. "What?"

"All right, I'll confess. Remember I told you I thought your friend Hammi was top notch. My instincts weren't wrong. As soon as he noticed the names of a few of his police colleagues listed in his copies of the ledger pages he did a marvelous, wonderful thing—he made extra copies and hid them at home. He told me last night. I immediately raced to his house and picked them up. Only you, me, and Hammi know they exist. This will be our secret weapon, partner."

The End

ACKNOWLEDGEMENTS

Thank you to my family and friends for their encouragement and support. I am especially grateful to my children, Nic and Rachel.

I don't know what I would do without the helpful comments, suggestions and diligence of my mother-in-law Sylvia Curran who proof read and edited initial versions of the book. You are the greatest!

I feel extremely fortunate that one of the first people to read an earlier version of this book was the thoughtful and understanding book reviewer/author Nickie Anderson. Her encouragement, criticisms and suggestions motivated me to take her advice and seek the services of a professional editor to polish the text.

Thank you editor/author Kelly Hashway. Your sharp editorial eye and thoughtful comments amazed me. You thoroughly exceeded my expectations.

Of course, I am also very grateful for the encouragement provided by readers of my previous novels, the Socialite 1 series.

ABOUT THE AUTHOR

Martin Renaud lives near Vancouver, British Columbia with his two children. Learn more about his current and future projects and leave comments at:

www.facebook.com/socialitebooks.

Also available in print and ebook formats:

Socialite 1

Unknown to a small community in Mission British Columbia, an alien family from the planet Zozia has been living in their midst for many years. They came to Earth to marry their beautiful daughter Elle Amis to a human and send them to Zozia to save the planet from extinction. The alien family, the Amis, are unaware that a well known public figure is also from the planet Zozia and is creating havoc with the world's communication systems.

Socialite 1 Book 1: Bees to Benny
Socialite 1 Book 2: Mission to Mission
Socialite 1 Book 3: To Humanize
Socialite 1 Book 4: Unless Rules

www.ingramcontent.com/pod-product-compliance
Lightning Source LLC
LaVergne TN
LVHW020652110826
845149LV00012B/1972

* 9 7 8 0 9 8 7 8 5 1 6 9 7 *